MURDER
AT THE GREENBRIER

MURDER
AT THE GREENBRIER

GREG JOHNSON

Kindle Direct Publishing

Murder at The Greenbrier

This is work of fiction. While the settings are real, the names, characters and incidents are products of the author's imagination. Any resemblance to persons living or dead is entirely coincidental.

ISBN: 979-8-9943200-0-6 (paperback)

ISBN: 979-8-9943200-1-3 (ebook)

Cover design by Mary Baldwin, Havenbrook Media

Kindle Direct Publishing (KDP)

Contents

Don't it always seem to go
that you don't know what you've got 'til it's gone.

- Joni Mitchell

Chapter 1 The Bellman

From the window of his suite overlooking The Greenbrier's north entrance, Mordecai Oakes surveyed the formal garden bursting with spring colors five stories below. There were some advantages to being a paraplegic, he considered. One was that hotels tended to give him superior accommodations like this, rooms that looked like they were reserved for visiting heads of state. He hadn't expected such regal treatment – he was just a professional loudmouth. Well, he was a commentator for Fox News, pretty much the same thing.

Oddly, the hit-and-run that had confined him to a wheelchair three years earlier had turbocharged his media career. Before that fateful day he was just a naysaying weatherman, railing against the notion that human-induced climate change was an established scientific fact. Now he was the Stephen Hawking of climate change denial, delivering his unvarnished contrarian opinions from a high-tech wheelchair. The conservatives thought he was a prophet. The environmentalists thought he was a pompous ass. All he knew was that he was worth a lot more than he used to be, thanks to his media exposure and his book deals.

The American Meteorological Association had invited him to their convention at this grand Southern resort to debate Hayes Hancock, a liberal firebrand whose Chicken Little views on global warming echoed those held by most of the AMA members. They were billing this little confrontation as The Great Climate Change Debate, but since his peers seemed to have closed minds on the subject, he knew his real job was entertaining them. They were expecting him to serve as Hancock's punching bag and toss out a few zingers while he was being pummeled. His chance of being declared the winner of this sham battle was about the same as General Custer's at Little Bighorn.

He was used to entertaining groups that wanted their prejudices reinforced - conservative think tanks, Republican PAC's, coal and oil execs. Addressing his professional brethren on climate change was going to be a challenge. He planned to use his opening statement to take them on a little historical journey and point out some of the wildly erroneous "facts" scientists used to accept without question. Hopefully they'd get the point: just because a bunch of elitist eggheads share a rosy consensus about something, it doesn't mean it's true.

He rolled over to the antique writing desk where he'd been jotting miscellaneous one-liners in his notebook. He made a note to point out that in 2007 Mr. Inconvenient Truth himself, Al Gore, had predicted that by 2013 there wouldn't be any ice left at the North Pole. The last time he checked, there were still a few cubes.

He had stayed in more than his fair share of hotels, but The Greenbrier was refreshingly different. An elegant jewel tucked in the West Virginia mountains, the resort's gleaming white exterior gave no clue to the extravagant burst of color inside. He'd learned that during a 1950's makeover, the hotel had given free rein to Dorothy Draper, a wildly creative New York designer. Her affinity for bold colors and mismatched patterns prefigured the psychedelic 60's but somehow looked tastefully stylish. Over the decades her signature decor had become synonymous with this one-of-a-kind property. Following the designer's death in 1969, her acolyte, Carlton Varney, had turned embellishing on his mentor's style into his own lifelong project.

Another chapter in The Greenbrier's storied history that captured Mordecai's attention was the secret bunker the Eisenhower administration had buried deep in the hillside behind it, where Congress was supposed to hole up and conduct business in the event of a nuclear attack. Hidden behind a 28-ton blast door in the hotel's exhibition hall, the facility had been secretly maintained by the federal government until 1992, when a Washington Post reporter had outed it. The decommissioned Cold War relic had become a popular tourist attraction, and Mordecai had signed up to tour it after his debate.

He heard a knock on his door and he rolled over and answered it. He found himself face-to-face with a young-looking bellman wearing gloves and an expectant look.

"Hello, Mr. Oakes," the bellman said brightly. "I'm the one who called you earlier. I'm here to take you to the green room."

Mordecai glanced at his watch. "Aren't we a little early? This shindig doesn't start until two."

"They don't want the audience to see you before it starts," the bellman explained. "They want me to bring you in the back way, so you can make a big entrance when they introduce you. We're using the service elevator. Are you ready, or would you like me to come back in a few minutes?"

"I'm not opposed to making a grand entrance. I guess I'm as ready as I'll ever be. Let me grab my papers."

The bellman insisted on pushing him, so he flipped the freewheel lever and disengaged his chair's motor. They navigated a hallway wallpapered with lime stripes and pink rhododendrons, and they arrived at a padded service elevator twice the size of the mahogany ones the guests used.

Mordecai gave the lift a once-over. "The Meteorological Association finally has me where they want me," he observed. "A padded cell."

Five minutes later they entered the enormous main kitchen, roughly the size of a football field.

"Are you giving me a kitchen tour?" Mordecai asked.

"No, sir, we're just passing through," the bellman explained.

"Look, I appreciate your help, young man, but you don't need to push me. I may not look like it, but I'm a pretty self-sufficient guy. That's why this chair has a motor. Just lead the way and I'll follow you." Mordecai re-engaged his wheelchair's motor and followed the bellman past a long row of prep stations, into an industrial corridor lined with ancient metal pipes, an area of the posh resort the guests never saw.

"I signed up for the Bunker tour this evening," Mordecai told him. "Will I have any trouble navigating it in my wheelchair?"

"No, sir, you won't have to worry about that."

"I have a hard time believing the government had a secret fallout shelter here for 30 years without anyone knowing about it."

"The Bunker's huge," the bellman said. "You only see part of it on the tour. It was built to hold 1100 people. It even had a clinic and pharmacy."

"Surely your staff knew about it. It sounds too big to hide."

"They say only the top managers knew. The workers who maintained it had a repair shop where they worked on the hotel's TV's. That was their cover. There was a secret passageway between the shop and the Bunker."

"Very clever - and that's not something I usually say about the federal government. Of course, that wouldn't work nowadays. Nobody fixes a TV anymore. You junk it and get a bigger one."

"True," the bellman agreed. "Before we get to the green room, I want to show you something special."

"What it is?"

"A surprise. We need to go outside."

"Outside?" Mordecai puzzled.

"It won't take long. We're almost there."

"What did I do to merit this backstage tour?"

"You're a celebrity!"

Mordecai was used to attention, he actually loved it, but he was mildly suspicious of the fawning treatment this bellman was giving him. "Are you just sucking up to me so I'll give you a big tip?" he asked accusingly.

"Oh no, Mr. Oakes," the bellman protested as they emerged on a sunlit delivery dock. "We're just trying to make your stay at The Greenbrier memorable. You've got a lot of fans."

"I've got plenty of haters, too. That's the price I pay for being a public figure. But just between you and me, all that ranting and raving I do on TV is just an act. I'm not really an asshole, I just play one. In fact, let me give you a little something to remember me by." He reached in his coat pocket, pulled out a ballpoint pen and offered it to him. "This is one of the Montblancs I use to write my commentaries. Take it - it's yours."

"Wow," the bellman accepted the gift. "Thanks."

"You're welcome. Now do me a favor. When you hear people talking shit about me, tell them you met me and I'm really a nice guy."

"Okay," the bellman agreed.

Mordecai glanced at his surroundings. "What are we doing out here? This looks like some kind of delivery dock."

"This is where our culinary staff makes the ice sculptures for the banquets and weddings," the bellman explained. "There are two refrigerated rooms, one on the left and one on the right. The one on the left is where they manufacture the ice blocks. The one on the right is a walk-in freezer where they keep the sculptures until they're ready to use them." He opened the door on the left and ushered him in.

"I should have brought my winter coat," Mordecai reacted to the temperature drop. "They didn't tell me I'd be touring a refrigerator."

The bellman pointed to three stainless-steel sinks in the middle of the room. "Those are giant ice cube trays. Each one holds a 300-pound block of ice. Once they're frozen, they lift them out with a hoist. If they're working on a really big sculpture, they fuse two blocks together. They put them on a dolly, wheel them out on the dock and start carving them up with chainsaws. Then they use chisels and torches to turn them into sculptures. They used to make a sleigh with reindeer for the front lawn at Christmas, but the winters have gotten a lot warmer, so they don't do it anymore. Did you know the past three years have been the warmest ones on record?"

This sounded like a loaded question, one Mordecai chose to ignore. "If I were a sculptor, I believe I'd work in marble instead. I couldn't bear to watch my masterpieces melt."

"I'll show you some of the finished ones," the bellman offered.

They exited the refrigerated room and crossed over to the other side of the dock. The bellman opened the door of the walk-in freezer and a cloud of frost billowed out. As it cleared, Mordecai saw an angel, a swan, an eagle, two interlocked hearts, and a butterfly perched on a leaf. "Very impressive," he surveyed the artwork. "You've got some talented people here."

The bellman ushered him into the freezer.

"My God, it's cold in here," Mordecai complained.

"Mr. Oakes, do you have a cell phone I could use for a minute? I need to let people know we're on our way to the green room."

Mordecai retrieved his iPhone from his coat pocket and used the facial recognition feature. "Here you go," he handed it over. "Hurry up. I'm freezing my balls off."

"Enjoy the climate change, Mr. Oakes," the bellman said. He exited quickly and latched the door. The ancient walk-in had been there for decades, long before manufacturers thought about equipping walk-ins with escape handles. He gave the door a tug to make sure it was secure, and, with a satisfied look, he hurried back into the hotel.

No one could hear Mordecai Oakes' frantic screaming, pounding and clawing. In addition to being very cold, the old freezer was very soundproof.

Chapter 2 News in Colonial Hall

Brendan Bell checked his watch. It was 1:45 and his ten Environmental Studies students were missing in action. They were operating on Eastern Teenage Time, distracted by The Greenbrier's endless smorgasbord of amenities. Greenbrier River High School's partnership with the resort meant he could take advantage of opportunities like this. Instead of spending another day in the classroom, his seniors were attending a debate with the members of the American Meteorological Association. His wife Greta was a concierge, and she had arranged for box lunches and a few other freebies. All he had to do was herd cats.

Hayley and her out-and-proud friend, Hudson, were getting their wrinkleless young faces refreshed at the spa. Jude and Santiago were bowling. Zoey, Genesis and Rylee were visiting boutiques, admiring all the clothing and accessories they couldn't afford. Joseph and his girlfriend Skylark were supposedly getting ice cream at Draper's Cafe, but they were probably looking for an empty bedroom. Brendan's main concern was Gunner, who functioned on the high end of the autism spectrum and was roaming the hotel by himself. Gunner's mother was a doctor at The Greenbrier Clinic and his family lived on the grounds, so at least he knew his way around.

In a strange way Gunner was his star pupil, laser-focused on the subject of man-made climate change. His obsession with saving the planet, coupled with his penchant for inappropriate behavior, resulted in some awkward scenes. Lately he'd been standing by the recycling bins in the school cafeteria, outfitted in rubber gloves, snatching the trash from people's trays and making sure the items ended up in the proper receptacles. Gunner had been seeing a therapist who was trying to polish his social skills. He didn't really care about other people, but he was learning how to pretend like he did.

Brendan spotted his students winding through the mass of conventioneers filing into Colonial Hall.

Hudson reached him first. "Hey, Mr. Bell. I got my eyebrows waxed."

Brendan eyed him curiously. "Congratulations, Hudson. That's always a big step in a young man's life."

"You're being sarcastic, aren't you?"

"I wouldn't dream of it."

"We didn't shoplift," Zoey reported.

"That's comforting news, Zoey."

"Those clerks were watching us like hawks."

Brendan turned to Santiago, whose immigrant Filipino parents worked in the hotel's housekeeping department. "Have you seen your folks?"

"Not yet."

"I guess that's a long shot with 2000 employees."

Skylark's jaw dropped. "Two thousand people work here?"

"Actually, it's more than that in the summer," Brendan informed her.

"When I finish college, I'm coming back and running this place," Santiago vowed.

Jude eyed him skeptically. "Wouldn't it be awkward to be your parents' boss?"

He shrugged. "I'll give them raises and they won't care."

Brendan noticed his star pupil was missing. "Has anyone seen Gunner?"

"I'm right behind you, Mr. Bell," Gunner spoke up. "I came from over there." He pointed to the red-carpeted grand staircase that swooped down dramatically from the floor above.

"Gather round, troops," Brendan motioned them into a huddle. "Listen up. We're guests of the Meteorological Association and The Greenbrier, so we need to be on our best behavior. No talking during the debate. If it's boring, pretend it's not."

"It won't be boring," Gunner felt sure.

Brendan turned to him. "Gunner, we know Mr. Oakes is going to say some outrageous things that will rub us the wrong way, things we know simply aren't true. Please don't overreact. His job is to argue with Mr. Hancock and our job is to listen. Got it?"

"Keep my big mouth shut," the young man translated.

"Exactly." Brendan turned to the others. "Even if some of the people sitting around us get worked up, we're not going to join in the fray. Right?"

Jude gave him a salute. "Sir, yes, sir!"

"Okay. Follow me."

They entered the hall and claimed their reserved seats near the front of the room. As the proceedings got underway, the Association's president introduced the high school students as special guests. She followed this with another announcement. "It doesn't look like we're going to be starting on time," she broke the assembly the news. "Mr. Oakes isn't here yet. We've been trying to reach him, but we haven't had any luck."

Jude leaned over to his teacher. "He probably chickened out," he said in a low voice. "He doesn't want to face a bunch of people who know he's full of shit."

Brendan put a finger to his lips.

"As you know, Mr. Oakes is a controversial figure," the AMA president continued. "Our surveys show that 97% of our members believe climate change is the preeminent crisis of our times, and we're running out of time to address it. But that still leaves 3% who hold other opinions. Our planning committee felt we need to offer them an opportunity to air their views, and that Mr. Oakes is an ideal spokesperson. I'm afraid we don't have anyone else we can ask to fill in for him. We'll give him a few more minutes. If he doesn't show up, we've asked Mr. Hancock to share some of the points he intended to make. If Mr. Oakes can't join us today, we apologize to those of you who signed up for the session hoping to meet him or get a book signed."

Hudson turned to his teacher. "This totally sucks. We've been watching this crazy ass dude's commentaries for weeks, and now he's a no show."

"Look at it this way, Hudson," Brendan tried to help him reframe things. "You've missed a day of school, you've gotten to run around a world class resort with your friends, and you've had a free spa treatment."

"True," the boy considered.

Brendan studied his student curiously. "Sometime you'll have to explain the benefits of eyebrow waxing to me."

Hudson gave him a thumbs up, and they settled back in their seats for whatever came next.

Chapter 3 Frozen Stiff

Twenty-four hours later, on Friday afternoon, Shanice Waters visited the walk-in freezer on the hotel's loading dock to take a few more pictures of her butterfly. Ice carving was one her culinary apprenticeship's requirements, and even though she was a Brooklyn girl who had never touched a chainsaw, a chisel or a torch in her life before she arrived in West Virginia, she'd quickly picked up the basics. Her first major effort, a 250-pound butterfly perched on a leaf, was scheduled to grace a wedding reception in the Cameo Ballroom on Saturday.

Joey Russo, one of the other apprentices, had noticed that "ice" was part of her name and he'd started calling her Shan-*ice*. She didn't mind; she liked to think it reflected her cool-headedness. Besides, Joey was cute in that curly-headed Italian boy sort of way, so she let him get away with shit she wouldn't take from the others.

Her cool-headedness was put to the test when she opened the freezer and saw a man's body sprawled on the floor next to a fancy-looking wheelchair, a leather tote bag and some scattered papers. She bent over and poked him ever-so gingerly. He felt like a frozen slab of beef. Horrified, she backed out quickly without noticing her masterpiece in icy shards on the floor. She fumbled for her phone and speed-dialed the first person she could think of, Ben Curry, the Executive Chef.

Chef Curry was in the main kitchen, sampling a lobster bisque on the evening menu. He glanced at his phone and took the call. "Yes, Shanice?"

"We've got a BIG problem, Chef. There's a dead man in the freezer."

"What?"

"There's a dead man in the freezer," she repeated, hardly believing her own words as she struggled to keep her cool.

"Which freezer?"

"The one with the ice sculptures."

There was a pregnant pause as the chef tried to wrap his head around this. "Are you sure he's dead?"

"He's frozen stiff and he's not moving or breathing."

"Don't touch anything, Shanice. Stay put. I'll call Security."

"I'm not touching anything! There's a wheelchair, too, Chef. One of those electric ones."

"Where?"

"In the freezer with the man!"

"I'm on my way."

As he dashed off, he turned back to his saucier. "More sherry, Raoul," he called over his shoulder.

Chapter 4 The Wolfe Pack

Twenty miles away, in the picturesque hills of northern Greenbrier County, *New York Times* reporter Zac Wolfe was polishing off dinner at his parents' farm, the 160 rolling acres where he'd grown up mending fences, baling hay, driving tractors and chasing stray cattle. He'd lived in New York City for nearly 15 years now, but his wife Abby had recently returned to Lewisburg, the Greenbrier County seat, to care for her mother, Annie, who had Alzheimer's. Their 12-year-old son Connor had opted to make the move with his mother. They were hoping this long-distance arrangement was temporary, until they could figure out some better way to deal with the situation.

Zac was spending a few days in West Virginia with his wife and son. He'd brought Connor up to the farm for the weekend to give him some quality time with his paternal grandparents, who were pushing 70 but hale and hearty. Connor had grown up used to the rhythms of city life in New York, and he was a little dubious about this whole farming thing.

"Can we go to a movie tonight?" he asked his father.

Zac glanced up from the cornbread he was using to sop up what was left of his brown beans. "Depends on the movie."

"Are you too old for the new Spider-Man? It's at the Cinema Eight."

"Who's ever too old for the Marvel Universe?" Zac replied.

"Me," Jordan Wolfe said.

Connor turned to his grandfather. "Grandma's old as you are, Grandpa, and she likes Spider-Man," he pointed out. "Don't you, Grandma?"

"I love Toby Maguire," his grandmother Debbie said.

The boy made a face. "He was a few Spider-Mans ago. Toby Maguire's like a senior citizen now."

"You have something against senior citizens, Connor?" his grandmother teased him.

"Not really." He turned back to his father to press his case. "We should do something fun tonight," he said.

"You don't think hanging out at your grandparents' farm is fun?"

"E-I-E-I-O," the boy replied unenthusiastically.

"The apple doesn't fall far from the tree," his grandfather observed.

"I like farming, Dad," Zac insisted. "I just like journalism better."

"You like people better than cows," Connor interpreted.

"Most of the time." Zac felt his phone vibrating. He glanced at it and saw he was getting a call from Buzzy Adams, the Director of Security at The Greenbrier. Buzzy was one of the few high school buddies he'd kept up with over the years. He'd never understood how the class's most dedicated party animal had ended up as the resort's top cop.

"Hey, Buzzy."

"Hey, Zac-Man. You in New York?"

"No, I'm at the farm in Frankford. Connor and I are spending the weekend here."

"Good timing, bro."

"Why's that?"

"We've had a celebrity murder at the hotel."

"Seriously?"

"Have you ever heard of Mordecai Oakes?"

The name didn't ring a bell. "Can't say I have."

"He's a commentator for Fox News. Well, he was."

"I only watch Fox for sports, Buzzy. I love their sports coverage, but I can't take their news division. They're factually unreliable."

"Oakes was their point man for climate change denial," Buzzy elaborated. "Someone stuck him in one of our walk-in freezers."

"Holy shit."

"We've got it on the security footage. It was either one of our bellmen or somebody dressed like one, but you didn't hear that from me. This place is crawling with law enforcement. They haven't alerted the media yet. They're waiting for his son to get here and make a positive ID and notify the family."

"Doesn't Fox know about it?"

"Not yet. The word's spreading like wildfire with our staff, so it's probably just a matter of time. One of the culinary apprentices found him in the freezer this afternoon. He was supposed to headline a debate on climate change in Colonial Hall yesterday, and he didn't show up for it. We're sure it's Oakes. He was a paraplegic, and his wheelchair and debate notes were in the freezer with him."

"Are you telling me I'm the only journalist who knows about this?"

"At the moment. Thought I'd give you a heads up."

"This is going to be huge, Buzzy. Can I access the crime scene?"

"I can get you close, but I can't promise you access. Bring your media credentials and your charm. You'll need both if you're going to try to talk your way past the yellow tape. Meet me in front of the medical clinic and we'll slip in a back way so you won't have to deal with security at the main gate."

"I'll be there in 45 minutes. Thanks."

Connor had been listening to his father's end of this conversation with growing dismay. "We're not going to the movie, are we?"

"I'm sorry, Connor, but something really big has come up. I've got to go over to The Greenbrier."

"What's the really big thing?"

"There's been a murder at the hotel. That's all I can tell you."

"That person's dead. I'm still living."

"We'll catch the movie tomorrow. I promise. This is my job."

"Your job sucks."

"Sometimes it does, but the world doesn't operate based our preferences. Get used to it, buddy."

Jordan Wolfe stepped in. "Connor, will you help me close up the hen house and put the tractor in the shed?" he requested.

"You're trying to make me forget about the movie, aren't you?"

He raised his hands in mock surrender. "You caught me red-handed, kiddo. Did it work?"

"No."

\+ \+ \+

The Greenbrier Clinic occupied a low hillside near the hotel. The medical facility looked like a stand-alone building, but it was connected to the hotel for the convenience of the guests who liked to sandwich annual physicals between time at the golf course and spa. Zac found Buzzy waiting there as promised. "I thought you'd be wearing a uniform, Buzzy," he said. "You actually look semi-respectable."

"The Director of Security gets to wear a suit and an ear piece and act like the Secret Service. It's just cosplay, but it makes people think I'm important."

"Are you armed and dangerous?"

"I could take you out in a heartbeat. But that's been true ever since kindergarten. Follow me."

They walked down the hill beside the clinic and surveyed the chaotic scene at the loading dock. The Greenbrier specialized in discretion, and this evening discretion meant that an ambulance and an array of vehicles from the State Police, the Greenbrier County Sheriff's Department and the White Sulphur Springs Police Department were parked near the delivery entrance, out of sight of the guests.

"Is the hotel full?" Zac asked.

"We were," Buzzy replied. "We were hosting the American Meteorological Association. The convention was over this morning and they're all gone, except Mr. Oakes, who will be departing shortly. Well, I guess technically he's already departed. By the way, I saw your brother-in-law standing outside Colonial Hall with some of his students yesterday. They were going to the debate."

"Brendan loves field trips. He's an outdoorsy guy. He hates being stuck in a classroom even worse than the kids do."

"Wait until they hear why their speaker didn't show up."

"Do you realize how much homework you're giving me, Buzzy? I've never heard of Mordecai Oakes. Now I've got to pull an all-nighter researching him and cobbling together a story."

"I guarantee you'll hate everything about him."

"Why?"

"You're a Libtard."

"Unlike you, I've evolved beyond my redneck roots. I'm surprised you're letting the *Times* break the story."

"I'm not letting the *Times* break it. I'm letting my bro Zac."

"I appreciate that."

"We're bracing for a media shitstorm. If something interesting develops, I'll try to make sure you hear about it first."

"I appreciate that, man. This is too late for the print edition, but they'll run it online as soon as I submit it. More people read the paper online anyway. I'll have to come up with something more substantial for Sunday."

"Think it'll make the front page?"

"Definitely. You don't find dead TV personalities in hotel freezers every day.

Chapter 5 A Helpful Encounter

The West Virginia State Police had cordoned off the crime scene, and, despite Zac's best efforts, they wouldn't let him past the tape. The Criminal Investigation Unit's lead investigator, Sergeant Wendy Lavender, had shared what little they knew with him. What she didn't bother to mention was some key information Buzzy had already shared: a security camera had recorded the perpetrator wheeling his victim into the freezer. Zac knew he couldn't publish this quite yet without blowing his friend's cover. Buzzy was a valuable inside source, and protecting his source was a priority.

Soon satellite trucks from up and down the East Coast would be beating frenzied paths to White Sulphur Springs, West Virginia. Zac enjoyed some advantages the other media hounds didn't have: his friend Buzzy, and having grown up in the community. His sister Greta and some of his former high school classmates worked at the resort. They ran departments, parked cars, prepared elaborate meals and crafted multimillion-dollar vacation homes for The Greenbrier Sporting Club's well-heeled members. Sure, the victim's Fox News colleagues had known him personally, but he had a backstage pass to this sprawling complex that ran like its own small city.

He couldn't get anywhere near the freezer, but his consolation prize was an encounter with Oakes' 24-year-old son, Oliver. Surprisingly, the young man was a whitewater rafting guide at Adventures on the Gorge in neighboring Fayette County. Sgt. Lavender had alerted him to Oliver's presence, pointing to a lanky, bearded, distraught-looking young man pacing the hallway. He was wearing what looked like his rafting outfit - shorts, sandals and a neon green Patagonia t-shirt. Zac approached him and offered his condolences. River rats weren't usually teetotalers, and he asked Mordecai's son if he could use a drink. His hunch played out, and they headed to the Lobby Bar, a clubby-looking setting where burnished wood and earth tones replaced the hotel's omnipresent lime greens, pineapple yellows and tomato reds.

Oliver eyed the bar's other patrons. "I think I'm violating the dress code."

"Given the circumstances, I'm pretty sure they'll forgive you," Zac said.

A server appeared. "What's your pleasure, gentlemen?"

"Smooth Ambler Contradiction, on the rocks," Oliver requested the local bourbon. "Make it a double."

"And for you, sir?"

"I'll take a Mojito." Hemingway's favorite was Zac's usual drink, and one was his self-imposed limit when he was working. He'd learned the hard way that alcohol in general, and rum in particular, failed to improve his writing, even if it had worked wonders for Papa Hemingway.

"How much of this conversation is going to end up in the paper?" Oliver asked pointedly. "Look, man, I'm a nervous wreck. If I say something stupid, I don't want everyone on earth reading it."

"I'll only use what you tell me I can," Zac promised. "I'd rather get to know you and feel like I can call on you when I need information. I talked with my editor. I'm going to be here for a while, following this investigation while the police work on it. I live in New York but I grew up here. I happened to be around this weekend, visiting my family. My wife's mother has Alzheimer's, and Abby and our son Connor moved back here last September to take care of her. I feel like I've abandoned them to pursue fame and fortune in the big city, but it's just a temporary arrangement."

"Yeah, well, if you want to know about being abandoned for fame and fortune in the big city, I'm your guy."

"When's the last time you saw your dad, Oliver?"

"Wednesday, believe it or not. I hadn't seen him for months, and then he called out of the blue and said he'd signed up for some big debate at The Greenbrier so he'd have an excuse to get together with me. I came over here and we had steaks at Prime 44. He wanted to let me know he'd drawn up a new will and named me his executor."

"Does your family know about your father's death?"

"His fiancée's the only one who knows so far. She doesn't exactly have the best relationship with the rest of us. The police are counting on me to let the rest of the family know before they hear it on the news. I should be making calls instead of sitting here with you."

"His fiancée?"

He rolled his eyes. "Calista Martin. She's 26. Dad was 53. She's a cross between a caregiver, a housekeeper and a hooker. They were getting married next month."

"Not your ideal stepmother?"

"Not my ideal anything. I've never trusted her. When they couldn't find him at the hotel, they called her this morning in New York and asked if she'd heard from him. She hadn't, and she called me, freaking out. I mean, I get it. People in wheelchairs don't usually pull disappearing acts, and Dad loved an audience way too much to miss a chance to grandstand. When they found him this afternoon and told her, she went hysterical."

"I think if they found me in a hotel freezer my wife would be hysterical, too," Zac tried to imagine it.

Their drinks arrived. Oliver grabbed his bourbon and tossed down most of it in a gulp. "Man, I can't believe this. I mean, he was perfectly fine two days ago."

"Were you and your father close?" Zac asked.

His sigh spoke volumes. "Not really. We had issues. His Fuck the Environmentalists crusade didn't help anything. We argued about it every time we were together. Dad was a scientific thinker. He had a degree in meteorology, for Chrissake. I can't believe he bought all the crap he was spewing on TV, but he wasn't going to admit it. I think his goal was getting rich, and he'd found a way to do it. When he went to work at Fox, he reinvented himself for that crowd, if you know what I mean."

"Folks who want their conservative beliefs reinforced?"

"Or their paranoia. He wasn't all that popular until the hit-and-run turned him into a tragic figure. His wheelchair became his pulpit. He was still the same opinionated blowhard, but all of a sudden he had a fan base and book deals. Have you seen his new one, *Apocalypse Postponed*?"

"I haven't seen any of his books," Zac admitted. "I'll probably skim them online before I write this story."

"He's in his wheelchair on the cover! I mean, they could have used a headshot or a graphic or something, but he knew how to milk the disability bit. Dad was all about the Benjamins."

"His online bios are pretty skimpy. Can you tell me more about your family?"

"I can tell you why the bios are skimpy, but I don't want all this stuff in the paper."

"Just let me know what you don't want me to use."

"Dad and Mom grew up in Indiana and they met when they were working at a station in Indianapolis. Mom was the news anchor and Dad was the weatherman. My sister Layla and I were born there. She's three years younger than me. Dad was always chasing better jobs in bigger markets and we bounced around from place to place. Mom just wanted to settle down and have a more normal family life, but Dad was restless. Finally, eight years ago, he landed his gig with Fox News in New York."

"I read that your mother died six years ago."

Oliver shifted uncomfortably in his chair. "I don't know if we should be talking about this," he voiced his misgivings. "I definitely don't want it in the paper."

"Okay, it won't be."

His eyes narrowed. "How much can I trust you?"

"A hundred percent."

He fortified himself with another swig. "Mom committed suicide. She filled the bathtub in our apartment with warm water, slit her wrists and bled out. Layla came home from school and found her. I was a senior in high school and Layla was a freshman when it happened."

Zac was momentarily speechless. "I didn't know that, Oliver," he said quietly. "I'm sorry."

"Now you know why there's not a lot of stuff about the family online. Mom was smart, she was talented, she was beautiful. Back in the day, when they were working together, she was more popular than Dad and she made more money. He couldn't handle the fact that she was so much better than him in every way. They argued all the time and she was unhappy. His version is she was mentally unstable. If she was, it was because she was married to a self-centered asshole who drove her over the edge."

"Strong words."

"Strong feelings. He told us she killed herself because she had some kind of cancer, but we never really bought it."

"How's your sister?"

"Layla's messed up on drugs. She's been to rehab three times."

"Where is she now?"

"New York, with her wannabe actor boyfriend, Declan. She was always hitting Dad up for money. When he realized what she was spending it on, he stopped giving it to her. They got so hard up they rode the Amtrak here last month to bum money off me so they could cover their rent. I mean, I love my sister, but she's a fuckin' mess."

"How'd you end up in West Virginia?"

"I had to get away from the drama. I went to Dickinson College in Pennsylvania, then I moved here. None of my friends know I'm related to the dude on Fox. Fortunately, he couldn't make it to my graduation. It would have totally blown my cover."

"You can always move to Costa Rica."

"Yeah, I might have to."

"Did you grow up with money?" Zac asked him.

"Are you kidding? Local TV people don't make shit. Dad just started raking it in the past few years, after his accident. When he told me about his new will, he said he was worth four million, counting the equity in his co-op on the

Upper East Side. Fox didn't pay him all that great, but it gave him a lot of exposure. Most of his money came from his book advances and royalties, and his speaking gigs. He got 500K from Mom's life insurance. He used it to make the down payment on his co-op on the Upper East Side and pay for my college."

"If there were such hard feelings between you and your dad, why would he make you his executor?" Zac dug a little deeper.

"Good question," he said. "I wondered the same thing. I think I got the honor by default. He hated lawyers and he didn't have friends like normal people do. He said his old will left everything to Layla and me. The new one supposedly leaves half to Calista and the other half to us, with Layla's part in a trust so she can't blow it."

"Does Calista know about the will?"

"She knows he was updating it and he was meeting with me about it, but I don't think she knows the specifics. I only know what he told me. He gave me a copy in an envelope, but I haven't opened it. I didn't have any reason to. Guess I'd better read it."

"Does Layla know?"

"Definitely not. She would have called me to bitch about Calista getting half. We're not exactly besties with her."

Zac saw trouble brewing for Oliver and Layla and their 26-year-old almost-stepmother. Homicide investigators like to follow the money. Even if they were as innocent as lambs, they were potential suspects. He had plenty more he wanted to ask this young man, but he decided he'd better give him some space so he could make his phone calls. He motioned for the check and stood up. "I appreciate your time, Oliver. If you don't mind, I'd like to stay in touch. This first piece I'm writing will just cover the basics about your father's death. I'll have a more detailed follow-up story on Sunday. I'd like to call you for more information if I can."

"I'll probably be on the phone all night with relatives, and then I'm going into hiding for a couple of days," Oliver let him know. "I'm scheduled for rafting trips this weekend, so reporters won't be able to reach me unless they chase me in kayaks. But you seem okay. I'll give you my number. Text me a link to your article, and I'll read it. If I'm okay with it, I'll keep in touch."

"As the next of kin, don't you and your sister have to make the funeral arrangements?"

"Yeah, but since it was a homicide the state medical examiner in Charleston has to do an autopsy. Seems kind of pointless since they know how he died, but I guess it's the law or something. I don't see us having some big memorial service. Dad was a public figure, but Layla and I are pretty private. We'll probably just have him cremated and scatter his ashes on a melting glacier in Greenland."

"Nice."

The young man's expression changed. "I just thought of something else he said on Wednesday. I took him back up to his room and when I was leaving, he said, 'I know you and Layla don't think much of your old man, but I'm going to do something that'll make you proud of me.' I don't have a clue what he was talking about. I guess I never will."

"You think he was talking about your inheritance?"

"No. We'd finished talking about that. He seemed like he was talking about something else."

"Interesting," Zac reacted. "Before you go, I have one more question." He hesitated, but as a reporter he had to ask. "Can you think of anyone who might have had a reason to want to kill your father?"

"You mean besides Calista, Layla, me, all of Mom's relatives and everyone in the Meteorological Association and environmental community? No, not really."

Chapter 6 Speaking of Irony

Through several layers of sleep Zac heard his phone ringing. He groped across the bedside table, cracked an eyelid and saw his brother-in-law was calling. He was pretty sure he knew why.

"Hey, Brendan," he croaked. "Do we have to talk now?"

"Yes, Zac, we do. I was peacefully going about my Saturday morning routine. I fixed a mug of coffee and crawled back in bed with my iPad to read the news. The first thing I saw was your story about the guy I took my students to see on Thursday. He was murdered at the hotel!"

"Yeah, I heard you were there."

"Where'd you hear that?"

"Buzzy saw you. Does Greta know about it?"

"We're on speakerphone, Zac," his sister made her presence known. "I want to know how my brother in New York knows more about what's going on at my workplace than I do."

"Because I'm not in New York, I'm here. I picked up Connor and brought him to the farm for the weekend to visit with Mom and Dad. Then Buzzy called and this thing landed in my lap. I was at the hotel until midnight, and then I worked on the story into the wee hours. If I sound flaky, I've had three hours sleep."

"You don't sound any flakier than usual," Brendan assured him.

"Do they know who killed him?" Greta asked.

"Nope. They were loading him in the ambulance when I got there. This thing is going to get barrels of ink and hours of air time, but right now all they have is a stiff in a freezer. It's what we call a developing story, which means we'll run a lot of filler about him while law enforcement tries to sort it out."

"I'm sorry poor Mr. Oakes suffered an agonizing death," Brendan offered, "but as an Environmental Studies teacher I'm not going into deep mourning."

"I'd never heard of the guy until yesterday," Zac admitted.

"Count your blessings. He was a shill for the fossil fuel industry."

"So I gather," Zac said. "He was preaching to the choir on Fox."

"I teach kids who think climate change is the most important issue of our times, and I happen to agree. I took them to the debate so they'd realize there really are people who turn a blind eye to all the science. I wanted them to see what they're up against. Oakes had a following because he was entertaining, but he shoveled all the usual bullshit. *The greenhouse effect is just an unproven theory. What we're seeing is a natural cycle that's been going on for centuries. Even if the world seems like it's getting a little warmer, it's only temporary and nothing to worry about. We can't even predict the weather for the next few days but all these climate alarmists think they can predict it for decades to come. Yada, yada, yada.* But he had some good one-liners, I'll give him that. You don't see a lot of folks in wheelchairs on TV, so he had that going for him."

"His son Oliver is a rafting guide in Fayette County," Zac said.

"You're shitting me."

"Nope. I met him last night. Seems like a nice guy. He doesn't think his father was a true believer. He thinks he was an opportunist who adopted his environmental views when he realized he could cash in on them."

"He was probably getting kickbacks from the oil and coal barons," Brendan speculated.

"On the contrary, Oliver said most of his dad's money came from his book sales and speaking gigs."

"Maybe, but I'll bet the fossil fuel lords were his biggest fanboys."

"Did you take Connor to the hotel with you?" his sister asked.

"No, I left Connor at the farm with Mom and Dad. He wanted to go to a movie, but this little murder got in the way."

"So you came here to spend the weekend with your family, and you went off and did your journalist thing?"

"Greta, please. It's my job. You make it sound like I'm engaging in some kind of criminal activity."

"Connor's a great kid, Zac. He deserves more quality time his father."

"As much as I hate to get lectures about child rearing from my childless sister, I totally agree. That's one reason I've arranged with my editor to stay here and work on this story. I'm going back to the hotel today because I promised her a follow-up for Sunday. I can take Connor along, but I'm afraid he's going to be bored to death. Is there something we can arrange to occupy him at the hotel while I'm 'doing my thing', as you so eloquently put it?"

She gave it some thought. "What about falconry?"

"What's that involve?"

"Riding a bus from the Greenbrier Outfitters shop to the site. They give you a history of hunting with birds of prey, and then a live demonstration. They even let you put on a glove and hold the birds. They've got falcons, hawks, eagles and owls. I've never done it, but the guests always come back raving about it."

"Connor watches Animal Planet, so this might be right up his alley. Since I can't go with him, can he bring a friend?"

"They don't let unaccompanied children do this, Zac."

"What about his favorite aunt? Can you take him?"

"It's expensive."

"Can't you just arrange it with your friends at the hotel?"

"I don't own The Greenbrier, brother dear, I just work there. Brendan had me 'arrange' lunch and entertainment for his students on Thursday. I can't keep begging for freebies. I can get away with it once a year, not once a week."

"Okay, I'll pay for you and Connor."

"Really?"

"Really."

"Aren't you going to ask how much it costs?"

"No, because then I'll change my mind. Is it in the morning or afternoon?"

"Either one. Your choice."

"Going back to sleep is probably a lost cause, so we might as well do it this morning."

"Fine. I'll meet you in the lobby at 10:30. Bring your best credit card."

"Thanks, Greta. You'll always be my favorite sister."

As he stretched out in bed, Zac realized he wasn't going to have any trouble falling back into the arms of Morpheus. He was about to ask Siri for a wake-up call when his phone rang again. This time it was Buzzy.

"Hey."

"The circus is rolling into town," his friend reported. "Satellite dishes are blooming like sunflowers in Kansas. Just the B teams so far. The A teams are still on their way from the major cities."

"I don't want to join the circus, Buzzy. I just want to talk with Sgt. Lavender again, and maybe the apprentice who found Mr. Oakes in the freezer."

"I can do you one better. Wendy's coming to my office at 11:15 to review the security footage. Want to sit in?"

"*Wendy*, huh?"

"She told me to call her that. I detect a certain chemistry."

"Earth to Buzzy. Just because a woman tells you her name, it doesn't mean she has the hots for you."

"We'll see about that."

"She won't mind if I turn your little private rendezvous into a ménage à trois?"

"It's not her footage, it's the hotel's," Buzzy reminded him. "She'll probably seize it for evidence, but right now it's on a thumb drive in my office."

"Don't give it to her before I get a chance see it."

"You mean before your competitors know it exists?"

"Exactly."

"I like your killer instincts, Zac-Man."

"I'd rather play offense than defense."

"I find you highly offensive."

"Thanks, Buzzy. That's the nicest thing you've ever said to me."

\+ + +

Zac and Connor were on route to the hotel in Zac's Jeep. Connor had reacted favorably to a close encounter with birds of prey, and Zac wished he could accompany him, but the situation was what it was.

"Dad, why did you become a writer?" his son asked out of the blue.

"I'm a journalist, Connor."

"Yeah, I know, but why did you become one?"

"I've always been an observer by nature and I'm fascinated by irony. Do you know what irony is?"

"No."

"What kind of English student are you?" he teased him.

"One that hasn't had irony yet."

"Irony's when you expect something to happen and the opposite does. Or when you say one thing and you do another."

"Like when you cuss me out for swearing?"

"Exactly. The world is full of irony, and for some reason I've always noticed it. I can tell you something ironic that happened when you were three years old. I call it The Parable of the Nun and the Bartender."

"Tell me."

"It happened when I was in grad school at Columbia. Mom heard about a food festival in Little Italy and we decided to check it out. As soon we got there you announced that you needed to go to the potty, but there didn't seem to be any potties around. You were getting desperate and Mom saw a convent, where Catholic nuns lived. She knocked on the door and a wrinkled old nun who looked like a creature in a horror movie answered it. Mom explained our predicament and she asked the woman in her sweetest voice if you could use their bathroom. The nun seemed shocked that we would dare to even ask such a thing. She scowled and said, 'This is a private residence!' She literally slammed the door in our faces. We walked up the street and we came to a bar that wasn't open yet. We could see a guy mopping in back and Mom knocked on the window to get his attention. She explained the situation and he let us in to use the restroom. So, who was the Christian – the nun or the bartender?"

"The bartender."

"Exactly. That's irony. The world's full of it."

"I get it, but what does that have to do with writing?"

"For some reason I've always been tuned in to it. When I had writing assignments in high school, I always used it. The teachers thought I was a good writer and I ended up editor of the school paper. When I went to WVU, I started out as an English major, but all we did was read novels and short stories and talk about them and I was bored shitless. I wanted something more active. I switched to journalism so I could run around and talk to people. The summer between my junior and senior years I interned with an investigative reporter at the Charleston Gazette and that sold me on it. He wrote a nice letter that got me into Columbia, where he'd gone. And that's how your old man ended up in the journalism game."

"Do you ever think about quitting your job so you can live here?"

"I don't know what I'd do here. *The New York Times* is a world-class paper and I'm lucky to work there. Millions of people read the *Times* every day. I love my job. What would I do in West Virginia?"

"Run the farm. Grandpa and Grandma can't keep doing it forever. Uncle Brendan's not going to quit teaching and Aunt Greta's not going to leave The Greenbrier to raise cows."

Zac let out a sigh. "Do we have to talk about me, Connor? Let's talk about you."

"That's ironic."

"What?"

"You're a journalist, but you don't like people asking you questions."

"Touché."

"What does that mean?"

"It means you're a little shit."

The boy sat back with a contented grin.

Chapter 7 Video Date

Weekdays at The Greenbrier meant meetings and conventions. Weekends brought couples, families and wedding parties. This particular weekend the guests arrived in high spirits, only to find a chaotic scene. Camera crews dotted the front circle, and reporters were taping breathless descriptions of the horrific goings-on at "America's Resort". Zac and Connor made their way on foot around the circle, catching bits and pieces of their dispatches.

"… shocking homicide at this 200-year-old luxury resort known for its Southern charm …"

"… since its inception more than two centuries ago as a mineral spring where guests came to 'take the waters' …"

"… found lifeless in a walk-in freezer at this historic retreat that has hosted presidents, celebrities and royalty …"

"… popular television personality and author known for his controversial environmental views …"

"… the perpetrator and motive are still unknown …"

Zac had spent part of his working life wading knee-deep into media frenzies, but this was a first for Connor, who stared in wide-eyed wonder. "The man who died was well-known," his father explained. "He had a strange death in a glamorous place where murders don't usually happen. That's why there are so many reporters. Or to put it in Animal Planet language, you're seeing a pack of hungry wolves feeding on a carcass."

"That's gross, Dad," the boy reacted. "But aren't you kind of doing the same thing?"

Zac shot him a dirty look.

He shrugged. “Maybe you shouldn’t have told me about irony.”

\+ + +

Sergeant Wendy Lavender was perched like an owl on a stool in front of the computer screen in Buzzy’s office, waiting to scrutinize the security footage the resort’s tech department had cobbled together. She seemed mildly irritated that a representative from the nation's preeminent newspaper was perched on a stool beside her. “I think criminal investigations should proceed discretely,” she said to Zac. “Publicizing the existence of this video could work against us.”

Buzzy swiveled in his chair and faced her. “All the people who work here know we have security cameras, Wendy. That's a lot of people. It’s no secret there’s one on the loading dock. The person who committed this crime obviously knew we had cameras, too, because he managed to avoid all of them except that one.”

“If he was aware there was surveillance, why would he leave this kind of evidence?” the sergeant puzzled. “Even the clueless idiots who rob convenience stores know enough to wear ski masks or shoot out the cameras.”

“You’ll get a better idea when you see it,” Buzzy promised. He pushed the play button and offered a running commentary. “He’s wearing our standard bellman’s uniform. The jacket comes in long and short sleeve versions and he’s wearing the short sleeve model. You'll notice he's also wearing disposable black gloves. Disposable gloves have been an option for the bellmen ever since the pandemic, but most of them don’t wear them. He's obviously aware of the camera because he keeps his back to it most of the time. When he turns toward it, he lowers his head so you can't see his face.

“They’re having quite a conversation,” Zac noticed as the video showed a rear view of the bellman chatting it up with his intended victim. He leaned in closer. “It looks like Oakes took something from his coat pocket and gave it to him. Can we zoom in on it?”

“I can't,” Buzzy replied. “I'll see if our techies can.”

The sergeant squinted at the monitor. “We need a better view of his face.”

“Spoiler alert,” Buzzy broke her the news. “We don't get one.”

“Do you know all your bellmen?” she asked. “Would you recognize someone who isn’t on your staff?”

“Not really,” Buzzy confessed. “That's not my department. I don’t have a clue how many bellmen we have.”

“I’d like to question all of them on Monday,” she decided. “Can you round them up and set up interviews at 10-minute intervals starting at 9:00 o'clock?”

“Will do,” Buzzy said. “You sure ten minutes is long enough?”

“Long enough to flag the ones I might want to question at greater length.”

He gave her a thumbs up. “We’ll find an office you can use.”

Zac was jotting observations in his ever-present notebook. “He’s Caucasian. He looks about average height. From the way he moves, I'd say he's on the younger side, but that's hard to tell because people move differently. The jacket hides a lot, but it looks like he has a slender-to-medium build. He has blond hair, sort of longish like he needs a haircut, but I'll bet it's a wig.”

“*He* could be a *she*,” the sergeant suggested.

“Not to be politically incorrect or anything, but *she* walks an awful lot like a *he*,” Buzzy begged to differ. “I'm no expert, but I've had a few wives and girlfriends.”

They watched as the bellman escorted Oakes into the refrigerated room on the left side of the dock. They emerged a minute later, still chatting away as they crossed over to the freezer on the opposite side. The bellman opened the door with his left hand and pointed with his right, indicating the sculptures inside. They had a brief exchange, and then the bellman escorted his victim into the walk-in. He exited in short order, closed the door and gave the handle a tug to make sure it was secure. He slipped something into his pocket and hurried back into the building with his head bowed to avoid looking at the camera. The time on the video showed 12:47 p.m.

The trio stared pensively at the bloodless murder scene.

"So what do we think, boys and girls?" Buzzy broke their silence.

"I think he spent a lot of time casing the place," the sergeant said. "He may not have been one of your bellmen, but he knew how to get a uniform. He knew where your cameras were located. He knew people's schedules well enough to take a chance that no one else would be there."

"My money says he's not one of our bellmen," Buzzy was convinced. "It would be a slam dunk to identify one of our folks. Eliminate everyone who isn't white. Eliminate everyone who's too short or too tall or too heavy. Eliminate everyone who can prove they were somewhere else. But that's not to say he didn't work here at some point in the past. I'll have the bell captain take a look at the video and see what he thinks. James has been here for three decades."

"You've got to give the guy points for ingenuity," Zac said. "If anyone had happened on the scene, he could have aborted his mission, shown Oakes the ice sculptures and taken him on to his debate. He didn't leave any fingerprints or bloodstains, or probably any DNA, and he didn't use a weapon. If Oakes had been able to scribble an accusatory note, all he could have written was, 'The bellman did it', which we already know. Except he probably wasn't a bellman. The whole thing was well thought out."

"Oakes' cell phone is missing," the sergeant informed them. "It wasn't in the freezer and it wasn't in his room. That's probably what the bellman was slipping in his pocket when he left the scene."

"He didn't want his victim to be able to call for help or use the flashlight to get his bearings," Buzzy suggested. "Did you put a tracer on it?"

"Yes. Nothing turned up." She raised her hands in mock defeat. "All the things we usually rely on – fingerprints, ballistics, blood splatter, wounds, toxicology – are non-factors. We might find a few stray hairs, but they could be from a wig, or the victim, or the kitchen workers who use the freezer."

Zac decided to elaborate on his involvement for the sergeant's benefit. "I'm covering this because I grew up in

Greenbrier County and I happened to be here this weekend," he explained. "Homicides aren't my usual beat. I write human interest features, longer pieces that read more like magazine articles, but since I'm already here my editor's given me the green light to pursue it. This lends itself to the kind of longer format I usually work in. It's got a lot of interesting angles."

"Such as?"

He ticked them off on his fingers. "Oakes' environmental views, his association with Fox News, the fact that he was previously the victim of a hit-and-run. Then you've got The Greenbrier, which is an exceptionally posh setting for murder, and the death-by-freezing angle, which could be some kind of environmental statement. This isn't a run-of-the-mill crime of passion. Someone put a lot of thought into it. It's made to order for my kind of journalism. There's only one problem."

"What's that?" the sergeant asked.

"Good stories need beginnings, middles and endings. All I've got so far is the beginning."

"We'll see what we can do about finding you a middle and an ending," she promised.

"Thanks. I'll have to update the *Times* with any breaking news, but I won't be able to write the more definitive piece I'd like to write until there's some kind of resolution." He gave her his card. "I'd appreciate it if you'd call or text me if you run across anything you think I should know. I might even be able to help you. When it comes to interviewing people, I have some advantages over the police. I don't interrogate, I chat. Sometimes you get more information that way."

The sergeant accepted his card. "We don't play favorites," she ignored his charm offensive. "We're not going to tell the *Times* something we're not telling everyone else."

"Then I guess I'll have to conduct my own investigation," he decided. "Homicides aren't my thing, but I have a lot of experience asking people nosy questions. How much can I publish about what we just saw on the tape?"

"Can't you just say the West Virginia State Police Criminal Investigation Unit is in the process of analyzing the security footage?" she asked. "I'd prefer it if the bellmen don't know the specifics before I question them. When I finish my interviews with them, you can publish away. I've got a press briefing this afternoon and I'm not planning to mention the footage. If someone knows about it and brings it up, I'll say we're still reviewing it and we're not in a position to comment on it yet."

"Will I miss anything if I skip your briefing?" Zac asked her.

"A bunch of obnoxious people trying to out-yell each other."

"Surely you're not talking about my colleagues in the fourth estate?"

"I am, and don't call me Shirley," she couldn't resist the openintg. "In fact, call me Wendy. I'm not big on formalities."

Zac shot Buzzy a sidelong glance. "Works for me. I've always hated having to address someone as Your Excellency or Your Honor when behind the fancy titles we're the same pathetic human beings."

"You're full of radical ideas, Wolfe," Buzzy said.

"Radical ideas like equality, like the Founding Fathers envisioned?"

The sergeant smiled. "If they really were serious, we would have had Founding Mothers, too."

"My ex-wives would agree," Buzzy said. "For some reason I keep marrying militant feminists."

"Maybe they just turn militant when they have to deal with you," Zac suggested.

"I haven't even had a starter spouse yet," Wendy confessed. "This job keeps me too busy for much of a home life, and I don't want to be anyone's absentee wife or mother."

"Living with a police investigator wouldn't work well for a lot of guys," Buzzy tried to imagine it.

Zac slid off his stool. "While you two bemoan your love lives, this happily married man needs to go fetch his son."

Buzzy popped the drive from his computer and gave it to the Sergeant. "Zac asked me to give you this before his competitors get a chance to see it. He's not as dumb as he looks."

She accepted the drive. “It’s going to be interesting dealing with you two gentlemen.”

Zac looked at Buzzy. “Did you hear that? She called us gentlemen.”

“Yeah, I noticed,” Buzzy replied. “Obviously we can’t trust her judgment.”

\+ \+ \+

Fifteen minutes later Zac was standing at the hotel's candy shop counter, listening to Connor and Greta recap their falconry experience while he texted their whereabouts to his wife and parents.

Connor eyed his father's text. “Why do you use capitals and periods? No one does that.”

“Just another one of my bad habits, Connor,” he said. He turned to his sister. “Thanks for suggesting the falconry. I owe you one.”

“You owe me, too,” Connor reminded him. “Remember the Spider-Man movie?”

“There’s a word for your approach to dealing with your parents, Connor. It’s called badgering.”

“Why is it called badgering?”

“I have no idea, but you're very good at it.”

Chapter 8 Toasting a Murderer

On Sunday evening, as Zac and Connor returned to Lewisburg from the farm, Zac was thinking about Wendy Lavender's statement about not wanting to be an absentee spouse or parent, which was what he happened to be these days. His wife and son were happily ensconced in this picturesque, artsy little town while he was missing in action.

A few months earlier they were just as happily ensconced in their apartment in Astoria when Abby's father had died of a coronary embolism. As her mother tried to adjust to widowhood there were impossible-to-ignore signs of dementia. She was having trouble organizing meals and keeping track of her appointments and meds, and she kept confusing the TV remote with her cell phone. One day she walked into a neighbor's house, mistaking it for her own. After giving the situation a lot of thought, Abby had decided to quit her nursing job at Sloan Kettering and return to West Virginia to take care of her mother. Given the choice of accompanying his mother or remaining in New York with his father, Connor had opted to make the move to West Virginia. Now Abby was caring for her mother, catching up on her reading and singing with the Greenbrier Valley Chorale, while Connor navigated seventh grade and played Little League.

Zac had planned to join them twice a month, but he wasn't making the thousand mile round-trip as often as he'd imagined. To rescue things, either Abby needed to find another caregiver for her mother or he needed to find another job. Neither option sat well with them. They considered moving Abby's mother to New York, but she'd lived in the same house and town for decades, surrounded by her friends, and Abby thought the change would be too much for her. At least in Lewisburg she was somebody. And even if they had decided to move her to New York, their two-bedroom apartment was too small and they would have needed to find another one.

"Thanks for the falconry," Connor interrupted his father's musings as they pulled up in front of the house on Frazier Street.

"Glad you liked it, Connor. I've got a surprise for you next weekend, if it's okay with Mom."

"What is it?"

"If I told you, it wouldn't be a surprise."

"What if it's not okay with Mom?"

"Then you won't be disappointed since you don't know what it is."

"Tell me. I can handle disappointment. I get lots of practice."

Abby met them at the door. "Hey, guys. How was your weekend?"

"Eventful," Zac summed it up.

"I held a hawk," Connor reported.

His mother gave him a quizzical look.

"At the hotel," he explained. "Aunt Greta took me. The trainer held out food and it flew right past my face. I could feel the air from his wings. Then they let me put on a glove and hold him."

"Tell her the part you didn't like," Zac prompted him.

He made a face. "When we were coming back on the shuttle some lady said I looked like the boy in a movie called *Moonrise Kingdom*. Then she pulled up a picture of him on her phone and passed it around."

"That's what you get for looking like a movie star," his mother said.

"Yeah, a dorky one," he failed to see the compliment.

"It's your glasses and shaggy hair," Zac told him. "The good news is you're all set for Halloween. You just need to find a coonskin hat and a scout uniform."

"Great idea, Dad. I'll make my friends watch some crappy old movie and then I'll dress up like the guy in it so they can mock me."

"A) It's one of Wes Anderson's best movies, and B) you know I'm joking, right?"

He shrugged. "I can never tell if you're joking or just being stupid."

"I'm only stupid 7.8% of the time," Zac insisted.

Connor headed to his bedroom with the family's Bernedoodle, Rocky, in pursuit. Zac claimed a seat in the living room on the couch next to his mother-in-law, who was knitting. "Hello, Annie," he gave her a peck on the cheek.

"Well, hello there," she said pleasantly.

This sweet lady's social graces rarely failed, but he wondered if she knew who he was.

He watched her knit. "You're doing a nice job," he complimented her.

"Thank you, dear."

They'd seen a documentary about a country singer with Alzheimer's who could still play the guitar flawlessly, illustrating that as the disease progresses it affects regions of the brain differently. Obviously, the corner that controlled Annie Cooper's knitting ability was still magically intact.

"Do you have to get back to New York?" Abby asked him.

"We need to talk about that. Why don't we open a bottle of wine and sit out on the deck?"

They'd been an item ever since their junior year of high school, which had conveniently saved them years of agony playing the dating game. Given their long history, there was no doubt in their minds their relationship would survive their current awkward living arrangement.

They shared a fondness for wine and an aversion to drinking it from those oversized balloon glasses that struck them as cartoonish. They usually went for $15-$20 reds, but on special occasions they sprang for the higher end pinot noirs. They went in the kitchen and Zac opened the door of the pantry that doubled as their wine cellar and pulled out an $80 bottle of Merry Edwards pinot.

Abby eyed the pricey bottle. "Are we celebrating something I don't know about?"

“Possibly,” he said mischievously. He uncorked the bottle, grabbed two glasses and carried them out to the deck. They settled into chairs that overlooked the back yard and the neighboring estate that bordered it.

Abby pointed to the garden plot. “I'm planting Mom's vegetable garden this year, but I'm afraid it might be a losing proposition with all the deer that wander through,” she said. “Rocky manages to keep them at bay during the day, but we haven’t been able to convince him to stand sentinel at night.”

“You need an 8-foot fence,” Zac prescribed. “I can put one up.”

“When?”

“Soon. I take it you've heard about the murder at the hotel.”

“It's all people are talking about,” Abby said. “I read your articles yesterday and today.”

“Thanks to a tip from Buzzy, I'm the one who broke the story. As far as the *Times* is concerned, now I own it. I’ve arranged with my editor to hang around here and keep working on it.”

“For how long?”

“However long it takes.”

“Are we talking days, weeks or months?”

“Possibly.”

She smiled. “This cloud has a silver lining.”

“I'll be here this week, then I'll need to interview some folks in New York next week. After that I should be here most of the time, unless the story leads me elsewhere.”

“Well, well, well,” she said, raising her glass. “This feels like we're toasting the murderer, but whatever.”

“In other late breaking news, I’ve got the opportunity to take Connor white water rafting next weekend. I haven’t said anything to him because I wasn’t sure how you’d feel about it. Turns out Mordecai Oakes's son, Oliver, is a rafting guide in Fayette County.”

“I read that in your story,” Abby said.

“I met him Friday evening and I talked with him at length again on the phone yesterday. He’s an important source and I need to get to know him. He suggested going along on a rafting trip next Saturday on the Upper New River. He's got two slots open in an 8-person raft."

"How rapid are these rapids?"

"They're not for the faint-hearted, but we'll have life jackets and helmets. He controls the raft with oars. We just help out with paddling. I'm sure we'll be in good hands."

"I guess it's okay," she decided. "A couple of Connor's friends have kayaks and he's been asking about getting one."

"He should put in some time in his grandparents' hayfield to earn the money for it," Zac proposed.

"Bad idea," a voice said.

They turned and saw their son listening at his bedroom window.

"Are you eavesdropping?" Abby accused him.

"Yeah," he said with an impish grin. "I want to go rafting."

"You won't be going anywhere if you don't give us some privacy," Zac threatened him.

He retreated to the other side of his room and resumed a video game.

"This homicide is a major story," Zac continued. "Media outlets from all over the place are covering it. I'm lucky to have some connections the others don't."

"I have a request," Abby said. "While you're hanging around here, I'd like you to be more than the fun dad who takes his son on weekend adventures. I'd like you to share the parenting responsibilities, like helping with homework and going to teacher conferences and taking him to his ball practices."

"I'll share all the responsibilities, not just parenting," he promised. "I can cook and clean, too."

"I know you can, Zac. You used to do all those things before you started working at the *Times*. Once you went to work there, you were always chasing stories while I did everything else, in addition to holding a full-time nursing job."

"True," he admitted, "but now I only have one story to chase and better control over my schedule," he said. "I'll help with everything. I promise."

She arched a skeptical eyebrow. “Can I get that in writing?”

“I’ll have our lawyer draw up a contract.”

“Make sure to include the garden fence.”

“Done,” he said, and they clinked their glasses.

Out of sight, under his bedroom window, with Rocky curled beside him, Connor had heard enough. With a contented smile he crept back on hands and knees to his video game.

Chapter 9 Deserving to Die

Brendan's senior Environmental Studies class met in the early afternoon, but all morning students had been popping into his room to see what he knew about the murder. He decided to scrap his planned lesson and let them vent.

"We won't need Bill Gates today," he announced as they straggled in and claimed their seats. In lieu of the standard text, they were using Gates' *How to Avoid a Climate Disaster*, a book Brendan thought did a better job analyzing the world's environmental challenges. He knew Gates had later backpedaled on some of the book's content, but he wrote this off to the author's desire to balance himself on the precarious tightrope between the left and right.

"What did you think about Mr. Hancock's presentation on Thursday?" he asked them.

"Boring," Joseph said. "He just rambled on like a preacher. It would have been better if Mr. Oakes was there."

"Unfortunately, Mr. Oakes was preoccupied," Brendan said.

"Was it *cold-blooded* murder?" Hudson asked, stressing the words to make sure everyone got his joke.

"Yes, but it wasn't murder in the first degree," Brendan played along. "It was however many degrees the freezer was."

"Walk-in freezers are between zero and minus ten degrees Fahrenheit," Gunner volunteered, taking things literally as usual.

"How do you know that, Gunner?" Santiago was curious.

“I researched it. He froze to death in less than two hours. Hypothermia sets in when your body falls below 95 degrees. You start shivering, then you get tired and confused. You go numb and lose control of your muscles. When your temperature gets down to 82, you pass out. By the time it reaches 70, you’re dead. The lowest recorded body temperature anyone has ever survived is 56.7 degrees.”

“How do you remember all this random stuff, Gunner?” Hayley asked him.

“It's interesting.”

Genesis rolled her eyes. “Yeah, if you like gross things.”

“Freezing to death is better than burning to death,” Gunner offered his clinical opinion.

“Thank you for that post mortem, Gunner,” Brendan intervened. “I’ll be sure to consult with you when I’m ready for assisted suicide.”

“Okay.”

“I’m kidding.”

“Okay.”

They were graduating in a few weeks. Hayley, their academic superstar, had been accepted at her parents' alma mater, Duke. Hudson was heading to Virginia Tech. Santiago and Zoey were off to WVU. The senior counselor had tried to steer Gunner to a Marshall University program for students with Autism Spectrum Disorder, but after meeting two of the program's lower functioning participants during his college tour, he'd decided to enroll as a regular student. New River Community and Technical College would get a shot at turning Skylark into a cosmetologist and Rylee into a phlebotomist. Joseph's parents wanted him to go to work in the family's meat processing plant, but he was escaping life in the slaughterhouse by enlisting in the Navy. Genesis was on the managerial track at Starbucks. Jude would probably continue to devote his considerable entrepreneurial talents to the cannabis cultivation and distribution business that Brendan wasn’t supposed to know he’d been operating since ninth grade. Jude kept a tantalizingly low profile for a teenage drug lord; he drove a 20-

year-old rust eaten Ford F-150, but rumor had it he could afford a better vehicle than the Superintendent of Schools.

"I have a question for you," Brendan addressed the group. "There aren't any right or wrong answers, I just want your opinions." He paused for dramatic effect. "Did Mordecai Oakes deserve to die?"

There was silence.

"I'm not going to ask for a show of hands, because you may change your minds as we talk about it," Brendan said. "Does anyone have an opinion?"

"Yes," Gunner said.

"Yes, you have an opinion, or yes, he deserved to die?"

"Both."

Genesis raised her hand. "No."

"Why?"

"Because no one deserves to die."

"Hitler deserved to die," Joseph disagreed. "Osama Bin Laden deserved to die."

"Why?" Brendan pressed him.

"They were evil men. They had warped beliefs and they killed huge numbers of innocent people."

"Mordecai Oakes was a television personality and a writer," Brendan countered. "He may have had warped beliefs, but do you really think he belongs in the same category as Hitler and Bin Laden, Gunner?"

"Yes," Gunner was convinced. "He was poisoning thousands of minds. Maybe even millions."

"Gunner's right," Hudson agreed with his classmate. "If all those people's ignorant opinions keep society from accepting the reality of climate change and dealing with it, eventually the whole human race could go down the toilet. Oakes wasn't herding people into gas chambers like Hitler, but in the long run what he was doing could have turned out worse for more people."

Gunner was pleased someone else saw the larger picture. "The earth's atmosphere was his gas chamber."

"So does that mean he deserved to die?" Brendan returned to his original question.

“Deserve is a tricky word,” Hayley parsed the question like the lawyer she hoped to become. “Even if we think the world's better off without him, it’s not an excuse for vigilante justice. There’s a big difference between thinking someone deserves to die and killing them. If we follow that line of reasoning, it would be okay if one of us had done it.”

Brendan shrugged. “Maybe one of you did. I don’t know what you were up to before you got to Colonial Hall.”

Jude spoke up. “I confess. I did it with the candlestick in the library. Colonel Mustard and Professor Plum helped me put him in the freezer.”

Brendan smiled. “Thank you, Jude. It took a lot of courage for you to admit that. I’ll notify the police immediately.”

Chapter 10 Bellmen and Chefs

Sergeant Lavender was pleased to learn The Greenbrier only employed two dozen bellmen, a manageable number. She'd spent the morning interviewing a parade of impeccably-mannered luggage handlers - young, old, black, brown and white. Their polished manners made sense; when earning your living depended on your ability to charm strangers, you got pretty good at it. None of them struck her as a potential suspect. Most claimed, convincingly, that they'd never even heard of the victim before the murder.

Her most helpful conversation was with James Argyle, the elegant silver-haired bell captain who'd been schlepping baggage around the resort's labyrinthine corridors for thirty-five years.

"Mr. Argyle, it's going to come out in the next day or two that the person who put Mr. Oakes in the freezer was dressed as a bellman," she told him. "We have it on the security footage."

"Yes, I know," he revealed. "The Director of Security showed me the footage and asked me to keep it quiet. Personally, I don't believe the person in the video was one of our men, Sergeant. Do you think it was?"

"No, but we can't rule it out yet. I want to explore a few thing with you."

"Certainly."

"Let's talk about your uniforms. Where do you get them? Do you take them home and launder them yourselves?"

"No, we have a uniform shop downstairs. The word 'shop' makes it sound like a store, but it's just a place where they keep the uniforms and clean them and do minor repair work."

"You drop off the ones you've worn and pick up clean ones?"

"That's right."

"What if someone wanted to steal a uniform. How could they do it?"

He gave this some thought. "I suppose they could break into the shop, but that really wouldn't be necessary. They keep the clean ones in plain sight on racks out front, and everyone has an assigned number for their uniform. Mine is number 12. If the attendant is helping someone at the counter, a person could slip in and grab a uniform without being noticed. It wouldn't be hard."

"Have any of your men complained about their uniform being missing?"

"No, but they wouldn't tell me. They'd tell the people at the shop. You should check with them."

She pointed to his brass name tag. "Do all your men wear name tags?"

"Yes. We're expected to."

"Would it be possible to steal one?"

This gave him pause. "People do forget them from time to time. We keep some generic ones that say 'Bellman' in the bell stand by the front desk, where the guests check in. If you knew where they were and no one was looking, you could help yourself."

"That's helpful information, Mr. Argyle. It sounds like a person would have to be familiar with the workings of your department to know about those tags."

"Yes, but I'm sure they could order something similar online," he pointed out. "You can get anything on the Internet."

"True," she conceded. "Did you notice anything out of the ordinary when you watched the video?"

"His shoes," Argyle pinpointed. "It looked to me like he was wearing black athletic shoes, not the dress shoes they prefer us to wear. I must say I've seen men get away with it once or twice - we're on our feet all day - but it's out of the ordinary."

“That's an excellent observation and we'll follow up on it,” the sergeant promised. “Next subject. Suppose you wanted to escort someone in a wheelchair from Mr. Oakes's room to the loading dock where the freezer is. What route would you take?”

“You’d take an elevator to the main floor, and then you could go through the Exhibit Hall or the main kitchen.”

“Suppose you wanted to avoid the security cameras?”

“Then you'd avoid the Exhibit Hall. The entrance to the Bunker is there. Part of it is leased to a company that warehouses documents for major corporations. There are more cameras in there than anywhere else at the hotel, except the casino. They’re continually monitored.”

“So it would make more sense to go through the kitchen?”

“Yes. There might be other ways, but those two come to mind.”

“I’ve strolled around the hotel and I haven’t seen many security cameras,” she said. “I didn't see any in the corridors where the guest rooms are. I noticed them by the entrances and the front desk, and some on the lower level, where the retail shops are. But for the most part, The Greenbrier doesn’t seem to have a lot of surveillance.”

“Honestly, Sergeant, I’ve never paid much attention to it. But if you think about it, this is a vast property – thousands of acres and over 700 rooms. Some of them are in row cottages and houses that aren't even connected to the hotel. We can’t have cameras everywhere, can we? How many would it take? Two hundred? Five hundred? And how many people would it require to monitor them? There’s been a resort on this property since the late 1700’s. We’ve welcomed hundreds of thousands of guests and we've rarely had any serious crimes. We have minor disturbances from time to time, but The Greenbrier is a very peaceful, idyllic place. A little bit of heaven on earth. You don't need surveillance in heaven.”

\+ + +

Buzzy had arranged for Zac to interview Shanice Waters, the apprentice who had discovered Mordecai Oakes in the freezer. Executive Chef Ben Curry had insisted on sitting in.

"You keep glancing at our toques," Chef Curry noticed.

Zac grinned. "I've always wondered why chefs wear them."

"Tradition. These funny hats have been around for centuries. They don't serve any practical purpose, except maybe keeping hair out of food, but they're iconic. They're symbols of our profession and we can't really abandon them."

Zac accepted this explanation and turned his attention to the chef's young protégé, who was sitting on the edge of her chair. "Thanks for taking the time to meet with me, Shanice. I'm sure you're a very busy young lady."

"I'm nervous," she confessed. "I've never talked to a reporter before."

"I'm not going to put anything in the paper or online that you don't want," he assured her. "And if you want to reword something you say, that's fine. This isn't sacred scripture. Writing's just edited thinking. We can keep editing until it says what you want."

"Good." She sat back and relaxed a bit.

"I'm going to record this to make sure I quote you correctly," he let her know. He clicked Voice Memos on his iPhone, his go-to app for interviews.

"I hope you don't mind my sitting in," the Executive Chef said. "I don't usually hover, but this is an unusual situation, to say the least. We think we've prepared our apprentices for anything they might encounter in this line of work, and then something like this comes along."

"I don't mind at all, Chef. In fact, I'd like to use what you just said." He turned back to the young woman. "I'm with *The New York Times*, Shanice," he explained in case she hadn't been informed. "I'm working on what's probably going to be a series of stories about the homicide. The way you discovered Mr. Oakes makes a natural opening. That's why I want to talk with you. First of all, do you mind if I use your actual name?"

She gave a little shrug. "I am who I am."

"Tell me a little about your background."

"I'm 22. I'm from Brooklyn."

"I live in New York," he shared. "Astoria. If you could stand in the middle of Central Park and throw a rock across the East River, it would land near where I live."

"Bet you don't have murders in your neighborhood," she said.

"Not really. So many theatre people live there, they call it 'Actoria'. I hear a lot of the creatives live in Brooklyn, too."

"That's true. My brother Dantrell's a stagehand. He runs with the gay crowd. They come to our house to watch the Tonys and they carry on like it's the Superbowl."

He laughed. "I promise not to use that in my story."

"Dantrell would love it. People think if you live in New York, you see murders all the time. I never saw a dead person in my life before Friday."

"We're sorry this happened to you Shanice," the Executive Chef said. "Would you like to talk with a counselor? Do you need a few days off?"

"I'm not a wimp, Chef."

"I know that. Wimps can't cut it in this program. I just want you to know that if this is bothering you, we want to help."

"Thanks. I'm okay. I think."

"What brought you to The Greenbrier?" Zac was curious.

"Growing up, I used to watch all the cooking shows - Gordon Ramsey, The Great British Baking Show and all those things. I'd try to make some of the recipes they made. I did culinary in high school and after I graduated, I went to the Culinary Institute in Hyde Park. A Greenbrier chef came and spoke to us about the apprentice program, and I decided to apply. I probably won't end up famous like some of the people who've worked here, but it's definitely making me a better chef."

"You're going to be featured in *The New York Times*," Zac said. "There's your first 15 minutes of fame. I've got a hunch the editor might want a picture of you by the freezer."

"Finding dead bodies isn't what I want to be famous for."

"Maybe a picture of you cooking would be better," Zac reconsidered. "I don't make those calls. A photographer will come and take a couple of hundred pictures and they'll end up using a very small number of them. At least that's the way it usually works."

"Our apprenticeships are for people who've gone through culinary school or had work experience," Chef Curry explained. "We expect them to arrive with a mastery of the basic kitchen skills. It's a three-year program that combines formal training with work in all our kitchens, everything from butchering to buffet work to haute cuisine. It's very intense. We're the Parris Island of the culinary world. I've seen exhausted apprentices sleeping in closets between shifts. I'm prejudiced, but I don't think there's a better program of its kind in the country. We only accept 5 or 6 applicants a year."

"What's the most valuable thing you've learned?" Zac asked her.

"Taste everything," she said without missing a beat.

Zac laughed. "I was expecting something more profound."

She shrugged. "Guess I'm more of a doer than a thinker."

"You should give yourself more credit, Shanice," Chef Curry chided her. "You've got a pretty good head under that toque."

"Let's go back to last Friday," Zac said. "Walk me through it. What were you doing in the freezer?"

"I made an ice sculpture for a wedding reception. I took some pictures when I was working on it, but I wanted to take more before they used it for the reception."

"Unfortunately, we lost all the sculptures in the freezer," Chef Curry revealed. "Apparently Mr. Oakes knocked them over when he was struggling, and the police had us cut the power so they could photograph the crime scene. What was left of them melted."

"What was your sculpture?" Zac asked her.

She pulled out her phone and scrolled through a series of pictures that detailed the metamorphosis of a block of ice into a butterfly on a leaf.

"Very impressive," he admired her artistry. "If I tried that, it would look like the West Virginia Chainsaw Massacre."

"You start with a chainsaw, but you do most of it with a chisel and a torch."

"Okay, so you wanted pictures of your butterfly. What was your reaction when you opened the freezer door?"

"We're always pranking each other. I thought someone was playing a joke on me and it was a dummy. Then I poked him and I just knew he was real." She shivered at the memory. "I keep thinking how helpless that poor man must have felt, trapped in that pitch-black, ice-cold room, knowing he was freezing to death. Someone must have really hated him."

"I'd like to use that in my story."

"Go for it." An odd look appeared on her face. "He came through the kitchen on Thursday," she remembered.

"Who?" Chef Curry asked.

"Mr. Oakes. There was a bellman with him. I was there when they came through. I didn't pay it any mind because folks come through all the time."

"Were they touring the kitchen?" Chef Curry asked.

"No, just going through it."

"When was this?" Zac asked.

"Lunch time. We don't serve lunch in the main dining room, but some of us were working on the convention buffet."

"Did you notice anything about the bellman?"

"Like what?"

"What did he look like? How old would you say he was?"

She shrugged. "I don't pay the bellmen any mind. They're kind of like wallpaper around here."

"I guess that's what he was counting on," Zac said. "Have the police interviewed you?"

"Only about a dozen times. I don't know what more to tell them. I opened the door, I saw the man on the floor, I poked him, then I called Chef and told him about it."

“You’ve said a couple of things I’d like to use,” Zac let her know. “Any idea what you’ll do when you finish your apprenticeship?”

“I’d love for Shanice to stay here, but she’s got other plans,” Chef Curry said.

“I interviewed at The River Cafe in Brooklyn, and they offered me a position,” she said.

“The River Cafe is Michelin-starred,” the Executive Chef elaborated. “It's a gorgeous restaurant with a spectacular view of the Manhattan skyline. This is typical of the offers our graduates get. We supply staff for kitchens and front of house all over the world. I have no doubt Shanice will have a brilliant career.”

“But no more dead bodies,” she said. She raised her hands and pushed an imaginary freezer door, and hopefully this chapter of her young life, closed.

Chapter 11 Teacher of the Year

Zac delivered Connor to Hollowell Park and climbed into the bleachers to watch his Little League practice. He'd never been much of an athlete himself, and as he watched his son participate energetically in the stretches, high knees and sprints, he suspected he must have inherited a stray sports gene from some distant branch of the family tree.

His brother-in-law walked over from the parking lot and joined him in the stands.

"Hey, Brendan. Glad you could come by."

"My pleasure," Brendan said. "I played Little League back in the day. I was our team's reserve-reserve-reserve pitcher. The coach said I had a unique style."

"Funny, that's the same thing the choir teacher said about my singing," Zac recalled.

"Unfortunately, sometimes our personal limitations clash with our dreams," Brendan observed.

"You must be doing something right, Brendan. I saw your name on the marquee in front of the high school. You're the Greenbrier County Teacher of the Year!"

He shrugged it off. "I just teach what I believe in."

"You must be good at it."

"I had a lively discussion about the late great Mr. Oakes with my seniors today," he deflected the praise. "I asked them if they thought he deserved to die."

"That's an odd question," Zac opined. "What'd they say?"

"The first one to offer an opinion was Gunner, who's on the high end of the autism spectrum. Gunner said he thought Oakes deserved to die because he was 'poisoning minds'. High school's basically a popularity contest and Gunner's the designated oddball, so I didn't expect anyone to agree with him, but Hudson did. Hudson's gay and he has a strong independent streak. He came out to his Baptist preacher father when he was 13, and ever since then nothing's held any terror for him. He doesn't really care what people think of him. He got his eyebrows waxed while we were at the hotel."

"Your super power is understanding your students," Zac said.

"Teenagers aren't hard to understand," Brendan insisted. "They have runaway emotions, raging hormones, poor impulse control and hideous judgment. Other than that, they're a joy to be around."

"You're making me look forward to Connor's teenage years," Zac said as they watched him round the bases. "I'm in the process of rearranging things so I can be here for him. The next thing you know he'll be 20, and if I've missed his ball games, his driving lessons, his prom and all his other triumphs, he'll remember me as his father who was never around."

"You left out his car accidents, his sports injuries, his experiments with alcohol and drugs, and his questionable relationships."

"Nah. None of that stuff's going to happen to Connor."

The team moved on to hitting, throwing and catching. "This looks a lot more organized than when I played," Brendan noticed. "We spent a lot of time standing around. This coach has set up stations so they're always practicing something."

"He emailed us last night and told us what they were doing today," Zac said. "He seems a little OCD, but I've got a touch of that myself and I like to think it's a plus. Keeps me on task."

"Have you heard anything else about the murder?" his brother-in-law changed the subject.

"What everyone is about to learn, and Greta probably heard at work today, is that the hotel has security footage of someone in a bellman's uniform wheeling Oakes into the freezer."

"No shit? Have they IDed him?"

"No. They're assuming it was a disguise. You can't make out the guy's face in the video..Apparently, a lot of folks had it in for poor old Mordecai, so it's going to take a while to whittle down the list of suspects."

"I can't believe we were actually there while this was going down," Brendan said. "It adds another indelible memory for my senior students." He hesitated. "I'd like to talk with the person in charge of the investigation. How do I go about doing that?"

"The lead investigator is Sergeant Wendy Lavender with the State Police. She works out of Beckley. Why do you want to talk with her?"

"I don't want to go into it."

"But I'm your brother-in-law."

"My brother-in-law happens to work for a major newspaper. I'll explain it later, Zac."

"Get out your phone and I'll airdrop her contact info."

He pulled it out. "Is the F.B.I. involved?"

"Not yet. I don't think this falls in their bailiwick. It's not terrorism, it's not organized crime, it's not civil rights. It's just a local homicide, even if the victim was a public figure. I think the State Police see it as an opportunity to prove their mettle. I'm sure they're going to be interviewing some folks up in New York, and I intend to beat them to it."

"The Big Apple," Brendan reflected on his only time there. "The traffic's insane. It took us an hour to get across the George Washington Bridge. One afternoon Greta went shopping and I took off to see Pelham Bay Park because I'd read it's three times bigger than Central Park and it has trails and water views. I got stuck in the gridlock, I got lost and I never found Pelham Bay Park. Presumably it's there somewhere."

"Next time leave your car at home and I'll show you how to use the Metro," Zac offered. "The subway's one of my few true areas of expertise. Once you understand it, you can get around pretty quickly."

"Has Abby been back up there since she moved here?" Brendan inquired.

"No. She isn't willing to leave her mother in someone else's care."

"How's Ms. Cooper doing?"

"She's fine physically, but she comes and goes mentally. I try not to dwell on it. Alzheimer's is an endlessly depressing subject. It's a long, slow trip downhill. Being around someone with it is a reminder that no matter how well we try to take care of ourselves, the bodies and/or the minds that have served us so well for so long betray us in the end."

Brendan studied him thoughtfully. "Your life's complicated, bro."

"Yeah, it is," he agreed. "I'm working on uncomplicating it. I think I need to switch from journalism to writing non-fiction books. If you write books, you can live pretty much anywhere."

"Non-fiction is going to be your escape hatch from the news industry?"

He shrugged. "It worked for Woodward and Bernstein." He had the germ of an idea, but he was afraid it would jinx him if he said any more.

Chapter 12 Pretty Damn Spongy

He'd always been curious about his IQ, but he'd never taken a test. He knew that your Intelligence Quotient doesn't measure how much you know, but how readily you pick up on concepts and use them, how good of a sponge your brain is. The average IQ fell between 90 and 110. Bright was 130, genius 160. But suppose he took a test and the results said he was just average? He'd pulled off the perfect crime. Didn't that prove his brain was pretty damn spongy?

Lots could have gone wrong, but by the time he'd worked it out, he had contingency plans for his contingency plans. He knew the hotel had walk-in freezers because they kept enormous stores of food. When he spotted a chef wheeling an ice sculpture along a hallway, he realized there had to be a freezer somewhere that wasn't accessed very often, where they kept these fragile works without having to worry about them being knocked over, or absorbing odors, or melting from workers constantly opening and closing the door. An online search turned up an old Greenbrier Valley Quarterly article about the hotel's ice carving operation. It described a culinarian chiseling away at a block of ice on a loading dock, the room where the blocks were manufactured, and the freezer where the sculptures were stored. He'd roamed the hotel's perimeter until he spotted the dock, and when no one was around he scoped things out. The old freezer had enough room for a wheelchair and it lacked an escape handle. The next step was figuring out how to get Mordecai Oakes inside it.

He'd studied the bellmen closely enough to know he could pass for one of these porters. He'd seen one of them wearing disposable gloves, a perfect accessory to prevent leaving any stray fingerprints. If he showed up at Oakes' room in the right uniform with the right story, the TV commentator wouldn't have any reason to doubt his authenticity. But to intercept him, he needed to know where he was staying. He figured he would probably arrive the day before the event on an afternoon flight at either the Lewisburg airport or the Roanoke, Virginia, airport. In any case, The Greenbrier would meet him with a shuttle equipped for the mobility impaired and ferry him to the hotel. All he had to do was stake out the front entrance where the shuttles pulled up, or the lobby where the guests checked in, and keep an eye peeled. When Oakes arrived, he could discretely follow the bellman who escorted him to his room. If a stray kitchen worker showed up on the loading dock while they were there, he could just give Oakes a tour of the carving operation and take him on to Colonial Hall.

Fortunately, everything had gone just like he'd envisioned. He'd left his victim in the freezer, ducked back into the hotel and retrieved the backpack with his clothes that he'd stashed behind stacks of toilet paper in a restroom cabinet. In the privacy of a stall, he'd changed out of the uniform, smashed Oakes' cell phone with a ball peen hammer he'd brought along for the purpose, and stuffed everything in the backpack.

Later that evening he'd driven to a remote stretch of the Greenbrier River and hurled the phone into the water. He'd helped himself to a firepit in a fishing camp and burned his uniform and wig. The police could spend days combing through the hotel's trashcans and dumpsters, and even the county landfill; they wouldn't find any evidence of his crime.

He supposed he should feel some remorse for taking another person's life, but it was hard to feel sorry for a loudmouth asshole who was trying to convert people to ridiculous beliefs. The only thing that had given him pause was when Oakes had presented him with the Montblanc pen. This little act of generosity from the man he was about to kill had taken him by surprise. He'd started to ditch it in the river, but he decided to keep it as a souvenir.

All in all, everything had gone brilliantly. What the hell - maybe he would take an online IQ test.

Chapter 13 Person of Interest

Brendan Bell and Wendy Lavender were sitting in rocking chairs on the porch of the Presidents' Cottage Museum, surveying The Greenbrier's steepled wedding chapel on the lawn below them. The sergeant had suggested meeting at the high school, but Brendan didn't want his students seeing him consulting with law enforcement. What he wanted to discuss was too delicate.

"This beats meeting in a classroom," the officer observed. "All we need now are mint juleps."

"My wife Greta's a concierge," Brendan told her. "She can make it happen."

"I'm kidding. The State Police don't take kindly to drinking on the job."

"Zac Wolfe gave me your contact information," Brendan explained. "Zac's my brother-in-law."

"I'll try not to hold that against you. I'm not a big fan of the media."

"Zac's a good guy."

"I'll take your word, but I've had negative experiences with others."

"I've got a concern, Sergeant," Brendan got down to business. "I know the Greenbrier County prosecuting attorney and I started to talk with him about it, but I decided you might be a better place to start."

"I'll let you know if I think you need to share your concern with him."

"I teach Environmental Studies at Greenbrier River High. I brought my seniors here on Thursday for the debate. There are ten students in the class. One is a young man named

Gunner Hoke, who functions on the high end of the autism spectrum."

"Asperger's?"

"We don't call it Asperger's anymore. Turns out Dr. Asperger wasn't your kindly family pediatrician. He was a Nazi sympathizer who sent his young patients off to hospitals where they experimented on them."

"Ouch."

"Instead of honoring him for identifying the syndrome, now we just say someone's 'on the autism spectrum' or 'on the spectrum'. I don't know how much you know about autism, but it comes in more flavors than Ben & Jerry's. It's common for people on the higher end to have some kind of obsessive intellectual or artistic interest. I don't know when it started, but Gunner's obsessed with climate change. He lives, breathes, eats and sleeps like the world's going to end tomorrow if he doesn't take some sort of direct action. In a way, he's the best student I've ever had. He's totally focused on the subject. But he's humorless and intense, and his social skills leave a lot to be desired. A therapist has been trying to help him to improve them. He can fake it when he has to, but if you know Gunner, you can tell it's just an intellectual exercise. He's just not very interested in other people. He's not a warm and fuzzy guy."

"It sounds like he wants to save humanity but he doesn't particularly care for humans as individuals."

"Exactly."

A middle-aged black couple strolled over and paused in front of the Presidents' Cottage Museum.

Brendan spoke up. "There's some interesting stuff in there, but there are some old murals celebrating the joys of antebellum plantation life you might find …"

"Offensive?" the woman filled in the blank.

"I was going to say questionable, but offensive is probably a better word," Brendan agreed.

"We can handle it," the woman assured him. "I teach African-American History at Howard University and I'm interested in that sort of thing. Who knows - I might even take some pictures and use them in a class." They started inside and the man turned back. “I’m curious - why are the police guarding this museum?”

Wendy laughed. “I guess it looks that way, but we’re just sitting here chatting.”

“Oh. Sorry for the interruption.” And with that, the couple disappeared inside.

“Back to last Thursday,” Brendan picked up the thread of his story. “We got to the hotel around eleven and we had an early lunch. I gave the kids time to run around and enjoy themselves before the debate started. They went off in twos and threes to do things, but Gunner was roaming around by himself. That's par for the course since he doesn’t really hang out with the others or have friends. I don’t have any idea where he was or what he was doing between 11:45 and 1:45.”

“What are you suggesting?”

“I don’t know if I’m suggesting anything,” Brendan admitted, “but I can’t stop thinking about it. When we were prepping for the debate, I had the students watch Oakes's commentaries and we talked about his views. All these kids are environmentally attuned, and they saw him as a leader of the enemy camp. When we were talking about him after the murder, I asked if they thought he deserved to die. I know that sounds like a strange question, but I was just trying to jump start a discussion. Gunner immediately said he did, which was fine. But then without prompting he started sharing all this detailed technical information about death by freezing. He knew the temperature of walk-in freezers, the stages of hypothermia and how long it takes for a person to freeze to death. Someone asked him how he knew all this stuff and he said he researched it.”

“Did that raise any concerns for his classmates?”

“Not really. Most of them have known Gunner for years and they tend to write him off.”

“How old is he?”

“All my seniors are 18. I remember Gunner turned 18 in March because his parents gave him a used Tesla for his birthday. He’s the only student in our school who drives a Tesla. Maybe that's common in Beverly Hills and Silicon Valley, but not in rural West Virginia.”

"Are you suggested Gunner Hoke might be a person of interest?"

He squirmed in his rocker, uncomfortable with the label. "I don't know if I'd go that far," he waffled. "I just don't know. He's pretty zealous when it comes to climate change."

"Is he capable of devising an elaborate plan?"

"Absolutely."

"Would he have had access to the hotel to plan things?"

"Total access. His mother's a doctor at The Greenbrier Clinic and his father's a financial consultant in Lewisburg. They live here on the grounds in Creekside, one of the Sporting Club neighborhoods. Gunner has a gate pass and he can come and go anywhere on the property. His younger sister plays sports and the parents go to her games. I get the impression Gunner's left on his own a lot."

The sergeant weighed all this. "Let's assume this young man was involved. If I interview him and he thinks he's a suspect, it might prompt him to destroy any evidence. If he was researching death by freezing prior to Thursday and I question him, he'll probably erase it from his search history. Actually, anyone smart enough to pull this off has probably already erased it or used a computer somewhere else, like a library. In any event, we'd have to get a search warrant to take his phone or his laptop or tablet."

Brendan winced. "I'd rather not create all that commotion. This is probably much ado about nothing. Why don't you interview all the students who were at the hotel so Gunner doesn't think he's being singled out? You could pull them out of class one at a time and ask them if they noticed anything unusual when they were here. Then if you think he's a person of interest, as you say, you can do whatever you need to do to follow up."

She thought about it and nodded slowly. "I can do that. If I save Gunner for last, you can keep an eye on him and see if he seems nervous, or if he grills the others about what I asked them when they come back."

"I'm struggling with this, Sergeant. I feel like I'm betraying one of my kids. Gunner's probably just a young eccentric, quirky but harmless."

"Have you shared your concerns with your brother-in-law?"

"No, and I'm not planning on it. This is probably just a figment of my highly overactive imagination. If you don't mind, I'd like to keep it between us for now."

"I share everything with our investigative team," she let him know. "But I'll just let them know that I'm questioning some students who were at the hotel to see if they noticed anything unusual. Do I need to call your principal?"

"Yes. I'm sure he'll be fine with it. You don't need parental permission since they're all legally adults. I don't want anyone knowing we've talked, so please don't mention my name. The class meets every day at one o'clock."

"I'll be there tomorrow."

"I appreciate it, Sergeant. A couple of the kids are pretty chatty, so you could be there a while. Oh, one more thing. I don't want you to think I'm singling out Gunner because of his diagnosis. I've had other students with autism, and some of them were very sweet kids. Gunner's just not as endearing. You'll see what I mean when you meet him. His peers tend to ignore him because he doesn't make an effort to relate to them, or care about the things young people usually care about. He lives in his head."

"It sounds like you've spent a lot of time thinking about this young man."

"I think about all my students. It's gratifying to have one who's so engaged. This is the first time I've had someone whose passion for environmental issues equals my own, but I worry that in Gunner's case it's an unhealthy obsession."

"Thanks for sharing your concern, Mr. Bell. I'm looking forward to meeting him."

"You'll probably end up deciding I'm the crazy one, Sergeant."

"There's always that possibility," she agreed with a smile.

Chapter 14 Action Hero

As Zac drove into Adventures on the Gorge, he saw that the rafting company where Oliver Oakes worked was a full-service resort, with cabins, camping, restaurants, bars and a pool complex. If whitewater wasn't your thing, you could zipline, mountain bike, rock climb, paddleboard, fish, hike or play paintball.

Oliver had called the night before to postpone their rafting trip. After reading his father's will he decided he needed to make a quick dash up to New York to talk with his sister Layla and his father's ex-fiancée, Calista Martin. Zac wanted to catch him before he left.

They were meeting for lunch at AOTG's flagship eatery, Smokey's on the Gorge. The restaurant perched like an eagle's nest on a New River cliffside. He found Oliver waiting for him on the deck, looking his usual outdoorsy self in his guide apparel, with a pair of high dollar sunglasses dangling from his neck. He liked this young man instinctively, but he reminded himself that he might have been involved in his father's death. He had motive, method and opportunity, as they liked to say in the TV procedurals. He blamed his father for his mother's suicide and he stood to inherit a life-changing chunk of change. He knew when Mordecai was going to The Greenbrier, and he lived close enough to have made reconnaissance trips to plan the crime. On the flip side, he didn't seem interested in money, and he couldn't have passed himself off as a bellman without his father recognizing him, so he would have required an accomplice. His gut instincts told him young Oakes wasn't involved, but his gut wasn't always right.

He grabbed a seat, scanned the menu and slid it aside. “You’ve probably got this memorized, Oliver. Any recommendations?”

“You can’t go wrong with the wings or the smoked turkey,” he suggested. “And try one of the Bad Shepherd beers. It's a Charleston brewery.”

“Breweries are springing up like wildflowers in West Virginia,” Zac had noticed.

“It's not just here,” Oliver reacted. “I was in Alaska last year, and every little crossroads had a brew pub. I don’t know how they all stay in business. They probably don't.”

“Speaking of businesses, Adventures on the Gorge looks successful,” Zac observed.

“Wildly so,” Oliver agreed. “Folks come here from all over the country. Other countries too. Adventure’s the operative word. If you’re looking for a quiet spot to commune with nature, you're better off somewhere else. We even have weddings. You can rent this restaurant and deck and exchange your vows overlooking the Gorge.”

“So the adventures range from whitewater to marriage?”

“Pretty much.”

“Connor's bummed about our rafting trip being cancelled.”

“Sorry to bail on you, man. I promise I’ll make it up. When I read the will, I knew the shit's gonna hit the fan. Dad drew up the new one assuming he was getting married in a few weeks. The will refers to Calista as his wife, Calista Oakes. But since the wedding’s not happening, she’s not going to be his wife, and that’s never going to be her name. I haven’t talked with a lawyer, but it seems to me since they weren’t married, she gets zilch.”

Zac imagined the awkward conversation between Oliver and his would-be stepmother. “I’m sure she’ll readily agree,” he said, tongue in cheek.

“Yeah, right.”

A young woman with a lot of frizzy hair bounced over. “Hi, guys. Are we ready to order?”

"I'll take the turkey sandwich and the Bad Shepherd IPA," Zac took Oliver's suggestion.

"No problem."

Oliver held up two fingers. "Times two."

"No problem," she repeated.

As soon as she was out of earshot Zac said, "I'm glad bringing us lunch isn't a problem for her, since it's basically her job. By the way, *The New York Times* is footing the bill for this."

"Damn. If I'd known that I would have ordered a steak."

"Has Sergeant Lavender been in touch?" Zac asked him.

"Oooh, yeah. She was waiting when I came off the river on Sunday. She had loads of questions, but something about being grilled by an officer with a gun on her belt doesn't exactly make you want to bare your soul."

"I hope you're feeling more talkative today," Zac said. He noticed Oliver's gaze wandering to the table behind them.

"Oh my God!" a woman yelled. "Somebody please help!"

In a flash Oliver was out of his seat and by the time Zac turned to see what was going on, his companion was pounding an elderly blue-faced man between his shoulder blades with the butt of his hand. A chunk of something flew out of his mouth and landed on the table. Minor chaos erupted as the woman hovered over her gasping partner and staff rushed tableside. Oliver waited for the man to catch his breath and regain something closer to a human color. He waved off their profuse thanks and rejoined Zac.

"Ho hum, another day in the life of a superhero," he said, reclaiming his seat. "The dude was in panic mode. He had his hands on his throat and his eyes were bugging out. We're all certified in first aid and CPR, but we don't usually have to administer it in the restaurant."

"Why didn't you use the Heimlich?" Zac wondered.

"That's the old protocol. Now you whack 'em on the back, and if that doesn't work, then you use the Heimlich. You can crack ribs with the Heimlich, so it's not supposed to be your first intervention."

"I gave a guy CPR once," Zac related. "One of the workers on my folks' farm grabbed a live wire and he passed out."

"Did it work?"

"He didn't buy the farm. He's still working there."

"You lucked out, man," Oliver said. "Most of the time CPR isn't enough to save someone."

Their food arrived and they attacked it with gusto. Zac was increasingly curious about Mordecai's fiancée. "Tell me more about Calista," he requested.

"What do you want to know about her? I don't know much."

"How did they meet? What's she like?"

"After the hit-and-run he went to Rehab. When he came home his insurance paid for a home health agency to help with personal care. Calista was one of the providers, or whatever you call those people. Next thing we knew, she'd moved in with him. That was two-and-a-half years ago. In January they announced they were getting married. You can't accuse him of falling for the same kind of woman twice. She's the opposite of Mom in just about every way."

Zac shared a formula he'd heard somewhere. "Supposedly the rule of thumb for winter-summer relationships is no younger than half the older person's age plus seven."

Oliver did the math. "In that case he should have found someone at least 32. Calista was 24 when she met her Sugar Daddy."

"Was their relationship sexual or was she more of a companion and caretaker?"

Oliver made a face. "I have no idea. Layla might know."

"Is your sister still using drugs?"

"I don't know where that stands at the moment. Can't say I blame her if she is. I mean, we're literally orphans now, and we've lost both of our parents in tragic ways. I need to let her know she's getting an inheritance, but the bank's going to be managing it. 'Layla, the good news is you're coming into some money. The bad news is when you want any of it, you'll have to go to the bank and act like a dog begging for table scraps.' I mean, I know you can't hand someone with drug issues a million bucks and expect things to turn out well, but she'll be pissed."

"Suppose she gets clean and stays that way?"

Oliver shrugged. "Then hopefully they'll recognize she's capable and cut her some slack. I'm just glad he left me out of that deal - I wouldn't want to be the one doling out money to her."

They saw a trio of rafts snaking down the river far below, and the New River Gorge Bridge in the distance. Once a year, on the third Saturday in October, hundreds of BASE jumpers are allowed to parachute 900 feet from the bridge. Rescue personnel cruise the river in jet boats, plucking out the unfortunates who miss the dry land they're supposed to target. Adventure sports had transformed sleepy Fayetteville into a mecca for adrenaline junkies. Once upon a time Fayette County's young people could only look forward to working for the coal industry or moving away. Now they were opening outfitting stores, rigging ziplines, teaching rock climbing and paddleboarding, hosting Boy Scout Jamborees, baking artisanal pizzas and leading strings of nervous Nellies across the Gorge on the narrow catwalk under the bridge.

"What brought you here, Oliver?" Zac was curious.

"Like I told you before, I wanted to get away from all the family crap."

"But why West Virginia?"

"I was in the Dickinson Outing Club. We came here on a rafting trip and I got to talking with some of the guides. They were free spirits and world travelers, and they had friends all over the place. I kept thinking, *I want to be one of these people.* I like the outdoors and it seemed like a way to have a life of my own."

"Do you have a significant other?" Zac pried a bit more.

He smiled. "I've had others, but I guess they weren't that significant. No one I've wanted to settle down with. Some of the ladies in this line of work are, um – how shall I put it – a little restless and on the wild side? I'd like to end up with someone tamer. Not *too* tame. Just not someone whose idea of a good time is beating the guys at the bar in arm wrestling."

"You're such an old-fashioned guy, Oliver."

"Maybe in some ways," he agreed. Oliver seemed to remember he was talking to a reporter and his expression grew more serious. "What are you doing with all this stuff I'm telling you? You're not putting it in your story, are you? Why'd you come over here today?"

"Two reasons. First, I'm gathering background so when I start writing, things make more sense. Second, I want to interview Calista and Layla and I'm hoping you'll pave the way for me and give me a heads up about what to expect. Now I know when I meet Calista, I'll probably get an earful about what a bastard Oliver Oakes is."

"No doubt. Maybe you should talk to her before I do."

"When are you going?"

"Tomorrow."

"You'll see her first. I'm not going to New York until next week. I'm going to try to convince my wife to take a break from caring for her mother and come along. We need some quality time. Can you give me Calista and Layla's contact info and let them know they'll be hearing from me?"

"Sure, but after I break poor Never-Going-to-Be-Mrs. Oakes the news about the will, she'll be so pissed she probably won't talk to you."

"Maybe," Zac saw the possibility. "On the other hand, it might give her the opportunity to vent. I'm interested in her take on your dad. She lived with him for a couple of years, so she knew him pretty well."

"You might end up having more of a conversation with her than I've ever had," Oliver conceded. "For some reason, having a bimbo stepmother my own age never quite sat right with me."

The couple at the next table got up to leave. They gathered their things and came over. "We've taken care of your lunch," the man announced. "It's the least we could do. I really appreciate your quick action, young man. That's never happened to me before and I hope it never happens again.

What's your name? I want to write a letter to the management and commend you."

"Gary Donnelly," Oliver replied.

"Well thank you again, Gary."

"You're welcome. Thanks for lunch."

"Our pleasure."

They watched the couple head for the exit. "*Gary Donnelly*?" Zac puzzled. "I know you're a superhero, but do you have a secret identity?"

The river guide shrugged. "Oakes isn't a common name and I don't want them to connect me with the guy in the news."

"Understandable," Zac said.

"Can you wait a bit before you blow my cover?" Oliver requested.

"If I'm the only journalist you're talking to, I can be very patient. That includes bloggers, vloggers, podcast hosts, YouTubers and other busybodies."

"Deal," Oliver gave him a fist bump. "You're the only reporter I'm talking to. My confidant. My Lois Lane."

Zac rolled his eyes. "Let's not go that far."

Chapter 15 Death of a Tradition

Chef Curry met weekly with his apprentices to track their progress and offer general guidance. His current crop of future chefs ranged in age from 20 to 28, and in temperament from high-strung to Zen-like. He was justifiably proud of the program; over the years The Greenbrier apprenticeships had produced graduates who ran top restaurants or had their own successful food-related enterprises. He worked them mercilessly, but they were entering a demanding profession that often required working to exhaustion under intense pressure. If they couldn't cut it now, they wouldn't cut it later.

This morning's meeting was going to be a departure from their usual confabs. The Executive Chef had been giving some thought to pulling the plug on one of the program's honored traditions, and traditions at The Greenbrier didn't die quietly. They were sitting around a table by his office in the main kitchen.

Shanice walked in. "Ice-ice-baby," Joey Russo welcomed her. "You bring any frozen treats from the freezer?"

She gave him the finger. It was their first group meeting since her infamous discovery and she hoped she wasn't going to be the main topic.

"Ice is what we're going to talk about," Chef Curry said as Shanice took a seat. "Ever since the apprenticeship program started, we've had ice carving as part of it. I've always thought the sculptures added a touch of class to our events. But for the past year or so I've been questioning whether training our culinarians in this Old World skill is really worth all the time and effort we put into it. It's not something you're going to be called on to do in most of the places you'll work."

He could see from the curious looks he was getting that they were wondering where this was heading.

"Lately we've had the weather working against us. Winters are warmer, and we can't count on late December and early January being cold enough for us to be able to work on pieces out on the loading dock. So, after giving it a lot of thought and talking it over with management, we've decided to shut down the carving operation for now. You could end up being the last group to master this skill at The Greenbrier. We're no longer going to offer ice sculptures as an option at our receptions and events."

"Well, damn," Adam Wiley was disappointed to hear this. "Now that I've gotten pretty decent at it, we're scrapping it."

"Sorry, Adam," Chef Curry said, "but what we charge guests for the sculptures doesn't reimburse us for the time and effort we put into making them. As added amenities go, it's a loss leader, like the horses and carriages. Ice sculptures look good in pictures, but they aren't very cost effective."

"They make molded forms you fill with water and freeze," Jeannette Byrd offered. "Instant sculptures. Can't we just use those?"

The Chef sighed. "We could, Jenny, but that's like using prepared food instead of cooking from scratch. The Greenbrier prides itself on doing things artfully, and there's nothing artful about filling a mold with water, sticking it in the freezer and putting the result on a table. Our guests wouldn't know the difference, but we would."

Shanice had a sneaking suspicion. "Chef, does this have anything to do with what happened last week?"

"Yes and no," he admitted. "I've been thinking about it, and this made me think a little harder. Be honest – are any of you looking at jobs where you'll be required to create ice sculptures?"

No one spoke up.

"How many of you are disappointed?" the Chef asked.

They all raised their hands.

"How many of you are relieved?" he continued.

They all raised their hands again, and there was laughter.

"You mean my butterfly was the last ice sculpture anyone's going to make here?" Shanice asked.

"Possibly," the Chef said. "I'd like to say we could have an Icetravaganza where everyone could make a final piece, but given the fact that our production room and freezer are shut down, that's not going to happen."

"I'm still listing it as a skill on my resume," Adam decided.

"Go for it, Adam. I'm sure there's a nice restaurant in Fairbanks or Oslo that will be thrilled to have you."

Chapter 16 The Best Laid Plans

It was one o'clock and as Brendan's seniors trickled in, they were surprised to find a State Trooper conferring with their teacher. They exchanged puzzled looks and whispered theories.

"You're busted, man," Santiago whispered to Jude.

"Nah, they've got bigger fish to fry," the young cannabis lord said as he eyed the officer suspiciously. "I hope."

Hudson sidled up to Joseph. "This better not be more active shooter training," he whispered. "When they show us the best places to hide, they don't realize the future shooter's taking notes."

After they had taken their seats, Brendan introduced their guest. "This is Sergeant Wendy Lavender of the West Virginia State Police. Sergeant Lavender is in charge of the homicide investigation at The Greenbrier. She and her team are in the process of interviewing people and gathering evidence. I'll turn things over to the Sergeant and let her explain why she's here."

"Thank you, Mr. Bell. I understand that your group was at the hotel on the day of the murder. I'm hoping you might have seen something when you were there that could help with our investigation. I believe you were enjoying some free time while the person who committed the crime was escorting Mr. Oakes to the freezer. The Meteorological Association members were at a buffet, and they weren't roaming around the hotel like you were, so they were less likely to have seen anything. I realize this is a long shot, but I'd like to talk with each of you for a few minutes in the conference room by the guidance office. Mr. Bell will send you one at a time. Before we get started, do you have any questions?"

Genesis raised her hand. "What do you think we might have seen?"

"The most obvious thing is a person in a wheelchair. Less obvious are people who didn't seem to be where they should have been, or who were acting suspiciously. By now it's been well publicized that the person who put Mr. Oakes in the freezer was dressed as a bellman. We've ruled out the hotel's actual bellmen, but if you happen to have seen one with blond hair, I'd be very interested in hearing about it."

"How old was he?" Joseph asked.

The Sergeant shrugged. "We aren't sure. From what the camera captured, I'd say he's closer to younger than older, for what that's worth."

Brendan spoke up. "I have a suggestion, Sergeant. Most of the students were doing things in pairs or groups, and you're likely to hear the same things over and over. Instead of questioning them individually, why not talk with them in the groups they were in? I remember that Hayley and Hudson were at the spa."

"Jude and I were bowling," Santiago offered.

"Joseph and I had banana splits at that restaurant by the casino," Skylark volunteered.

"Draper's," Joseph remembered the restaurant's name.

Brendan glanced at Zoey. "Who were you were with, Zoey?"

"Rylee and Genesis. We were just walking around the shops, looking at things."

"Who does that leave?" Brendan asked, knowing the answer.

Gunner raised his hand.

"Okay," the Sergeant said. "It looks like we have a trio, three duos and a solo. That's how I'll meet with you. Mr. Bell can decide the order he wants to send you. I'll see you shortly."

"Do we have to do this?" Gunner asked after she exited.

"No," Brendan replied. "Do you have a problem with it?"

"I don't see the point."

"She explained the point, Gunner," Jude said. "We were running around the place the same time the murderer was. We might have seen some random thing that could help them. What's not to understand?"

"I didn't see anything."

"We all think we didn't, but when she asks us questions, we might realize we did," Jude countered. "What's the big problem?"

Gunner turned to their teacher. "Can I go to the restroom?"

"Go, Gunner," Brendan dismissed him with a wave of the hand and turned his attention back to the others. "Skylark and Joseph, why don't you go first and tell the Sergeant about your banana splits?"

Joseph gave him a thumbs up and they followed Gunner out of the room.

"Gunner's not coming back," Hudson predicted. "He's getting an E.D. and signing out."

"What makes you say that?" Brendan asked.

"You don't take all your stuff with you when you go to the restroom."

The best laid plans of mice and men, Brendan thought with a sigh. He shouldn't have given his Person of Interest such an easy out. He hoped the Sergeant found the others informative, or at least entertaining.

\+ \+ \+

Brendan was alone in his classroom when Wendy Lavender returned from her interviews. "What happened to Gunner?" she wanted to know.

"Apparently he went to the school nurse and said he had stomach cramps and diarrhea and he needed to go home," a dismayed Brendan reported. "How did it go with the others?"

She smiled. "They tried their best to be helpful. Let's see - I learned that their prom is the weekend after next, in the same hall where the debate was taking place. I also learned that four of them had never been to The Greenbrier until the other day."

"You'd be surprised at the number of locals who've never been there," Brendan said. "Because it's pricey, some people think of it as a playground for the rich. That may have been true in the past, but nowadays you see bus tours pulling up for lunch, and motorcycle clubs in their leathers waiting for the Bunker tour. The Greenbrier's expensive, but they have to charge what they do to be able to pay hundreds of staff and keep the place looking like it does. I wouldn't want to have to foot the electric bill. Hell, my salary probably wouldn't cover what they spend on toilet paper."

"Half of your students seem middle class and the other half seem to have humbler roots," the sergeant observed. "But I guess that describes West Virginia in general."

"True," Brendan agreed. "On one had you've got Santiago, whose parents immigrated from the Philippines and work in the hotel's housekeeping department. On the other hand, you've got Hayley and Gunner. Hayley's mother is a trial lawyer. Gunner's mother is a gastroenterologist."

"The gastroenterologist's son has stomach problems?"

"If he does, it's probably from worrying about being questioned by the police. For whatever reason, he doesn't seem to want to talk with you."

"I don't give up easily. I might pop back in tomorrow or the next day and catch him off-guard."

"Help yourself."

Her expression became more pensive. "You know, I realized something when I was talking with these kids," she shared her reaction to meeting them. "My work puts me in contact with a lot of young people who are bad actors, and I don't mean in the high school musical. It was good to meet some with aspirations. Hayley's bright. Hudson's witty. Zoey wants to be able to afford the fancy clothes she saw in the boutiques. They made a strong impression on me. You've got a pretty intelligent group of young people here."

"Did Jude say what he's planning on after graduation?" Brendan was curious.

"Horticulture," the sergeant reported. "He said he has greenhouses where he raises plants and flowers. He seems like a very enterprising young man."

Brendan suppressed a smile. "He certainly is."

"A lot of the young people I deal with leave me feeling relieved that I don't have kids," she confessed. "But these students actually made me regret it a little."

"I love my job," Brendan told her. "Maybe the subject matter I teach attracts a certain kind of young person, but the slackers don't usually sign up for my class. My wife and I don't have children either, but in a way working here makes up for it. These kids recharge my batteries. I don't mind spending hours every day with teenagers. They're an interesting subspecies."

The sergeant gave him a skeptical look. "I'm having a hard time buying your premise that a high school student would develop an elaborate plan to murder Mr. Oakes because of his position on climate change," she leveled with him. "What kind of teenager would kill someone they've never met for philosophical reasons?"

"I know, I know - I'm probably bonkers for even thinking it," Brendan conceded. "Gunner's odd, but that doesn't mean he's homicidal. I'm sure you'll find more promising suspects."

"I still want to talk with him," she said. "I'll let you know what I think."

Chapter 17 Travel Arrangements

Abby Wolfe was convinced that no one could care for her mother as well as she could. It was more than her nursing background; there were plenty of nurses. But when you added her lifetime of experience with the patient, and her concern for her, she was irreplaceable.

Alzheimer's had turned an active woman into a passive shadow. Once, Annie Cooper had run community events, cooked for church suppers, served on the board of the Greenbrier Valley Theatre, played pickleball, solved crosswords and sudokus, and traveled with friends to Broadway shows. That Annie had left the building, never to return.

Caring for her mother was a full-time job, one that prevented Abby from working outside the home. Her only breaks were her Tuesday night Greenbrier Valley Chorale rehearsals, when Connor kept an eye on his grandmother, with orders to call if there were any problems. The only issue had been when she decided her electric range was gas and she was convinced the pilot light had gone out. He had to hide all the matches in the house to keep her from trying to light it.

Zac knew that convincing Abby to leave her mother in someone else's care for a few days was going to be a hard sell, but he'd come up with a plan he thought she'd buy. They were working on dinner in the kitchen when he sprang it on her. He looked up from the bourbon and maple glaze he was stirring together for their grilled salmon. "How would you like to go to New York with me next week?" he asked nonchalantly.

“I’d love to, but you know I can’t,” she said what he was expecting to hear. “I don't have anyone I can trust with Mom.”

“I know someone,” he said with a hint of mystery.

“Who?”

“My mom.”

It was obvious from Abby's thoughtful silence that it had never crossed her mind to recruit her mother-in-law as a respite caregiver. “Your mother?”

“Yep. I talked with her about it. She can come Sunday afternoon and stay until Friday.”

“Can I go to New York, too?” a voice called from the family room.

Abby went to the door. “Connor, do you have to eavesdrop on all our conversations?”

“No,” he said. “Only when they're interesting.”

“Aren’t you supposed to be doing your homework?”

“I’m multitasking. I'm doing my homework and I'm eavesdropping.”

“I’d prefer you to monotask.”

“Okay, I’ll just eavesdrop.”

“You’re not missing a week of school, Connor,” Zac said flatly. “End of discussion.”

“What discussion? We didn't even have a discussion. Who’ll take me to baseball practice?”

“Uncle Brendan.”

“It sounds like you've got this all planned out,” Abby couldn't help noticing. “Are you sure your mother's up for this? Do you think she can manage Mom?”

He stopped mixing his glaze and looked her squarely in the eyes. “Seriously, Abby? We’re talking about a woman who can wade into a muddy pasture in the middle of the night with chains and lube and pull an inverted calf out of a cow. This’ll be like a vacation for her.”

Connor appeared at the kitchen door. “Do Grandma and Grandpa have to help cows have calves?”

“Only when there are problems,” his father explained. “Ideally you put them in a barn to give birth, but sometimes nature has her own plans.”

"Can't they just call the vet?"

"Vets aren't enthusiastic about coming out in the wee hours for things that are fairly routine. Even if they will, they don't always make it on time."

Connor imagined the scene. "Do Grandpa and Grandma have to stick their hands inside the cows?"

"Yes, but they wear rubber gloves."

He reacted with a tortured face. "I'm definitely not a Future Farmer of America."

"Do your homework, Connor," his mother ordered. "Your father and I are trying to have a conversation."

He lingered in the doorway. "You want to go to New York, don't you, Mom?"

"I wouldn't mind," she admitted. "It would be a nice break."

"I wouldn't mind either," he said. "I could see my friends. You could take me to the Museum of Natural History or the Met. That would be more educational than being in school. You want me to be well-educated, don't you?"

"Do your homework, Connor!" Abby shooed him away with a gentle shove. "I swear, you're like a hundred-pound gnat."

"A hundred-and-six," he corrected her.

Zac brushed his glaze on the salmon steaks. "You've got to give the kid points for tenacity," he said. "But he hasn't mastered the finer points of manipulation. His attempts are too blatant."

"Unlike his father's subtle ones?" Abby asked.

"It sounds like I've convinced you to go on this trip."

"Let me talk with your mother. When would we leave?"

"Sunday. We can fly from Roanoke to LaGuardia in the afternoon. While we're there you'll have to entertain yourself part of the time because I need to interview Mordecai Oakes' fiancée and his daughter. I'd like to see the police report about the hit-and-run that paralyzed him, too. Ideally, I'd like to talk with Oakes's colleagues at Fox News, but I don't know if they'll cooperate with a rival news organization. What I'm saying is our schedule's going to have to be pretty flexible."

"No worries," she said. "I'm a big girl, Zac. I can take care of myself. I can look up some of my friends. If they aren't available, I'll go shopping, or go the Guggenheim or the Whitney. But I suspect you might be overestimating your mother's interest in moving in here for a week."

Zac laid the salmon on the counter and faced her. "Mom's totally in favor of this trip," he informed her. "Ever since we've been living 500 miles apart she's been fretting about our marriage. She was thrilled when I asked her."

"Hmm - in that case I'd better call my secret lover and tell him I won't be around next week."

"I'll call mine, too. She was hoping to run around the city with me, but I'll just buy her some expensive jewelry to make up for it."

Connor reappeared at the kitchen door wearing a thoroughly confused expression. "What?"

Chapter 18 Ecoterrorism 101

Brendan studied his seniors' expectant faces. "We're talking about something a little different this week," he informed them. "We've spent the past two semesters talking about the environmental challenges your generation will face, and we've been using *How to Avoid a Climate Disaster* as our roadmap. Gates suggests some specific steps we need to take to try to turn things around. But it depends on whether our society has the political will to take them. Some very powerful companies want to maintain the status quo, or at least stall things for a few more decades. They're remarkably generous when it comes to supporting the elected officials sympathetic to their cause. Many of these politicians represent districts where their constituents' livelihoods depend on the fossil fuel industries. Some environmentalists are so frustrated by this that they've been willing to take some pretty drastic steps to try to get people to focus on the bigger picture. So, we're going to talk about *ecoterrorism*. Does anyone know what that is?"

Zoey's hand went up. "Violent actions to try to save the environment? Like blowing up a bulldozer to stop logging in a forest?"

"Exactly."

"I wouldn't call that terrorism," Jude differed. "Can you really terrorize some billion-dollar company that knows they're going to win in the end? I mean, you can get on their nerves, but I don't see them quaking in their boots."

"The F.B.I. calls it domestic terrorism," Brendan informed him.

"What about the protestors who chain themselves to trees or lie down in front of trucks delivering pipes for gas lines?" Santiago asked. "Are they terrorists?"

"No, they're just batshit crazy," Joseph opined.

Brendan waited for the laughter to subside before he continued. "I could start by telling you about a book called *The Monkey Wrench Gang* that launched the ecoterrorism movement. Instead, I'm going to start by telling you about three high school students in Virginia who went on a rampage in the name of the environment in 2002, young people not unlike yourselves. They were members of the Friends of the Earth Club at Freeman High School in Henrico County."

He had their attention.

"These three young men didn't think mainstream organizations like the Sierra Club and the Nature Conservancy were having much impact on saving the planet. They felt they needed to do something more dramatic to call people's attention to the environmental issues in their area. They thought change might come about more quickly if corporations felt threatened economically. They were especially upset about the development taking place just west of Richmond, in an area not far from their school called Short Pump. The name Short Pump dates back to a tavern that was there in the early 1800's that had a water pump with a short handle."

"Isn't that where R.E.I. is?" Hudson asked.

"Yes," Brendan said. "And Whole Foods, L.L. Bean, an Apple store and a few hundred other shops and restaurants. Not to mention apartments and townhouses. How many of you have been there?"

Half the students raised their hands.

"Until a couple of decades ago that area was farmland. Our three young heroes, and I use the word loosely, were upset that all this countryside was being turned into suburban sprawl. I have to admit that some of the stores there now are kind of cool, and my wife and I enjoy shopping and eating there. But what these three young men saw were dozers and cranes tearing up farms. For three months they became ecoterrorists by night. They tried to blow up a $270,000 construction crane, but the wick they fashioned from an American flag and tucked in the crane's gas tank didn't work, so they poured sugar in the tanks of the other construction vehicles. They did $26,000 worth of damage to some new homes that were under construction, and they removed the For Sale signs and burned them in the street. They managed to delay the construction project by two months. To discourage people from buying gas guzzlers, they used acid to etch the windshields of 25 SUV's at a car dealership, and they did the same thing to three more parked in front of their owners' homes. They gave similar treatment to a McDonald's window, and filled the restaurant's door locks with glue."

"Did they get caught?" Jude asked.

"Yes, they were caught," Brendan said. "In 2004 they pled guilty. They were sentenced to state prison and had to pay $200,000 restitution. They did all this damage in the name of the Earth Liberation Front – ELF. Have any of you ever heard of ELF?"

Gunner raised his hand.

"What can you tell us about ELF, Gunner?"

"They want to stop development," he said. "They attack property."

"Exactly. The people involved are hard to catch because ELF isn't a formal organization. At least it wasn't back then. They didn't have elected leaders or meetings. A lot of the time the people involved didn't even know each other. You could burn down someone's corporate headquarters, and if you claimed you did it in the name of the Earth Liberation Front, ELF was presumed to be responsible and the F.B.I. considered it domestic terrorism. Law enforcement didn't have a good way to go after this kind of extremist organization because it wasn't even really an organization. ELF was more of a philosophy, and it's hard to catch a philosophy."

"It sounds like they were crazy in some ways, but smart in others," Hayley observed.

"True," Brendan agreed. "But what did our three young heroes ultimately accomplish?"

"Zilch," Hudson said. "They pissed off a bunch of people and got their dumb asses locked up. Meanwhile the construction companies collected their insurance money and finished their projects, and the car dealership collected its insurance money and popped new windshields in the SUV's and sold them."

"They should have tried suing the developers instead," Hayley suggested. "Maybe they were destroying the habitat of some endangered species."

"I suspect they lacked that kind of patience and long-term thinking, Hayley," Brendan replied.

"Why did you call them heroes?" Skylark asked.

"I used the word facetiously because that's how they saw themselves," Brendan explained. "I see them as young people with good intentions who weren't thinking very clearly. I know it's hard for you to imagine teenagers not thinking clearly, but occasionally it's been known to happen."

"I'd love to know what they talked about in the Friends of the Earth Club meetings that made them think it would be a good idea to do all this crap," Jude said. "They should have arrested the teacher who sponsored the club. There should be a law against misleading the stupid youth of America."

"I think it's called contributing to the delinquency of a minor," Brendan supplied the legal terminology.

They were interrupted by a knock on the classroom door. Sergeant Lavender poked her head in.

"It's our favorite State Police officer," Brendan announced.

"Did you catch the murderer?" Santiago asked her.

"I'm afraid the wheels of justice don't turn that quickly, Santiago," she replied.

"Still sniffing around for clues at the scene of the crime?" Jude asked.

"And elsewhere." She turned to Brendan. "Mr. Bell, one of your students left early the other day and I missed the chance to talk with him. I was hoping to catch up with him today."

"Gunner, would you like to go with Sergeant Lavender?" Brendan invited him.

An awkward silence ensued. "Not really," he said. "This is an interesting discussion. I don't want to miss it."

"How about when class is over?" Brendan proposed.

"I have Calculus. It's my worst subject. I missed it the other day when I went home and I'm behind. I can't miss another one."

The sergeant saw where this was heading. "I'll tell you what, Gunner," she said, pulling out a business card and handing it to him. "This is how you can get in touch with me. I can work around your schedule. Call or text me and we'll set up a time that's good for you. It doesn't have to be here at school. I can meet you anywhere. Can you do that?"

He stared at the card. "Okay," he said unconvincingly.

"Thanks for your cooperation the other day," she said to the others. "I appreciate your help." With a wave, she vanished as quickly as she had appeared.

"I have a question, Mr. Bell," Hudson said as the sergeant's footsteps faded in the hallway. "If the person who killed Mr. Oakes had written ELF on the freezer, would the F.B.I. consider it domestic terrorism?"

"Absolutely," Brendan replied. "The Feds would descend on The Greenbrier faster than the Holy Spirit on a Pentecostal church."

"So all we have to do to be official terrorists is vandalize something and write ELF on it?" Joseph inquired.

"I'm pretty sure it has to be something worse than smashing mailboxes," Brendan said. "But please don't try this at home. This isn't an ELF recruitment seminar."

"Does ELF still exist?" Zoey wondered. "We weren't even born when those guys did all that stuff."

"I was curious about that myself, Zoey," Brendan replied. "I Googled the Earth Liberation Front. They have a website. It's mostly tips on how to live a low-impact, environment-friendly lifestyle. I didn't see any bomb-making tips. It's been a while since any attacks have been attributed to them."

"Sounds like they've become the kind of organization they used to look down on," Jude noticed the irony.

"I'm giving you an assignment for tomorrow," Brendan said. "Some of you know that my brother-in-law, Zac Wolfe, writes for *The New York Times*. A couple of years ago he tracked down one of the young ecoterrorists I just told you about and interviewed him. He's older and wiser now. But because he's a convicted felon he can't own firearms, he can't serve on a jury and he can't run for public office. For a while he lost his right to vote, but that right was later restored in Virginia. Now any legal resident who isn't incarcerated can vote."

Joseph shook his head ruefully. "All because he signed up for the wrong club at his school. If he'd signed up for chess or robotics, he wouldn't have a prison record."

"When you read Zac's article, you'll learn that he actually helped start the club," Brendan said. "As far as we know, except for those three students, the other members weren't devoting their free time to terrorism. I was curious about whether Freeman High School still has a Friends of the Earth Club. I did an online search and, believe it or not, they do. At any rate, I'd like you to read Zac's article for tomorrow."

"Where do we find it?" Hayley asked.

"I'll give you the link. I know you're not supposed to use your phones in class, but you can start reading it now. If you don't finish it here, finish it at home and we'll talk about it tomorrow. I might give you a quiz about it."

"You always threaten us a with a quiz when you want us to read something," Hudson had noticed. "But you never give us one."

"Thanks for bringing that to my attention, Hudson. I'll see what I can do to remedy that situation."

Hudson saw his classmates' death stares. "I totally meant that as a compliment, Mr. Bell! That's why you're the Teacher of the Year!"

"Flattery will get you nowhere, Hudson."

The bell rang, and as the students filed out, Brendan motioned Gunner to his desk. "Are you going to give Sergeant Lavender a call?" he asked him.

"I have to study for my Calculus final. I hate it. I've got a D. If I don't pass, I might not graduate."

"Good luck with that, Gunner. Please try to find time to talk with the sergeant."

"I'll try," he said in a tone that suggested he had absolutely no intention of doing so.

Chapter 19 The Man from Fox 5

Zac and Abby had a love-hate relationship with New York City. Growing up in the Greenbrier Valley, they were used to friendly faces and wide-open spaces. When they moved up north for Zac's stint at Columbia, they were unprepared for The City That Never Sleeps, or even takes a short nap, and put off by the density, noise and expense. The people they passed on the sidewalk didn't even say hello or make eye contact. But as time went on, they came to enjoy being able to get around without a vehicle, have friends from exotic backgrounds, and order Pad Thai and have it show up at their door 20 minutes later. Dog lovers, they were fascinated by the variety of breeds, which were eclipsed only by the variety of owners at the other end of their leashes. By the time Zac finished school and went to work at the *Times*, and Abby landed her nursing job at Sloan Kettering, they hadn't exactly embraced city life, but they'd adjusted to it.

After spending Sunday night in their Astoria apartment, they grabbed some bagels at a local bakery, hopped the Metro and headed into Manhattan for a stroll through Central Park, where spring was underway. The cherry trees, forsythia and wisteria were blooming, and tourists were lining up at the boathouse to rent rowboats. Two hours later they emerged on the Upper West Side in front of the Museum of Natural History, and they decided to visit the Hayden Planetarium. Drifting through space always threw them out of their own orbits, and put the fragility of the planet and preoccupations of its eight billion inhabitants in clearer perspective.

"The earth seems a lot smaller when you leave the planetarium," Zac observed when they popped back outside.

“I know what you mean,” Abby agreed. “It turns you into a cosmic thinker for about five minutes, and then suddenly you're back in the rat race and the universe doesn't seem that important."

Late that afternoon, back at their apartment, Abby pondered restaurant options while Zac kicked back in his Scandinavian recliner and pursued his newfound interest in Fox News. He was surprised to see that the network seemed to have already found a replacement of sorts for Mordecai, a baby-faced meteorologist named Wyatt Carter, whose congenial vibe contrasted sharply with that of his predecessor, but whose views were strikingly similar. He did some quick research and discovered Carter was a weatherman at local Fox 5.

“They already have a new climate skeptic on Fox News,” he announced to Abby.

She failed to share his fascination with the Murdoch media empire. “How about Greek tonight?” she suggested. “We can go to Anassa.”

“Sounds good,” he agreed. He muted Wyatt Carter and turned his attention to trying to set up interviews with Calista Martin and Layla Oakes.

A few hours later, after too much wine and ouzo and a late-night ramble around their neighborhood, they stumbled back to the apartment and fell wearily into bed. The city never slept, but they did, soundly.

\+ \+ \+

Zac phoned Wyatt Carter the next morning. The meteorologist sounded surprised that a *Times* reporter wanted to talk with him. He invited Zac to drop by the Fox 5 studio on East 67th Street. Abby was meeting up with her friends, so they took the N train to 59th Street, said their goodbyes, and headed in opposite directions on the 6 train.

The Fox station was impossible to miss, with its marquee jutting prominently over the sidewalk. Zac presented himself at the reception desk and he was promptly ushered into the office of the man he’d seen on TV. He'd learned from Googling him that Carter was 33, only 4 years younger than himself, but his unlined face without any trace of a beard made him look younger. The meteorologist gave him a handshake and offered him a seat.

Zac explained his connection to the Oakes story while Carter listened with obvious interest and his loafered feet propped on his desk.

"I guess you know I was there when it happened," he said.

Zac was taken aback. "No. I just saw you on Fox News yesterday and I thought you might be worth interviewing."

"I always go to the AMA conventions," the man explained. "I'm on the planning committee that came up with the idea for the debate. Considering how things turned out, I'm feeling more than a little guilty."

"When did you start planning the convention?" Zac asked him.

"Last summer."

"When did you publicize it?"

"We had the schedule and workshops ready by December. We opened the registration in January."

"So whoever decided The Greenbrier would be a handy place to dispatch Mr. Oakes would have known months in advance that he was going to be there?"

"Sure," he said. "It was on our website."

"Was this your first time in West Virginia?"

"No, it was my third. Our planning committee visited the hotel a year ago to check it out and see if it was a good place for the convention. They wined and dined us, gave us vouchers for the casino, took us on the Bunker tour, sent us skeet shooting at the Gun Club and fly fishing with a guide. The whole enchilada. When a hotel knows you're thinking about bringing 600 people there, they go into major ass kissing mode."

"How long was your first visit?"

"Three days. I liked the place so much I brought my wife and daughters back in the summer. That was my second time there."

"Did Mordecai usually attend your conferences?"

"No, he was an inactive member. He was just there for the debate. We put him up in a VIP suite."

"Were your members upset that you were featuring him?"

"Not in the context of the debate. They thought they were going to get to see the gladiator kill the lion, with Hancock as the gladiator and Oakes as the lion."

"How well did you know Mordecai?"

"I didn't know him. We booked him through the speakers' agency that handled his appearances. I was looking forward to meeting him. I was one of the people Fox News called to sub for him after his accident. I liked the way he refused to parrot the conventional wisdom. In some ways he was kind of my role model."

"I gather you hold similar views."

"I was in total synch with him about all this climate hysteria – the pseudoscience and crazy energy mandates. He mocked the CEO's and celebrities who fly off to environmental conferences in their private jets, and he wasn't afraid to name names. He irritated the hell out of some powerful people. I figure they got tired of listening to him."

"Do you think his murder was orchestrated by someone who didn't like his views?"

"That's my theory anyway," he said with a shrug.

"Does Fox News see you as a replacement for him?"

This gave him pause. "I think they see me as someone who can keep the conversation about climate change going," he chose his words carefully. "Whoever did this was obviously trying to shut it down, and they're not about to let that happen."

This guy's smooth, Zac thought. "Are you going to continue working here at the local station?"

Carter swung his feet down from the desk and leaned forward in a way that suggested they were just having a little man-to-man chat. "I think they're testing the waters. Right now I'm shuttling back and forth between here and Fox News headquarters on 6th Avenue. If the ratings are decent, I'll probably end up over there."

"And go from local to national exposure?"

“Isn't that the name of the game, Zac?” Carter asked. “I don’t know how it works in the newspaper business, but in broadcasting most of us want the paychecks that come with a wider audience. If Fox offers me a shot, I’d be a fool to turn it down.”

“If they're looking for another meteorologist who doesn't believe in climate change, they must be fishing in a pretty small pond,” Zac ventured. “Maybe I'm wrong, but I get the impression there aren’t a lot of people in your line of work who share your views.”

“Let me give you a little background,” Carter offered. “Before Oakes came along, the folks who were doing the climate change commentary at Fox News were political pundits. They talked about it being a hoax and an excuse for the Left to push their socialist agenda. Mordecai was a game changer. The man had a degree in meteorology! He talked about the science! He was convinced human activity is too inconsequential to have much effect on the environment and he said so. He didn’t believe carbon dioxide plays much role in temperature variation. He talked about things like ocean temperatures and solar radiation cycles. He liked to point out that extreme weather events have been going on since the beginning of time, and he had plenty of examples. He spoke with the kind of authority you can have if making sense of weather patterns is your profession.”

Zac noticed Carter didn't add the conclusion he obviously wanted him to draw, so he supplied it. “And the powers that be don’t want to hand the issue back over to the pundits because they can't speak with the same authority?”

“Bingo.”

“Back to my original question. I don’t imagine there are many climate skeptics in your line of work. You must be one of the few people capable of taking the baton from Oakes.”

“There aren't many of us,” he admitted. “If you narrow it down to those of us who work in broadcasting, the pond's more like a puddle. I suppose I’m a handy choice because I live and work here and I already have a relationship with Fox. I'm a known quantity.”

"Based on what I saw on TV last night, you're more diplomatic than Mordecai was," Zac said. "Oakes was bombastic. He always went for the kill. My guess is that the folks who were attracted to his message will love you, but the ones who loved his grab-'em-by-the-balls personality are going to have a harder time seeing you as his worthy successor."

"I'm not into getting people fired up. I'd rather make them think."

"Did Oakes ever get death threats?"

Carter shrugged. "I wouldn't know. I've been questioning climate hysteria in deep blue New York for a few years now. People post shit about me, but no one's ever threatened me. Then again, I'm not the provocateur he was."

Zac leaned forward. "I have a favor to ask, Wyatt. I'd like to know if Mordecai ever received any violent threats. I'm sure you'd be interested in that, too. The suits at Fox probably don't want to share this information with the *Times*. I'm sure they'd share it with law enforcement, but I doubt if they'd want to share anything that newsworthy with a rival organization. If you discover there were threats, I'd appreciate it if you'd just text me one word – yes or no – and I'll try to track down the particulars. Even if I don't get anywhere, knowing he kept at it despite threats adds an element to my story. If I use it, I'll attribute it to an anonymous Fox insider."

Carter studied him curiously. "Why, exactly, should I help you?"

"Fair question. We're on opposite sides of the climate issue, but I think you're an articulate spokesman for your cause, and in the long run I think your less abrasive style has the potential to win more converts than Mordecai's."

"I appreciate that, Zac," he reacted to this ego stroke. "Are you telling me I have a friend at the *Times*?"

"Let's just say you have a helpful contact. Will that work?"

The meteorologist considered his request. "One word, huh?"

"Yep."

"Give me your card. I'm always open to making friends. You never know when you might need them."

\+ + +

For old times' sake Zac and Abby had decided to have dinner at Union Square Café. Their favorite eatery had relocated from 16th to 19th Street, and the refined-but-casual vibe seemed to have made the move successfully. They were reviewing the day's adventures over a Mojito and a Mule while they waited for steelhead trout and a duck breast.

"How was your day?" Zac asked.

"Emily and Quinn are native New Yorkers," Abby described her friends. "As far as they're concerned, if you can't see it from the observation deck of the Empire State Building, it doesn't exist. They think New Jersey and Connecticut are the far edges of civilization. It was interesting listening to them."

"How do they reconcile the fact that they have a classy friend from West Virginia who doesn't run around in bib overalls and eat deep-fried roadkill?"

"I'm not sure they've thought about it that deeply."

"What'd you guys do?"

"We took a walk on the High Line, and then we went to an Edward Hopper exhibit at the Whitney."

"Where did you have lunch?"

"Shake Shack."

"Wow, classic New York – the High Line, the Whitney, Hopper and Shake Shack."

"Glad you approve. How was your meeting with the weatherman?"

"I'm still processing it," he said. "Carter professed his undying admiration for Mordecai, but it's obvious he's a major beneficiary from his untimely demise. I'm still trying to figure him out. He's ambitious and cocky, but he's got a smooth veneer."

"You're describing half the guys in Manhattan."

"Yeah, I'm already tired of thinking about him. Let's talk about something else."

"Okay," she agreed. "When we were on the High Line, I couldn't help noticing how fit New Yorkers are compared to West Virginians."

"They walk everywhere!" Zac exclaimed. "They rush to the Metro and race up and down the stairs. They walk to the grocery and the laundry and restaurants. The kids walk to school. The laziest New Yorker gets more exercise in a week than a fitness instructor in West Virginia does in a month. Rural Americans drive everywhere. The kids ride school buses and they get their own vehicles as soon as they have their licenses. Have you seen the parking lots at the high school? They look like the parking lots at the Bristol Motor Speedway on race weekends. New Yorkers rely on their leg power. West Virginians depend on their pickups and SUV's."

"So true," she agreed. "Now that I'm living there I need to figure out how to get more exercise."

"I'll watch your mom if you want to start going to the track or the yoga studio or the aquatic center."

"That sounds like an offer I can't refuse. I'm going to like having a househusband."

"I'm not your househusband," he protested. "I'm a writer working from home."

"I prefer to see you as both."

"I'm trying to think of a clever reply, but here comes dinner."

The back waiter presented their dishes with practiced choreography as their server materialized tableside. "Would you like another drink or some wine?" she played the designated temptress.

"Sure, why not?" Zac caved. "Bring the wine list and we'll throw caution and our budget to the wind. Union Square Café is our favorite restaurant and we haven't been here in a while."

"Then you'd better save room for dessert," she said with a smile. "It's on the house."

Chapter 20 Second Thoughts

They say the criminal always returns to the scene of the crime, but he didn't have any desire to visit the loading dock or the freezer. He'd gone back to the river the day after the murder, when it dawned on him that camp owners sometimes monitored their property with security cameras. If that was the case, someone might have witnessed him using the fire pit. When he reached the rustic cabin and scoped things out, he was relieved to discover the place was decidedly low tech.

Two weeks had passed, and as far as he knew the police weren't making any headway. He imagined them looking for nonexistent fingerprints, footprints, DNA traces and cell tower pings. He'd powered his own phone off and left it in his backpack in the bathroom, and he'd destroyed Oakes' phone and ditched it where the only eyewitnesses were smallmouth bass, catfish and river otters.

He liked to think of himself as a good person, but now he was a killer who had committed murder, words he never imagined would describe him. He supposed technically he was an assassin because Oakes was a public figure. Assassins had bad reputations but good intentions.

He couldn't shake his curiosity about his IQ, so he'd taken three online tests. The results ranged from 109 to 141, reinforcing his belief that these stupid quizzes were just clickbait. The only way he could get an accurate estimate of his intelligence was to submit to testing by a licensed psychologist. He wasn't going to do that unless he decided to apply for Mensa membership.

The only problem with committing the perfect crime was that once you knew you could pull it off, you were tempted to keep going. There weren't any other crimes he wanted to commit, at least for now. Maybe there's wisdom in quitting while you're ahead.

Chapter 21 Pop Quiz

In seven years of teaching, Brendan had learned that when seniors are about to graduate it's a lost cause to try to get them to focus on academics. Their thoughts are on their prom, beach revelry, summer jobs, college orientations and family vacations. He liked to devote this time to Education Lite, when he set aside textbooks and let them talk about what they'd gained from his class, or anything else on their cluttered minds.

After they'd claimed their seats, he made an announcement. "Yesterday Hudson pointed out my habit of threatening you with quizzes, and then failing to follow up. In an effort to correct this, I'd like you to take out pen and paper, and we'll have one on the article I asked you to read."

"I was joking," Hudson offered lamely over his classmates' moans and groans.

"Okay," Brendan said. "Still, I'd hate for you to remember me as someone who lied to you."

"We don't care if you lie, Mr. Bell," Jude assured him. "We all lie."

"How many of you read the article?" Brendan asked.

All their hands went up.

"How many of you just lied about this?" he followed up.

Genesis raised her hand slowly, then Santiago.

"I started it in class but I forgot to finish it," she admitted.

"I didn't forget," Santiago confessed. "I figured we'd have a discussion and I could bullshit my way through it."

Brendan gave him a thumbs up. “Extra points for honesty, Santiago.”

Santiago reacted with a Cheshire Cat grin.

“Okay, here’s what I want you to do,” Brendan continued. “I want each of you to write a sentence about what you learned from the article. That’s all, one sentence only. Then I’ll ask you to read them. You’ve got two minutes.”

Like the contestants on Final Jeopardy, some hastily scribbled their answers while others gave it more thought. Seconds ticked by, with some barely finishing in time.

“Time’s up. You’ve probably figured out that there aren’t any right or wrong answers because you’re just sharing your opinions, and I can’t grade opinions. We’ll start with you, Skylark. What did you write?”

“A poem,” she said.

“I'm not surprised the class poetess wrote a poem. Go for it.”

She picked up her paper and read:

“The world will continue to turn
with little or no concern
that some of its residents
are batshit crazy.”

“I think you have a future as a poet, Skylark,” Brendan congratulated her.

“I stole the batshit crazy line from Joseph,” she credited her boyfriend.

“Everything's grist for the mill,” Brendan replied, a metaphor probably lost on all but one or two of his students. He turned to Zoey. “You're up next, Zoey.”

“People change,” Zoey read her two-word summary.

“Would you care to elaborate?”

“The guys who did the damage, they think different now that they’re, like, older and, like, went to prison. I mean, they still care about the environment and all, but now they know what they did was dumb. I mean, when you’re older you think different than when you're young.”

“Very true, Zoey. Fortunately, we all change. Jude, what did you write?”

"Environmentalists used to worry more about uncontrolled development than climate change," Jude recited.

"That's a good observation," Brendan said. "People didn't give much thought to the climate 15 or 20 years ago, except to complain about the weather. Santiago, are you ready to bullshit your way through the assignment?"

"Yes, sir."

"Go for it."

He cleared his throat and read, "Ecoterrorism is ineffectual."

"I think most of your classmates would agree. I'm impressed you used the word ineffectual. That's high-quality bullshit."

Santiago grinned. "I've had years of practice."

"That talent's going to help you in college."

"I'm counting on it."

"Genesis?"

Genesis picked up her paper and read, "Boys will be boys."

"Ah, yes," Brendan reacted. "The time-honored excuse for idiotic male behavior." He turned to the class introvert. "Rylee, would you like to share what you wrote?"

"Peer pressure makes people do things they wouldn't usually do," she said in a voice a few decibels above a whisper.

"Good observation," he praised her. "You think these young men were showing off for one another?"

"Yes."

Rylee was always so uncomfortable in the spotlight she made everyone else feel her discomfort, so he moved on. "Gunner, will you honor us with your insight?"

"Sometimes heroes go to prison for their beliefs."

"You really think these guys were heroes?" Jude asked him.

"Yes."

"How come?"

"They were warriors fighting to save the planet."

"That's an interesting perspective," Brendan said. "Would you be willing to do something extreme because of your beliefs?"

"Maybe."

Jude shook his head in disbelief. "Don't expect us to visit you in prison, man."

"I don't care," Gunner replied.

"Hayley, you're up next," Brendan invited the class valedictorian.

"They paved paradise and put up a parking lot," Hayley read.

Brendan laughed. "Unoriginal, but it fits with the theme."

"Developers believe construction equals progress," she expanded on the subject. "They think people should be happy when they build highways and apartment complexes and giant warehouses and big box stores surrounded by acres of asphalt. They think people who like nature more than this version of progress are extremists. I don't think the Short Pump guys were heroes, but I get what motivated them."

"I can see you want to write a treatise on the subject, Hayley," Brendan said. "Sorry I limited you."

"We have too many stores and parking lots, and not enough trees," she continued. "Our country is over-stored."

"Some stores are better than some trees," Hudson offered his opinion.

"Shop 'til you drop, Hudson," she came back at him.

"Your turn, Hudson," Brendan offered him the floor.

"When people feel passionately about things, they don't always think clearly," he read.

"Are you speaking from experience?" Brendan asked.

"I started to say they don't always think straight, but I thought I might be misinterpreted."

"Good catch. Joseph, you're batting last in the lineup. Any words of wisdom?"

He picked up his paper. "Once upon a time three clueless idiots set out to save the world."

"That's a good opening line for a novel," Brendan reacted. "Maybe you should write it."

"Twelve years of school and a teacher finally likes something I wrote," Joseph reacted.

"I'm sorry it's taken us so long to recognize your talent."

"You should get your brother-in-law to come speak to us, Mr. Bell," Hudson suggested.

"Zac's a busy guy," Brendan replied. "He's following the Oakes investigation and he's been running around interviewing people. I'll see if he has time to come by and talk with us."

"Cool," Hudson said. "I've never met a writer before."

"Let's continue our conversation about ecoterrorism," Brendan said. "Most people trace it back to a 1975 book called *The Monkey Wrench Gang*. Have any of you heard of it?"

"You mentioned it yesterday," Hayley reminded him.

"The author, Edward Abbey, was a part-time ranger at Arches National Park in Utah," Brendan told them. "He had a master's degree in philosophy from the University of New Mexico, one of those degrees we tend to think of as relatively useless. He wrote his master's thesis about when violence is morally justified. Abbey wasn't an ideal role model. He was a racist and a sexist. He was married five times and he cheated on all five wives. He was opposed to Mexicans coming to the United States, even legally. He took a dim view of Native Americans, too. But he wrote a couple of noteworthy books. *The Monkey Wrench Gang* is about four misfits in the desert Southwest who commit acts of sabotage against the forces they think are destroying the natural world. They wanted to blow up the Glen Canyon Dam because it restricts the flow of the Colorado River. After the book came out, Abbey became a cult figure. *The Monkey Wrench Gang* inspired the formation of groups devoted to eco-sabotage, like ELF and Earth First! The term monkey-wrenching became synonymous with ecoterrorism. Earth First!'s logo has a monkey wrench in it."

"Did the Short Pump guys read it?" Santiago asked.

"I don't know, but it influenced a lot of people back in the day. The main characters see themselves as eco-warriors. They go out at night and pour sand and syrup in construction equipment. Sound familiar?"

Heads nodded.

“Based on the way we think today, *The Monkey Wrench Gang* has some glaring faults. It's a comic romp with an underlying serious message. If you get caught up in it, the book can tempt you to want to engage in the kind of mischief the characters engage in. Even though Abbey is considered a major environmental writer, you’ll notice I haven't assigned his writings to you.”

“Was he a liberal or a conservative?” Hayley asked.

“He’s hard to peg. He was ahead of his time in some ways, and woefully behind it in others, especially in his views of women. I have the impression he was a cantankerous old desert rat. He was visionary on some issues, but myopic on others.”

“What’s myopic mean?” Gunner asked.

“Nearsighted. Not being able to see very far or very clearly. It’s a metaphor for being close-minded.”

“It was on the SAT,” Gunner remembered. “I missed it.”

“*The Monkey Wrench Gang* is credited with giving birth to ecoterrorism,” Brendan continued. “Before the book came out, environmental activists were pacifists who engaged in nonviolent protests like barricading roads and sitting in trees, things that tended to generate a little publicity and land them a couple of days in jail. Abbey’s book ushered in the age of eco-sabotage.” He fetched some notes from his desk and read from a list of some of the better-known acts.

“In 1996 ELF burned down a $5 million ranger station in Oregon. They thought the Forest Service was conspiring with the timber industry to destroy the woodlands. The following year they blew up a plant that slaughtered wild horses and shipped the meat to Europe.”

Joseph, who worked in his family's meat processing plant, winced.

“In ELF's most infamous act, they burned down $12 million worth of buildings at a ski resort in Vail, Colorado, including the lodge and restaurant. The resort was planning an expansion that supposedly threatened the local wildlife.”

This drew the attention of Hayley, whose family owned a ski condo at Snowshoe in Pocahontas County. "Did they close the resort?"

"They rebuilt it," Brendan reported. "Once again, the question is what does sabotage accomplish in the long run?"

"Nothing," Genesis said. "It's just pisses people off."

"Did they get caught?" Gunner was curious.

"The F.B.I. knew the names of the four people involved. They arrested three of them. The fourth is supposedly still hiding in Europe."

"Are they looking for him?" Gunner asked.

"Her," Brendan corrected him. "The culprits were two men and two women. I don't know if they're still actively looking for her. That happened a long time ago."

Jude spoke up. "They were probably sitting around bored one day, and one of them said, 'Hey, I've got an idea - let's torch the ski resort!' "

"Could have been," Brendan said. He returned to his litany of misdeeds. "In 2000 ELF set fire to three dozen SUV's at a Chevy dealership in Eugene, Oregon. They slid trays of gasoline-soaked kitty litter under the vehicles and connected them with rags." He looked up from his notes. "I'm not giving you arson tips, I'm just telling you how they did it," he clarified things. "In 2001 ELF set fire to the Center for Urban Horticulture at the University of Washington in Seattle, where genetic engineering research was supposedly taking place. They did $4 million worth of damage to the building. I said 'supposedly taking place' because they were misinformed. There wasn't any genetic work going on there."

"Oh, well," Hudson said. "We all make little mistakes."

"In 2004 they arrested a man who was involved in the arson. They offered him a plea bargain and he sang like a canary. He gave up the names of all the people who were involved."

"If he had a good lawyer, he's probably in the Witness Protection Program," Santiago speculated. "If he had a bad one, he was probably shanked in prison."

Brendan continued. "In 2008 ELF set fire to some McMansions in a Seattle suburb and did $7 million worth of damage to them. They were opposed to the development because it was near the headwaters of a salmon creek."

"What are McMansions?" Genesis asked.

"Can someone please tell Genesis what McMansions are?" Brendan requested.

"Expensive cookie cutter houses that look just like all the other ones in the neighborhood," Hudson explained. "It's what you get if you've got money but no taste."

"What do you get if you've got taste but no money?" Genesis wondered.

"A rich husband," Hudson suggested.

"You're full of helpful advice, Hudson," Brendan said. "In 2016 five members of a group calling themselves Climate Direct Action shut the valves on the Keystone Pipeline in Washington, Montana, North Dakota and Minnesota. They wanted to get arrested so they could use their trials to publicize the damage fossil fuels are doing to the planet. The Minnesota judge dropped the charges against two of them so they wouldn't have the opportunity to grandstand in court. The judges in the other three states didn't allow them to use their environmental views as a defense."

"It sounds like ecoterrorism peaked in the Nineties and early 2000's and since then it's kind of died down," Hayley noticed.

"True, but every now and then you still hear about an incident," Brendan said. "More recently a Canadian man was arrested for shooting up the pipeline and pump stations in North and South Dakota. He was sentenced to serve 25 years in prison and pay $2 million in restitution."

"All those protesters ever accomplished was turning people against their causes," Santiago shared his opinion. "They're doing exactly the opposite of what they think they're doing."

"Eco-saboteurs are easy to ridicule," Brendan agreed with him. "But if you look at things from their perspective, they're people who feel a strong connection with the natural world and are trying to preserve it. They're well-meaning but their actions are usually ineffectual. You're right, Santiago -

they never seem to achieve anything except getting themselves locked up."

"The guy who put Mr. Oakes in the deep freeze might be pioneering a new approach," Jude said. "If you can't beat 'em, kill 'em."

"That's an interesting observation, Jude," Brendan said. "Oakes' murder could represent a more extreme kind of ecoterrorism. And you had front row seats for it. Well, not quite front row because we weren't sitting in the front row in Colonial Hall and we didn't actually witness the crime. But you know what I mean."

They knew what he meant.

Chapter 22 An Ex-Fiancée

Mordecai Oakes' two-bedroom co-op was on East 75th Street on the Upper East Side, just a few blocks from the Fox station Zac had visited the day before. The woman who met him at the door wasn't the bimbo from Central Casting that Oliver had led him to expect. Calista was a wholesome-looking, short-haired brunette wearing glasses and an Acadia National Park T-shirt. Tanned and fit, she looked like she went on daily 5-mile runs through Central Park.

Calista had initially resisted Zac's interview request. With effort he'd managed to convince her that her perspective on Mordecai was valuable, and that the story of their relationship could help humanize him for people who had only known her late fiancé as a TV personality.

The third-floor apartment was open and airy, with off-white furniture, hardwood floors and area rugs with geometric designs. Zac assumed this lack of clutter was partly due to the owner's need to navigate the premises in a wheelchair.

"Am I younger than you were expecting?" Calista asked disarmingly.

"Not really," Zac replied. "Oliver told me about your age difference."

"Most women Mordecai's age couldn't have managed him without help," she pointed out. "When your partner's paralyzed from the waist down and he weighs 200 pounds, it helps if you're in good shape."

"I'm sure it does," Zac agreed.

She pointed to the dining table by a window overlooking the street. "We can sit over there. You want coffee or something?"

"Thanks, but I've already had 3 cups. I'm trying to get a handle on my addiction."

"Coffee's my thing, too," she admitted.

"Do you mind if I record our conversation? I want to make sure I quote you correctly."

She gave it some thought. "Yeah, I guess it's okay," she decided.

He set his phone on the table and activated Voice Memos. "Oliver told me you were one of Mordecai's caregivers after his accident."

"I worked for the Home Health Network," she explained. "I'm an LPN, but I didn't want to pull hospital shifts, so I decided to specialize in SCI." She could see from Zac's puzzled look that this nurse talk needed explanation. "Spinal cord injuries," she translated. "When Mordecai came back from rehab, I taught him how to self-catheterize. I helped him rethink the layout of this place, too. He had the bathroom remodeled with a roll-in shower and a handheld nozzle. He installed a safety valve to keep the temperature below 120 because he didn't have any feeling in his legs and he could have scalded himself and not even felt it. I convinced him he needed to take his phone in the shower so he could call for help if he needed it."

"I've never thought about those things," Zac admitted.

"Nobody does until they have to deal with it," she said.

"I'll bet he really appreciated you."

"Most of the time. Mordecai was a very proud man. He didn't want me around when he did his talks and his book signings because he didn't want to look like he needed help. He used to grumble about not needing a nursemaid. That's why I didn't go along on his trips and why I wasn't there when ..." Her lips started to quiver and tears welled in her eyes. "What kind of heartless asshole would do something like that to a person in a wheelchair?"

Zac felt his take on Mordecai softening a bit. It sounded like the man who came across as so cocksure of himself was struggling to project strength and independence. "I'm really sorry for your loss, Calista," he said softly.

She grabbed a Kleenex and dabbed her eyes. "I can't stop thinking about it. I've hardly slept."

"Do you have family here?"

She shook her head. "My mom and my brothers and their families live in Maine. My brothers have a hardware store."

"What brought you to New York?"

"Ever heard of Aroostook County?"

"No. Is that in Maine?"

"Yeah, way up by the Canada border. Aroostook's bigger than Connecticut and Rhode Island put together. It's mostly potato fields and wind farms and an abandoned Air Force base. Winters last forever. People who think it's cold here have never had to deal with the kind of weather like I did growing up. There's not much there for young people, unless you're into snowmobiling or ice fishing."

"So you went off in search of adventure in the big city?"

She nodded. "After I got my LPN."

"My wife Abby's a nurse," Zac told her. "She used to work at Sloan Kettering. Now she's caring for her mother, who has Alzheimer's." He didn't mention her M.S.N. degree, knowing that nurses who were tasked with delivering hands-on care didn't always appreciate the ones who outranked them in the medical hierarchy.

"Hospitals aren't my thing," Calista said. "I don't like all the bureaucracy."

"What kind of man was your fiancé?"

"Mordecai had two sides," she said. "The guy you saw on Fox wasn't the guy I knew. From the way he acted on TV, you'd think he was always running his mouth. He wasn't really like that."

"Oliver's not sure his father believed what he was preaching," Zac shared.

"That's probably the only thing Oliver and I agree on."

Zac decided to press the issue. "After the Dominion Voting Systems lawsuit against Fox, it came out that their commentators and producers didn't really buy what they were telling people about the 2020 presidential election being rigged. They were worried about losing viewers, so the network told them what they wanted to hear, even though the producers knew it was, and I'm quoting them, 'whackadoodle'. They wanted to protect their brand. That makes me wonder if Mordecai shaped his views to suit the Fox demographic. There aren't many meteorologists who believe climate change is a hoax."

"I don't have a clue what he really thought," she said. "I don't know if he believed in heaven or hell or voodoo or global warming. We never talked about that kind of stuff."

"What did you talk about?"

She shrugged. "Sports, what was for dinner, the workouts he did for his upper body strength, the places he was giving talks, our crazy neighbors, where we wanted to go on vacation. Everyday stuff."

"Did he watch Fox?"

"Constantly. He made notes about what people said in his little notebook."

"Do you have the notebook?"

She shook her head. "He always kept it with him. I guess it's in West Virginia."

"Did he ever get threats because of things he said on TV?"

"If he did, he didn't tell me. He wouldn't have wanted me to worry."

"Did he talk about Oliver and Layla much?"

This gave her pause. "Not really. They came around a lot after the accident. Once they knew he was going to be okay, we hardly ever saw Oliver, and Layla only dropped by when she wanted money. Mordecai knew they blamed him for their mother's death, but he didn't know what to do about it. Guess they had to blame somebody. He never got over Marianne's suicide. He could hardly talk about her. From what I know, after she died, he just buried himself in his work. He hired a housekeeper to clean the place and fix their dinner. Oliver went off to college, Layla fell in with the wrong crowd, and they had their own lives. My family's close. Mom and I text and Facetime. I talk with my brothers every week. I buy gifts for my nieces and nephews. Mordecai didn't just lose his wife – he lost his family. He was pretty lonely until I came along. The only thing that kept him going was his job, and he had to take time off from that after the accident." She hesitated. She seemed to remember that the person on the other side of the table was planning to write about what she was saying. "You're not putting all this in your story, are you?"

"I'm not into publicizing people's personal traumas and making their lives more complicated, if that's what you're asking," Zac said. "If I use any of what you're telling me, I'll find a way to soften it. I promised Oliver I wasn't going to write about his mother's suicide. I might change my mind, but if I do, it will have to be in a way he and his sister feel comfortable with it."

She gave him a hard look. "I hope I can trust you."

"You can trust me, Calista. It's interesting - Oliver said the same thing the first time I met him."

"You're a good listener. You seem more like a therapist."

He laughed. "That's the first time anyone's ever said that. I can't wait to tell my wife. She thinks I *need* a therapist."

"I bet you're wondering what I saw in Mordecai."

"I am, but I couldn't think of a nice way to bring it up."

"I'm not stupid. Everybody thinks someone my age couldn't possibly be attracted to someone his age. I got it from my family all the time."

"You don't have to tell me you're not stupid, Calista. You've already convinced me of that."

"I've got daddy issues," she put it plainly. "Our dad ran off when we were little. I guess he didn't want to be with Mom and he didn't want to pay child support, so he pulled a disappearing act. We don't have a clue where he is. Mom raised us by herself. My high school counselor pointed out that instead of having crushes on the cute boys, I had them on the men teachers. My attraction to Mordecai was probably the same deal. He needed me and I felt comfortable with him. My family thought I was totally nuts. Oliver and Layla thought I was taking advantage of their poor, naïve father. I get it, but there wasn't a naïve bone in Mordecai Oakes' body. To be honest, I spent more time with him and showed more concern for him than they did."

Zac wasn't expecting such confessional-level candor, even though most of the small-town folks he knew were open books like this; they didn't know how to be anyone but themselves. There were exceptions – the occasional shyster lawyer or corrupt politician, the kinds of characters who populated Grisham novels – but for the most part, the folks he'd grown up around were disarmingly honest. He wondered if Oliver had shared the contents of Mordecai's will with Calista, or confronted her about vacating the apartment. "Have you talked with Oliver lately?"

"Oooh, yeah," she said. "He's kicking me out. I've lived here over two years and suddenly I'm not trustworthy. Mordecai told me he was taking care of me in his will, but he didn't say how. Oliver doesn't think I should get what he wanted me to have because the will's written like we're already married. That's the bad news. The good news is that because Oliver's such a nice guy, he's offering me $250,000 not to take them to court."

"I don't have a dog in this hunt, Calista, but from Oliver and Layla's point of view it makes sense. You could keep each other tied up with legal maneuvering for years, with lawyers' fees eating away at the estate until there's not much left for anybody."

"My brothers say the same thing. Take the money and run. Come back home and work at the hardware store or start your own business."

"Is that such a bad idea?"

"Mordecai would want me to fight for it, but you've got to be really pissed off to keep that kind of thing going. Part of me says this chapter of my life's over and it's time to move on. But Aroostook County seems like my past, not my future."

"There's always Portland or Bar Harbor," he suggested. "Those are cool places."

"I'll go to Maine for a while. Wherever I end up, it's back to work. If this happened after the wedding, you'd be talking to a 26-year-old millionaire. But maybe I don't deserve it." She stared out the window pensively and then turned back to him. "Do you believe in karma, Zac?"

No one had ever asked him this before, and he gave it some thought. "I guess in a way I do and in a way I don't," he decided. "I think in the end people pretty much get what they deserve. The love you take is equal to the love you make, and all that. Then again, Mordecai didn't deserve a painful, lonely death. So maybe I don't believe in it. Thanks for giving me something to ponder."

"You're welcome."

"Would you mind showing me around the apartment? Sometimes little details catch my eye and I end up working them into a story. I've already decided to mention the shower renovation."

"There's really not that much to see," she said. They got up from the table. Zac grabbed his phone and followed her with the recorder running. The living, kitchen and dining areas flowed into one another. They went in the kitchen.

"I tried to talk Mordecai into redoing the kitchen with lower counters and cabinets," she said. "But he was worried if he ever had to sell the place, nobody would want it. He could reach part way across the counters and he could open the drawers and lower cabinets, but he couldn't reach the upper ones."

"Did he talk much about the accident?"

"He didn't remember it. That's not unusual with traumatic injuries." She led him into the living area. "He spent a lot of time in here watching sports and listening to music." She pointed to the wall-mounted Sony. "When it came to TV, he thought bigger was better. This one's 70 inches and he was already talking about getting a bigger one."

"What kind of music did he like?"

She rolled her eyes. "Jazz. Not my thing. At least I didn't have to listen to it when he wasn't around."

"What do you like?"

"Country. He hated it, but not as much as he hated rap."

"You can take the girl out of the country, but you can't take the country out of the girl."

"Something like that." She pointed to a closed door. "Want to see his office?"

"Sure."

"That's how he used the second bedroom. Nobody ever spent the night here except Oliver a couple of times, and he slept on the couch in the living room." They entered a room with a built-in desk and bookcases, an ego wall covered with awards, plaques and photos, and a freestanding fitness station. "This is where he wrote and worked out."

Zac studied the space. The awards were from conservative groups, and most of the pictures showed Mordecai smiling next to business-types. The desk was crafted to accommodate his wheelchair. The books were a hodgepodge; he seemed to have a thing for David Baldacci novels.

A framed photograph on the desk caught his eye. It showed the young Oakes family on the steps of the Lincoln Memorial, smiling for the camera, blissfully unaware that their collective future held suicide, drug addiction, disability and homicide. Marianne Oakes was glowing in a strapless summer dress, with her able-bodied, dapper-looking husband beside her. Oliver and Layla, who looked about 13 and 10, were standing on the steps below their parents. Zac was mesmerized; he took a picture of the picture. His gaze wandered to a ceramic jar next to it filled with identical ballpoint pens. He pulled one out and examined it. "Montblancs! These must have cost a fortune."

"They're fakes," Calista explained. "Mordecai's little joke. He got them from China, a hundred for 30 bucks. When he did signings and he met someone he liked, he'd give them one. They thought they were getting something valuable, but they aren't even worth 50 cents."

Zac studied the pen. "How can you tell the difference between the knockoffs and the real deal?"

"I asked him the same thing. He said the real ones have the word *Pix* and serial numbers on the gold bands. These don't have *Pix* on them and the numbers are all the same. Supposedly the real ones are made from some kind of special material. If you hold them up to a light, they look like dark red wine. These are just plain old black plastic."

"Can I have one?"

"Help yourself."

He gave the pen a test scribble. "Works just like a Bic."

"Bics cost more."

He poked around the apartment, made a few more notes and thanked her for the tour. He was tempted to ask if she had any theories about the murder, but he decided not to pursue the subject.

"I really appreciate your meeting with me, Calista," he said. "You're very kind and this has been really helpful. Good luck getting things worked out with Oliver and Layla."

"Thanks. I'll need it."

"Am I free to use the things you said?"

She bit her lower lip and gave it some thought. "Don't say anything about the $250,000 or Oliver kicking me out. That's between us. My brothers think this is just his opening offer and I can get more."

"My lips are sealed. I've learned not to publish things that upset my sources. Not only do they stop cooperating, they claim they never said what they said and I made it all up. I'd like to stay in your good graces."

"Just make me come off looking good."

"That won't be hard, Calista. You seem like a good person. I think Mordecai was very lucky to find you."

"Thanks."

\+ \+ \+

Zac and Abby rendezvoused in the Washington Square dog park. She'd picked up wraps and chips for their lunch, and they made themselves comfortable on a bench and ate while the dogs provided the entertainment.

"When you say New York City, a lot of people think of the Statue of Liberty or Times Square," Zac said. "I think of Washington Square, with the buskers and chess players and street performers. It's more of a neighborhood hangout than a tourist attraction."

“I always think of Central Park,” Abby said.

It was early afternoon and the sunshine and 70-degree weather left them feeling content to do next to nothing. They used to try to identify the dog breeds, but things had gotten out of hand with the Dandie Dinmont Terriers, Norwegian Lundehunds, and oodles of doodles, so they'd given up on this game. They finished their lunch and went for a stroll around the square, stopping to watch a man who was offering free haircuts.

“How was your visit with Mr. Oakes’ fiancée?” Abby asked him.

“Eye-opening. Calista wasn't the future trophy wife I was expecting. She's an outdoorsy-looking, down-to-earth young lady who seems like she'd be a more appropriate girlfriend for Oliver than his father. I like her. She was helpful. She's got me rethinking some of my ideas about Mordecai. She said I seemed more like a therapist than a journalist.”

Abby did a double-take. “What?”

“I told her you’d find that amusing.”

“Did you tell her your wife thinks you *need* a therapist?”

“That's exactly what I told her.”

An enterprising busker had wheeled a piano under the iconic marble arch, where he was doing a credible job on New York State of Mind. Abby stuck a couple of dollars in his bucket.

“Do we have anything lined up for tonight?” Zac inquired.

“I scored a couple of tickets,” Abby said.

“For what?”

“I was looking at Broadway plays, and then I saw that Lady Gaga's playing at Madison Square Garden. It might be a while before she makes it to our neck of the woods, so I got us tickets in the nosebleed section. We can scalp them if you’re not up for it.”

“You know me. I’m up for anything.”

“Good. Let’s start working on our costumes.”

He studied her, trying to decide if she was kidding. “On second thought, maybe there are some things I'm not up for.”

Chapter 23 Imitating Normal

Wendy Lavender was determined to ambush Gunner Hoke, who seemed to be doing his best to avoid her. She waved to the security guard at The Greenbrier's front gate, hung a right and hugged the property's eastern edge, winding her way through the Creekside neighborhood where his family lived.

The homes dotting the manicured grounds on both sides of Howard's Creek were picture-perfect, like everything else at the resort. She pulled up to the Hoke residence, a rustic townhome attached to a row of similar ones bordering the Old White TPC golf course. Gunner's black Tesla was in the pea gravel driveway. She pulled her cruiser behind it and climbed the steps to the covered porch.

Gunner answered the door and stared wordlessly at the officer, waiting for some explanation for her presence.

She gave him a warm smile. "Hi, Gunner. I was in the area and I thought I'd drop by and see if you have a few minutes to talk."

He looked like he was trying to make up his mind, so she tried another approach. "Is that your car?" she asked.

"Yeah."

"I've never seen the interior of a Tesla," she stretched the truth. "Will you show me yours?"

"Okay."

They left the porch and headed to the car. "It's a Model 3," he said. "It was pre-owned. It had 32,563 miles on it. People think Teslas are luxury cars, but it's pretty basic except for the computer system. My mother's Lexus has less road noise and a better sound system."

"I guess an electric vehicle fits with your environmental beliefs?"

"Gas-powered vehicles release 70 tons of carbon dioxide in the atmosphere in their lifetime," he recited. "The electricity to charge a Tesla releases 30 tons. If power stations switch to clean energy sources, it will eliminate all the emissions from electric vehicles. People claim that mining lithium for batteries is as bad as mining coal, but once the lithium is out of the ground, the environmental impact is over. When coal comes out of the ground the environmental impact is just starting."

"Most young men your age are less concerned with their vehicle's environmental footprint than whether it looks cool and how fast it'll go."

"This car takes off like a rocket," he told her. "Faster than any muscle car. Electrons travel from a battery to an electric motor a lot quicker than gas travels from a tank to a piston."

"Do you have a charging station?"

"We put one in the garage. The hotel has some by the north entrance."

"How far can you go when it's fully charged?"

"They claim 267 miles, but I haven't tested it."

Gunner slipped in the driver's seat and Wendy climbed in the passenger side. "It's so uncluttered," she admired the interior. "I guess you control everything with the computer screen?"

"Yes. It has way more features than a gas-powered car, but you have to know how to find them. Some of them are pointless."

"Like what?"

"You can make the road on the navigation screen look like a rainbow."

"That is pretty pointless," she agreed. "Unless you're trying to entertain a 4-year-old. Even then, they'd probably lose interest after 30 seconds."

"Do you know about fart mode?"

"No. How does that work?"

He started the car, pulled up an app with a whoopie cushion icon and pushed it.

"Wow, that's realistic," she marveled. "Some employee in the Tesla factory probably had to eat a can of baked beans to make that recording. What's the button that says Fart on Turn Signal?"

"When you engage the turn signal, it makes farting noises instead of clicking sounds."

"That would get old quickly."

"What else do you want me to demonstrate?"

"Nothing really. Do you have a few minutes? Can we go inside and talk?"

"Okay."

"Are your folks home?"

"Dad's at my sister's tennis match. Mom's still at the clinic."

She followed him into a living room with a vaulted ceiling, three skylights and a fireplace. The room opened to a screened porch facing the golf course. The row of townhomes shared a common backyard separated from the course by a line of oaks. Wendy took it all in. "This is beautiful, Gunner. Open and airy but very cozy."

"My parents' and my sister's bedrooms are down the hall," he pointed. "Mine's upstairs."

"I didn't see any signs of life when I drove through your neighborhood."

"These are mostly vacation homes," the young man explained. "Hardly anyone lives here year-round. The owners come for a week and then you don't see them again for months."

"It must be pretty lonely for a teenager living here on the grounds."

"Everyone at school thinks we're rich because we live at The Greenbrier. I tell them we have one of the cheap places, but they don't believe me."

"Price is relative, Gunner. I don't imagine your home is what most people call cheap."

"It is compared to the ones that cost four or five million."

"Are you happy here?"

He shrugged. "Everywhere I go people think I'm weird."

"Because you're on the autism spectrum?"

"I liked it better when they called us Aspies. Whatever you call it, I've got it. My brain has a different operating system than most people's. It works logically. I don't pick up social cues and I don't know how to act around people. I'm learning how to imitate normal."

"Are you imitating it now?"

"Yes. I'm looking in your eyes to show interest and interact with you. I'm giving you a chance to say things and I'm responding to what you say. If you say something that's wrong, I'm not going to correct you because you might be embarrassed."

"None of this comes naturally to you?"

"No. My therapist shows me pictures of people's facial expressions and tells me what they mean so I'll know how to react the right way. When they're happy and when they're mad and when they're surprised. There are 26 different expressions people's faces can have when they're angry."

"It sounds like a complicated way to live."

"I don't know why I have to do all the adjusting. I wish other people would just adjust to me."

"That's the problem with being in a minority, Gunner. Aspies aren't the only ones with that issue. I'm a woman working in a male-dominated field, supervising a bunch of guys who aren't exactly thrilled about it. I have to do plenty of adjusting, too."

They were standing in the living room. Wendy suspected that offering her a seat wasn't going to come naturally for him. "Shall we go out to the porch?" she suggested.

"Okay."

The weathered teak furnishings and green and white striped cushions echoed one of The Greenbrier's familiar motifs. Wendy helped herself to a rocker and Gunner took a seat in an armchair. "What do you remember about being at the hotel the day of the debate?" she got down to brass tacks.

"Everything. I have an exceptional memory."

"If you can remember 26 facial expressions for anger, your memory's a lot better than mine. What did you do during your free time?"

"I went to the room where the meteorologists had their exhibits and I looked at them."

"What did you learn from the exhibits?"

"The American Meteorological Association has known for decades that the world is getting warmer. They have research about the air and ocean temperatures, and charts and policy statements. I don't know why they were having a debate. Why would they invite someone to tell a bunch of lies?"

"They must have thought it would serve some purpose," she ventured. "What was your opinion of Mr. Oakes?"

"He was dangerous because a lot of people believed him."

"What was the harm of people believing him?"

"The main cause of climate change is greenhouse gases from cutting down forests, burning fossil fuels and raising livestock. If people don't believe these human activities are causing problems, they're not going to do anything about it. All the gases we're releasing are going to keep getting trapped in the atmosphere and build up, and the planet's going to keep getting warmer. The ice caps are going to melt, the oceans are going to rise, and we're going to have worse wildfires and tornados and hurricanes and floods. Whole species will die out. The world will gradually become less habitable for humans and we'll eventually become extinct, like the dinosaurs. People think fixing the climate will wreck the global economy, but if we don't fix it, there won't even be an economy."

"Not a rosy picture," she agreed. "I guess I haven't spent much time thinking about it."

"The future's going to happen whether we think about it or not."

"Gunner, the difference between you and the average person is that you not only think about it, you seem to care very deeply," she observed. "Why do you suppose that is?"

"Because I get obsessed with things."

She smiled. "Maybe the future of humanity isn't such a bad obsession. Do you feel like it's your role to help save the planet?"

"It's everybody's."

"One you take seriously?"

"Yeah."

"You're an interesting guy, Gunner."

"Thanks."

She was trying Zac Wolfe's approach, when he said sometimes people will tell him more than they'll tell the police because he didn't interrogate them, he chatted with them. Now that they seemed to be building some rapport, it was time for more pointed questions. She was about to ask one when the front door opened and Dr. Hoke burst in wearing a white coat and a worried look. She rushed to the porch.

"Is something wrong?" she asked the sergeant.

Wendy stood up. "Oh, no, nothing's wrong." She offered her hand. "I'm Sergeant Wendy Lavender with the State Police. I'm investigating the homicide at The Greenbrier."

"Yes?"

"I've been interviewing the students in Mr. Bell's class who were at the hotel to see if they noticed anything unusual when they were there. I missed Gunner the day I was at the school, so I'm just trying to catch up with him and finish my interviews."

"Gunner, did you notice anything at the hotel that day?" his mother asked him.

"I noticed everything."

"Well of course you did. But did you notice anything that might help the police?"

"I don't think so."

She turned back to Wendy. "I'm sorry if I'm a little edgy, but you don't expect to come home and find a police car in your driveway and an officer questioning your son. You never know what kind of trouble teenagers are going to get into."

“I’m not in trouble,” Gunner insisted. “She talked to everybody in the class.”

“I love your place,” Wendy switched gears. “It has such a comfortable feel.”

“We wanted a home, not a showroom,” the doctor said. “I like bright colors, but I didn’t want any of those chichi Greenbrier touches like birdcage chandeliers or checkerboard floors.”

“I'm in and out of a lot of homes with my job,” Wendy said. “This one feels right. I could live here.”

“Thank you, Sergeant,” the doctor was pleased to hear this. “Did you show her your room, Gunner?”

“No.”

“Gunner chose some interesting wallpaper for his room. Why don’t you take the Sergeant upstairs and show her?”

“Okay.”

Gunner climbed the carpeted staircase with Wendy in tow. The home was 1½ stories, and his bedroom was tucked under the sloping roof, with a lone dormer providing the only natural light. Because of the angled ceiling, the only sizeable wall was behind the bed. The wallpaper covering it was one of the most famous photographs in history, Earthrise, an image of the planet taken by an astronaut during a lunar orbit.

“I feel like I'm lost in space,” Wendy reacted. “It makes you realize how insignificant we really are.”

“And dumb,” Gunner added.

“Thanks for taking time to talk with me today, Gunner. There are a couple of other things I want to ask you, but I feel like I’ve been here long enough. Let's continue our conversation another time. Okay?”

“Okay.”

“By the way, I think you're doing a good job imitating normal.”

“Thanks.”

She glanced around the room. “I see you're a very organized young man. You even have your shoes lined up. I should hire you to organize my closets.”

"Okay."

"I'm just kidding."

"Okay."

On her way out she popped in the kitchen to say goodbye to his mother. “It was nice meeting you, Dr. Hoke. If I ever need a gastroenterologist, you’ll be my first choice.”

The doctor smiled. “How do you know I’m any good?”

“If you can make your home feel this comfortable, I'm sure you can make your patients feel comfortable, too.”

She laughed. “Good luck with your investigation. Are you making any headway?”

“I'd like to say yes, but, truthfully, I don't know.”

As she backed out of the driveway, she found herself hoping for his sake, and that of his family, that young Gunner wasn't involved in the homicide. On the other hand, she saw Brendan Bell's point. This young man had a strong dislike for the deceased, a reason to want him eliminated, intimate knowledge of the hotel, total access to everything on the grounds, and the smarts to have pulled the whole thing off.

Chapter 24 Hell's Studio

For the third day in a row Zac found himself on Manhattan's Upper East Side. This time he was visiting the NYPD's 19th Precinct, looking for information about the hit-and-run that had cost Mordecai Oakes the use of his legs. Lieutenant Gabriella Hernandez had fetched a slim file on the incident. For some reason the file included a clipping from the New York Daily News that had appeared the day after the accident. It read:

FOX COMMENTATOR INJURED IN HIT-AND-RUN

> Police from the 19th Precinct are looking for a driver who struck a pedestrian on East 75th Street on Tuesday, April 2, at approximately 2:05 p.m. and left the scene of the accident. Upon arrival, officers found Mordecai Oakes, 50, unconscious in the street near his East 75th Street apartment, with severe trauma to his body. Oakes, a meteorologist and commentator for Fox News, was transported from the scene to New York City Presbyterian Hospital, where he remains in critical condition.
>
> Police determined by questioning Joseph Silva, 36, a resident of the block who witnessed the accident from his apartment window, that the male operator of a dark color SUV traveling westbound at a high rate of speed struck Oakes as he was

crossing the street. The impact sent the victim flying in the air, landing some 25 feet down the street after bouncing off a parked car. The vehicle continued westbound on East 75th Street.

The investigation is ongoing by the NYPD Highway Patrol Investigation Squad. Anyone with information can contact the Crime Stopper's Hotline at 1-800-577-8477 or www.nypdcrimestoppers.com.

The police report was slightly more detailed. A CCTV camera at the end of the block, one of thousands in the city, had captured a navy-blue Toyota RAV4 hitting the victim and speeding off. Efforts to enhance the license had failed, leading them to conclude that the plate had been purposely obscured, possibly by a screen remotely controlled from the vehicle's interior. This suggested the attack may have been premeditated. Attempts to track the vehicle through the city with cameras were unsuccessful.

Zac laid the file aside and looked at the lieutenant. "Were any suspects questioned?"

"Not unless it's in the file," she said.

"I'm guessing the eyewitness who saw the accident from his window was probably paying more attention to the victim than the vehicle. All he seemed to remember was a white male in a dark SUV."

"It's not much to go on," she agreed. "Unless some new evidence comes to light, it isn't something we're likely to reopen."

"Maybe there is new evidence," Zac suggested. "The victim of the hit-and-run was murdered in West Virginia two weeks ago."

Lieutenant Hernandez's eyes grew wider. "Is this the man they found in the freezer? The weatherman?"

"The one and the same. Makes you wonder if the freezer was someone's unfinished business."

"Are there any suspects?"

"No serious front runners. I guess we need to find out if any of them owned a navy-blue RAV4 three years ago."

"That vehicle could have been rented or stolen," she pointed out. "Or the homicide could be completely unrelated."

He handed her the file. "I know. I was hoping your report contained some sort of helpful information. If there are any clues buried in here, besides the make of the vehicle and a white male driver, I don't see them."

\+ + +

Zac eyeballed the seedy 6-story Hell's Kitchen apartment building that gentrification had yet to reach. He climbed the steep stairs feeling like he was hiking in the Alps. He was sweating by the time he reached the fifth-floor studio occupied by Layla Oakes and her boyfriend Declan.

Layla answered the door. She looked thin and world-weary, a far cry from the bright-eyed girl in the picture on her father's desk.

"Hi, Layla. I'm ..."

"The dude from the *Times*," she cut him off. "I don't want to talk with you, but for some reason my brother thinks I should."

Zac was pleased to hear Oliver had run interference for him. "I know this might be hard for you, but I don't feel like I can write about your father without talking with the people who knew him best. I've met with Oliver a couple of times, and I spoke with Calista Martin yesterday."

She rolled her eyes.

"I hear you're not on friendly terms."

"What's your name again?"

"Zac."

"Well, Zachary – "

"Zachariah," he corrected her. "My mother got it from the Bible."

"Well, Zachariah, how would you feel if your father was planning to make a 26-year-old ho your stepmother?"

"Not very good."

"What'd she tell you?"

"That's between us," he wanted to keep their conversation confidential. "She seemed pretty honest."

"Apparently you bought it."

He could see this young woman wasn't blessed with her brother's laid-back personality and people skills. She still hadn't asked him in. "Do you mind if I come in?" he invited himself. "I'd like to record our conversation so I don't misquote you."

She studied him skeptically. "Sure you want to do this? I've got a potty mouth."

"I can work around that."

"Good fuckin' luck." She let him in and they claimed seats on the opposite ends of the sofa/pullout bed. He placed his phone beside a vape pen on the cluttered coffee table and turned on Voice Memos.

"I'm not into reporters," she said. "How's this work?"

"There's nothing to it," he promised her. "It's painless."

"Yeah, that's what my dentist always says."

"I live in Astoria," he eased into things. "I'm from West Virginia and I happened to be down there when your father died. I met your brother at The Greenbrier and we've been keeping in touch. I'm really sorry for your loss, Layla. I know this is an awkward time to ask you questions, but if I'm going to write about this, I need to get the facts straight."

"Awkward's nothing new for me. When Dad started making an asshole of himself on national TV, I didn't want anyone knowing I was his daughter. Oliver felt the same way. I'm surprised he's talking to a reporter."

"I think he just needed someone to vent to that night at the hotel, and I happened to be there. He told me quite a bit about your family, and I promised him I wouldn't use anything he didn't want me to mention."

"I can vent to my boyfriend. I don't need *The New York Times*."

"Oliver told me Declan's an actor."

"He's trying to get into the Actor's Studio," she explained. "He auditioned but he wasn't accepted. They let you try once a year. He gets another shot at it in July."

"Would I have seen Declan in the movies or on TV?"

"Probably not. So far he's just background talent. That's what they call the extras. Declan's way too hot for an extra so it's just a matter of time before he lands some bigger roles. He's out kayaking on the East River for some drug commercial now." She reached over to a side table and grabbed a photo. "Here's his headshot."

Zac studied the handsome young face, with piercing blue eyes that rivaled a Siberian Husky's. "If acting doesn't work out, he can probably make it as a model," he said.

"Yeah, right," she reacted. "Modeling's even tougher to break into than acting. They're both next to impossible ways to make a living. Believe it or not, this shithole is costing us 2900 bucks a month. We would have been kicked out a long time ago if Dad hadn't bailed us out."

Zac eyed the cramped quarters. "Seems pretty steep for what you get."

"It's the cheapest thing we could find. The average Hell's Kitchen studio goes for $4500. Declan thinks we should move into Dad's apartment, but Oliver says we've got to sell it because we can't afford to keep up the payments. Whatever we do, we've got to get rid of the ho first."

"When I was there, I noticed a photo on your father's desk," Zac related. "It's a picture of your family at the Lincoln Memorial in Washington. Everyone's beaming ear-to-ear. It made me think about all the trauma your family's been through, and how we never know what the future has in store for us."

She grabbed her vape pen, pressed a button, took a drag and exhaled. "I guess that's the cue to tell you my pathetic life story?"

He smiled. "How'd you guess?"

"I was born in Indiana, then we moved to Lubbock, Texas, then Macon, Georgia, then Philly, then here. We were like Army brats, except instead of military bases we hopscotched between TV stations. Oliver always made friends, but it was harder for me. Just about the time I'd finally make onc, we'd move again. Mom hated the moves and they argued all the time. The family in that picture didn't have many smiley days like that. Hell, we were probably faking it then. Oliver's always been kind of bulletproof. He shrugs things off. Shit gets to me."

"What did your parents argue about?"

"The biggest thing was Mom working. She wanted to go back to TV work, but Dad's supersized ego couldn't handle it. Our Aunt Jill says when Mom and Dad worked together at the station in Indiana, she was the star and she could have had a really big career. When we moved to Texas she wanted to keep working, but he was against it. Every move it was the same old thing. He was afraid her star was going to outshine his. She got depressed and she never pulled out of it. She wasn't as strong on the inside as she seemed on the outside. She should have ditched him and done her own thing."

"I appreciate hearing your take on things, Layla," Zac said. "It helps explain why you and Oliver weren't very close to your father."

"What I can't handle is the picture that's stuck in my head. I'm 15, staring at my mother's body in a tub full of blood. You know what it's like having something like that stuck in your head?"

"I can't imagine it."

"After she died, Dad tried to play Mr. Nice Guy with us, but we never bought it. He finally gave up and threw himself into his work. Oliver went off to college and I was kind of on my own."

Since she was being so nakedly honest, Zac decided to ask about her drug use. "Oliver told me you've struggled with drugs and you've been to rehab."

"Yep. I'm living proof the third time's not the charm."

"Does the fact that you've rehabbed three times mean you were trying to deal with it, or someone kept making you go?"

She took a fortifying drag and flopped back on the couch. "Here's the deal with drugs, Zachariah," she said, waving her vape pen as she spoke. "Part of you knows you're fucking up and you need to do something about it. But another part of you needs it. My reason's kind of obvious – Mom's exit scene. Drugs help me forget about it for a while."

"But aren't they kind of ruining your life at the same time they're helping you?"

"Yeah, that's the problem. No one's invented the perfect one. The one that makes you feel great and doesn't have any harmful side effects."

"What's come the closest?" he was curious.

"I'm still looking. Any suggestions?"

"I don't think journalists should prescribe drugs," he turned down the invitation. "What did you learn in rehab?"

"Something I would never have believed if I hadn't tried it: 12-Step groups actually help. Next question."

"New subject. Do you think your father bought all the stuff he said on TV and put in his books, or was he just playing to his audience?"

She wagged her head, like she was trying to decide. "I don't know. Does it matter?"

"If I'm writing about him, it matters if he didn't believe in what he was selling," he said. "Oliver thinks he was just trying to get rich. Calista claims they never talked about environmental issues."

She pursed her lips and gave it more thought. "The money part probably goes back to feeling like he wasn't a good provider," she said. "He was worried about putting us through college. Turns out he only had to pay for Oliver because I didn't go, but Oliver's school was expensive. He did a semester in New Zealand, and that wasn't cheap. After footing Oliver's bills and making the down payment on his co-op, he needed money. He had a chance to make it, and he started kicking ass with the books and everything. I don't know if he believed his own bullshit or not. Doesn't matter to me."

"You're young, Layla," he reminded her. "It's not too late for college."

"Maybe you should take a look at my high school grades before you pack me off," she reacted.

"School's not your thing?"

"I don't know what my goddamned 'thing' is. I guess right now it's trying to help Declan with his career."

"You're too good to be someone who lives off her father's money until she ends up dying from a drug overdose.

The way I see it, you can spend the rest of your life wallowing in self-pity or you can get over it."

"That's how you see it, huh? You make everything sound so simple. You have kids, Zachariah?"

"I have a 12-year-old son."

"What's he like?"

"He's so good at zeroing in on my faults and inconsistencies, he'll probably end up making his living doing stand-up routines about his weirdo father."

She studied him curiously. "Oliver's right - you're okay," she passed judgment on him.

"Okay's not hard to achieve, Layla. You should try it."

She cocked her head. "I hear they've got good drugs in college."

"The best," he promised her. "They're so good you won't even know you're there."

She smiled for the first time. "You are so completely full of shit."

He turned off his recorder and stood up. "See? I promised it would be painless."

"For you. For me it was a root canal." She followed him to the door, a few steps from the couch. "Before you go, I've got a question for you."

"What?"

"Who killed my father?"

"I don't have a clue, Layla. I wish I could tell you. I'm just a writer working on the story. What do I know?"

"Not much, apparently."

Chapter 25 Class in the Grass

Brendan had never liked the confines of a classroom. Occasionally, when the weather was cooperative, he held class in the grass. He figured if his students were going to talk about Mother Nature, they didn't always need to do it in a climate-controlled setting.

Gunner arrived at the picnic tables where they gathered for these confabs. He made a beeline for his teacher. "Sergeant Lavender came to my house," he reported.

Brendan was pleased to hear this. "Glad you two finally got together, Gunner," he said. "How did it go?"

"Okay."

"I'm not sure what that means."

"We didn't finish because my mother came home and they started talking. She said she's coming back."

"Good. I'm sure the Sergeant appreciates your help."

Gunner took a seat at one of the tables and Brendan turned his attention to Hayley and Hudson, who were stretched out on the lawn. "Are you two planning to join us?"

"You call this Class in the Grass," Hudson protested.

"No afternoon siestas, please," he chided them. "Don't let Class in the Grass turn into Yawn on the Lawn."

"We'll participate," Hayley promised. "We're too opinionated to keep our mouths shut."

He addressed the group. "I don't know how you managed to pull the wool over Sergeant Lavender's eyes, but you made a favorable impression on her."

"She's pretty friendly for a cop," Joseph offered his assessment. "You get the feeling you could talk her out of a speeding ticket."

"She's the head of the Criminal Investigation Unit," Brendan tried to put things in perspective. "She has more important things to worry about than someone doing 67 in a 55 zone."

"Try 82," Joseph said. His friends' heads swiveled.

"Did you lose your license?" Zoey asked.

"No. Since I'm going in the Navy, my lawyer convinced the judge to just let me give a talk to the Drivers Ed class so it wouldn't be on my record. Then she sent me a bill for $850. She has me on a payment plan."

"I think that's called the wages of sin," Brendan said.

"I think it's called sticking it to your client," Joseph had his own interpretation.

Brendan shrugged. "I'm not sure how to gracefully segue from Joseph's travails to today's lesson. Yesterday we talked about the radical actions some environmentalists have taken to get people to pay attention to their cause. Your consensus seemed to be that they haven't accomplished much. What I want to know is what you think your generation can do to help bring about the necessary changes."

"Do we have to speak for our whole generation?" Jude objected. "You should just ask us what we can do personally."

"Or what we'd like to see happen," Hayley further amended the question.

"Fair enough," Brendan decided. "What would you like to see happen, and how can you contribute?"

"I'm pessimistic," Jude shared. "We're talking about huge problems people are ignoring, and complicated solutions. For everything that needs to change, there's some big industry fighting it. Even the simplest things, like clothes. We manufacture too much clothing, we get rid of it too quickly and tons of it ends up dumped in landfills. Meanwhile the fashion industry keeps trying to convince us we need to constantly update our looks with crap 12-year-old Asians are making in sweatshops. The fossil fuel industry wants to preserve their right to pollute, the seafood industry wants to keep overfishing the oceans, and agribusiness wants to keep spraying poison on fields. There aren't enough people worrying about the bigger picture."

"Did you think about any of this before you took my class?" Brendan asked him.

"Not really."

"So I've turned an optimistic young man into a pessimist?"

"No, you've turned an apathetic young man into a realist. It's not your fault, Mr. Bell. You've just made me aware of stuff I would have figured out on my own sooner or later."

"Sounds like you're feeling powerless."

"What can we do?" Jude asked. "Email our legislators? I don't see that having as much influence as the contributions they get from lobbyists and their rich friends."

"What about the rest of you?" Brendan polled the class. "Do you all feel the frustration Jude is expressing?"

"It'll take a couple of generations for things to change," Hayley predicted. "Eventually people will see things differently because they'll have to. Someday we'll be the elected officials and the ones running the companies."

"By then it'll be too late," Gunner said. "We can't put the polar ice caps back on. They took millions of years to form."

Brendan turned to his most engaged student. "Gunner, it sounds like you're saying we've recognized the problem too late to be able to do anything about it. Solutions take scientific breakthroughs plus the political will to address the situation, and you see us barreling toward disaster faster than we can convince people we need to do something."

"Exactly," Gunner agreed.

"Is there a solution?"

"Smarter leaders," he suggested.

"Well that's not happening any time soon," Hudson said as he stared at the passing clouds.

"Solar and wind aren't magic solutions," Santiago added his two cents. "Gates' book says that to run the country on sunshine we'd need an array of solar panels as big as a whole state. We'd have to take all the tribal land from the Native Americans and turn it into solar farms. Solar power's not reliable anyway, because so far there's no good way to store energy for when the sun doesn't shine. Solar farms and wind turbines are okay, but they can't meet the world's energy needs. I mean, it probably takes a whole turbine just to power Zoey's hair dryer and styling brush."

She gave him the finger.

"I think the answer's some kind of nuclear - fission, fusion, whatever," Hayley voiced her opinion. "It's clean and sustainable. If we work out the safety and disposal issues, we can run the world with it. If the answer isn't nuclear, then it's some other technology we haven't perfected yet, like hydrogen cells or geothermal. Scientists will figure it out, but meanwhile the clock is ticking."

"It's just our luck we were born in desperate times," Hudson bemoaned his generation's fate.

"The Greek philosopher Hippocrates said desperate times call for desperate measures," Brendan said. "Step One is convincing people that as far as the environment is concerned, these really are desperate times. Until the majority of people believe it, any solution's going to be a hard sell. I spend my life preaching the environmental gospel to young people, but I'm afraid I'm not making enough converts to have much impact."

"I know one problem," Jude said. "The people who run for political office are always telling us that things are going to hell and we need to elect them to fix everything. People have gotten so used to hearing their bullshit and ignoring it that when things really are going to hell, no one believes it."

"That's very insightful, Jude," Brendan praised him. "You're saying it's the Boy Who Cried Wolf Syndrome, except instead of a flock of sheep, it's the Planet Earth that's getting eaten by the wolf."

"Oh, well," Hudson sighed as he continued watching the drifting clouds. "It was a nice planet while it lasted. It's a good thing we've got more important things to worry about, like the prom."

Chapter 26 A Fake Cop

Zac and Abby were mulling over how to spend their last full day in the city. The forecast was calling for late afternoon thunderstorms, and they were considering going to the New York Botanical Garden before the storms rolled in.

"There's one more person I'd like to interview before we leave town," Zac said to Abby. "Layla's boyfriend. Declan's a mystery man. I don't even know his last name. He's supposedly an actor. When the police start thinking about it, I think it will cross their minds that an actor could play a bellman."

Abby gave it some thought. "Wouldn't Oakes have recognized his daughter's boyfriend?"

"Depends on how well he knew him and Declan's acting chops. Layla said he's trying to get into the Actor's Studio. You've got to be pretty serious to even think about that. I mean, we're talking Marlon Brando, Al Pacino, Bradley Cooper, Julia Roberts."

"I think Al and Bradley could pass themselves off as bellmen," Abby reacted. "I'm not so sure about Julia."

"Don't underestimate Julia."

"The Botanical Garden's up in the Bronx," Abby pointed out. "Do we have time for you to interview Declan and then make it up there?"

Zac considered the logistics. "Probably not. Let me see if Declan's available. If I can't get together with him, we'll go to the Botanical Garden. If I can, we'll save it for next time. Maybe we'll go to the Central Park Zoo instead."

"So our last day in the Center of the Known Universe is coming down to either flowers or sea lions?" Abby asked.

"That's about the size of it."

A phone call to Layla revealed that Declan's last name was Delaney. Background work was keeping the aspiring actor busy; he was about to head over to Steiner Studios in Brooklyn. They agreed to meet for a few minutes in a park across the street from the studio before he reported to work.

\+ + +

At first glance, young Mr. Delaney impressed Zac as the kind of person who was so physically flawless that he'd probably been told since early childhood he should be in the movies. He was wearing a NYC policeman's uniform, which Zac found a little off-putting until he explained that today's gig involved marching a handcuffed actor playing a perp through a scrum of actors posing as reporters, into a make-believe courthouse. With luck he would end up with a few seconds of screen time in a TV pilot.

"Did you wear that uniform on the subway?" Zac was curious.

"Yeah, it's mine," Declan explained. "Production companies like it when extras have their own costumes because it saves them from having to rent them. I've got a few for standard roles, like cooks and cops and business types. I list them on my resume and they let me know if they want me to use them."

"Can't you get in trouble for impersonating an officer?"

"Impersonating an officer doing what - riding the Metro? I mean it's not like I'm sticking parking tickets on cars."

"You might be able score a free donut at Krispie Kreme," Zac suggested.

The aspiring actor flashed a smile worthy of a toothpaste commercial. "I'll take free anything," he said. "I'm making $29 an hour because I'm union. Joining SAG-AFTRA set me back 3000 bucks plus the yearly dues, so I've got to work my ass off just to recoup what I've shelled out."

“Whew,” Zac commiserated. “You're paying your dues literally and figuratively.”

“Acting's not easy to break into, even dumb shit like this. I'm giving it five years. If it hasn't turned into something by then, I'll have to come up with another idea.”

“How old are you, Declan?”

“Twenty-three. I get why you wanted to talk to Layla, but why me? That dude wasn't my father. I never even met the guy.”

“You never met Mordecai?”

He shook his head. “Nope. Never wanted to.”

“How'd you and Layla get involved?”

He hesitated. “I was her sponsor.”

“Her sponsor?”

“NA.”

“What's NA?” Zac asked.

“Narcotics Anonymous.”

“Oh.” He felt clueless for not picking up on this. “Can your romantic partner be your sponsor?”

“No, that's just how we met. Two months into it I decided I'd rather be her boyfriend. Your sponsor's almost like your favorite uncle or aunt, and I didn't want us to be like that.”

“I guess your sponsor has to be clean?”

“At least a year. I was clean 19 months when we met. I'm at 31 now.”

“Congratulations.”

“Thanks.”

“Oliver said Layla's still struggling.”

“Yeah, she's got issues.” He studied Zac suspiciously. “She gets these nightmares about her mother. I hope you're not planning to write about it.”

“No,” Zac tried to put his mind at ease. “In the end I'll run it by you guys to make sure I've got my facts straight and you're okay with it. I've written about a lot of people over the years and no one's sued me yet. If people are worried, I let them see my rough drafts, which is something most journalists won't even consider doing. I feel it's the least I can do in exchange for their cooperation. I'll give you guys a chance to read it before it's published, and if you're not comfortable with something, we can talk about it."

"What do you want to know? I don't mean to be rude or nothing, but I don't have much time."

Zac reached for his phone. "Mind if I record this?"

"Nope."

"First, tell me a little about yourself."

He reached for the satchel at his feet, pulled out a copy of his resume and handed it over. "This might help."

Zac gave the document a quick scan. "I'd like to know more than where you went to school, your singing, dancing and stage combat abilities, and your list of costumes."

"Like what?"

"Where are you from? What kind of family did you grow up in?"

"South Jersey. My dad works for the Postal Service and my mom teaches in a Montessori school. I've got two older sisters."

"And you were the cute little brother everyone spoiled?"

"Sounds about right."

"What's your family think about Layla?"

"They think I can do better."

"What do you see in her?"

"A good person who's had a rough life. I think she'll come out okay but it'll take a while."

"Are you on a rescue mission?"

"You can't rescue people from substance abuse. They have to rescue themselves."

"Is her father's death and the fact that her financial situation is changing going to help or hurt her?"

He shrugged. "Could go either way."

Zac saw that his prompts weren't eliciting much. Declan was supplying basic answers but he wasn't volunteering anything. He decided to dig a little deeper. "Oliver said you and Layla made a trip to West Virginia to borrow money from him."

This got his attention. "Oliver told you that?"

"He was talking about Layla's drug issues and how Mordecai cut her off when he found out where his money was going. He said you guys were in pretty dire straits when you came to see him."

"We were a month behind in the rent. Hitting up Layla's brother seemed better than getting put out on the street. I'm working my ass off, man. I even joined a group at Christmas that went around singing holiday songs in offices and stores. We're paying him back, it's just going to take a while. I thought this was a personal deal between him and us. Why's he telling a reporter about it?"

"Declan, pretty soon police investigators are going to be asking you much harder questions. The fact that Oliver and Layla and Calista stand to benefit financially from Mordecai's death makes them potential suspects as far as the investigators are concerned. The fact that you and Layla are an item puts you on their radar, too. They're going to want to know about the nature of your relationship, your finances, your movements over the past couple of months, your whereabouts at the time of the murder. From what Oliver told me, he and Layla had issues with their father. They were understandable issues, but when you combine that with the inheritance situation, the cops are going to be very nosy."

"Oliver and Layla didn't even know their dad had a will until the day before he died," Declan reminded him. "That's not enough time to come up with a murder plot and recruit someone to dress up like a bellman and stick him in a freezer. Whoever did it had to have been planning it for a while. How would Oliver know where some hotel's freezers were?"

"All good points, but they'll want to know if you and Layla were ever at The Greenbrier."

"We'd never heard of the place until this happened. We didn't know her dad was having some big debate there. It's not like she kept up with his schedule."

"What was Layla's relationship like with her father?"

"Limited."

"How limited?"

"He gave her a little financial help. The family sort of came unglued after Layla's mother died. Layla and Oliver didn't like the crap their dad was saying on TV and they pretty much kept their distance from him."

"Did you ever watch him?"

"Couple of times."

"You're an actor - what was your impression? Was Mordecai acting, or was the guy on TV the person he really was?"

He shrugged. "It's hard to say because I didn't know him. But if he was the same dude in real life, he would have been a big pain in the ass."

"Oliver and Calista think it was an act."

"Then it must have been a good one because he made serious money." He grabbed his satchel and stood up. "Gotta go. I'm still not sure why you wanted to talk to me."

"I want to get to know your family so I can tell this story better than anyone else."

"Whose side are you on?"

"Nobody's. I just want to follow it wherever it leads. Who knows - in the end I might take someone's side. I feel a lot of sympathy for Oliver and Layla and Calista. Mordecai's harder to figure out."

"Level with me, man. You really think the cops are going to be suspicious of me?"

"Cops are suspicious of everybody, Declan. That's the nature of their job. In their thinking, you're guilty until proven innocent, just the opposite of the way it's supposed to work. They come up with a theory and they get carried away trying to prove it. That's how innocent people get accused of things. The lead investigator is Sergeant Wendy Lavender. She seems fair, but either she or someone who works with her is going to show up and ask you a lot of very personal questions. She's not the type to try to pin something on an innocent person, so you shouldn't have anything to worry about."

"Good. I've never been accused of murder before."

"You're not being accused of it now," Zac assured him. "Just be ready to prove your whereabouts on the day it happened."

He thought about it. "I think I was walking down the sidewalk in a Kia commercial." He thought some more. "No, that was the day they found him in the freezer. The day it happened I was dancing in an ad for Hormel Chili Cheese Dip."

"And I think my job's weird."

The young actor grinned. "Later, man. Good luck."

And with a casual wave, Declan Delaney was off to be a fake cop.

\+ + +

Abby was waiting by the sea lion tank at the Central Park Zoo when Zac found her. "Have they fed them yet?"

"No, but they eat every two hours, like Connor. Speaking of our son, I talked with your mom this morning. She said he's expecting us to come back with some kind of fabulous gift as a guilt offering for not bringing him along on the trip."

Zac had an idea. "I saw a store on Fifth Avenue that sells drones," he said. "I've been kind of wanting one myself."

"Great. My husband and son can terrorize the neighbors."

"No, just spy on the ones sunbathing nude in their back yards."

The sea lions were racing around their open-air pool, entertaining themselves and the spectators watching through the pool's glass walls. "These guys are a lot more energetic than the ones we saw lounging on the docks in San Francisco," Abby noted.

"Their California relatives are probably exhausted from swimming around the bay, looking for food," Zac said. "These guys get the equivalent of room service at the Waldorf Astoria."

"Did you interview the actor?" Abby asked him.

"Yeah, but I don't think I'm a world class private investigator," he admitted. "None of the people I've met strike me as potential suspects. Calista, Oliver, Layla and Declan all stand to benefit from Mordecai's death, and theoretically any one of them could have orchestrated it. They just don't act like guilty people."

"Zac, you're a nice guy," Abby said. "People like talking with you and they show you their best sides, so they're not going to seem like the kind of schemers who would lock someone in a freezer."

"I think if I put them at ease, they're more likely to tell me things," he defended his approach.

"That doesn't mean the things they're telling you are true. Maybe you should start second guessing some of it."

"I'm trying to imagine a scenario that involves these folks. Let's say Oliver and Layla wanted to do away with their wealthy father because they blamed him for their mother's suicide. Let's say Declan, who claims he never met Mordecai, did the dirty deed. If that's the case, why would Oliver volunteer that Layla and Declan traveled to West Virginia to borrow money from him? He wouldn't want me to know they'd been anywhere near West Virginia. If it came to light that they traveled there before Mordecai's death and someone questioned him about it, *then* he would have come up with the alibi about them needing to borrow money."

"Makes sense," Abby agreed.

"Oliver seems content with his lifestyle, not someone who wants money so he can go off and do something else. Layla's a lost soul, not a criminal mastermind. And Declan's like every other aspiring actor we've known, busy paying his dues. He's proud of his sobriety and he seems to be trying to help his girlfriend. Bad guys are supposed to act like bad guys. None of these people do."

"What about Calista?"

"She already had access to Mordecai's money because she was living with him and about to marry him. What would have been her motive?"

"Maybe living with him was getting to be too much of a burden."

"She strikes me as someone who would have just walked away from the relationship. You'd think if money were her thing, she would have been more curious about the particulars of the will when he was working on it. Supposedly all she knew was that he was 'taking care' of her. She didn't know he was planning to give her half the estate until Oliver broke her the news. And how would she have known anything about a freezer at a hotel 500 miles away in a place she'd never been? Even if she hired a hit man, hit men shoot people, they don't dress up like bellmen and lock them in freezers."

"What about the weatherman?"

Zac hesitated. "Wyatt Carter wasn't on my radar until I happened to catch him on TV. I was looking for a back door into the Fox nation, and he's low enough on the totem pole that I thought he might talk with me. It worked, and he turned out to be a much better source than I was expecting. He was actually at the convention in White Sulphur Springs. He was one of the people who planned it and came up with the idea for the debate."

Abby's eyes grew bigger. "Really?"

"Yeah. He was in the right place at the right time. Suddenly he's their new climate hysteria critic. He's a true believer, but he's not a blowhard like Mordecai. He's a smoothie."

She gave it some thought. "I think you need to get out your little notebook and add 'Find out more about Wyatt Carter' to your To Do List."

Chapter 27 Revisionist History

Abby and Zac believed in traveling light, so it hadn't taken them long the next morning to throw their things back together for the return flight to Roanoke. They were standing outside the apartment with their luggage and a mini-drone, waiting for a ride to LaGuardia, when an unexpected call came from Calista Martin.

"Zac?"

"Hey, Calista. What's up?"

"Sounds like you're outside."

"We're waiting for an Uber. We're heading back to West Virginia."

"I'd like to talk with you again."

"I promise I'll keep in touch."

"I mean today. I don't know how much longer I'll be around."

"Is it important?"

She hesitated. "You can decide that. I lied to you about something."

"Can we talk about it on the phone?"

"I'd rather do it in person."

"Let me consult my wife." He covered the receiver. "Calista wants to see me again. She claims she misled me about something and she wants to set things straight."

Abby shrugged. "There's a later flight. Is your mother expecting us any certain time?"

"I told her we'd be back mid-afternoon, but I can tell her we'll be later."

"Fine with me. I'll rebook."

"Calista? Would you mind if we show up at your door with our luggage? Abby can entertain herself while we talk."

"I don't care if she joins us. She's a nurse, right? She knows how to keep things confidential. HIPPA and all that."

"Whatever you think. Can we come now? We'll just have the driver bring us to your place instead of the airport."

"Come on over. I'll make some coffee."

"Abby's a tea drinker."

"I don't have any tea."

"No worries. She always carries an emergency bag of Earl Gray Double Bergamot."

"Okay. I'll see you shortly."

Abby gave Zac a quizzical look. "What do you think she misled you about?"

He shrugged. "I don't know. Mordecai's will? Maybe she knew what was in it and she's afraid the police are going to give her a lie detector test. We'll soon find out."

\+ \+ \+

When people have something weighing on their minds, they don't always spit it out. That was the case with Calista, who made small talk while she busied herself fixing their drinks, fluttering around like a nervous butterfly.

Mordecai's airy Upper East Side digs represented a slice of New York life that Zac and Abby had never had the pleasure to taste. "All you have to do is walk down the street and you're in Central Park," Abby marveled.

"It's not one of those fancy places with a doorman and a skyline view, but the location's great," Calista replied. "I'm not sure what I did to deserve it. Nothing, I guess, but now I'm spoiled rotten."

Zac smiled. "That reminds me of Mae West's line, 'I've been rich and I've been poor. Rich was better.' "

"We never felt rich," Calista insisted. "I mean Mordecai was well-off compared to a lot of people, but he wasn't *Manhattan* rich. He worked hard to make the money come in faster than the bills."

"I'm sorry for your loss, Calista," Abby said.

The young woman stared at her a long moment. “Thanks. Fox sent me flowers, but everyone seems more focused on how he died than the people he left behind.”

“I know you're going through some big changes. I hope it all works out for you.”

Calista turned to Zac. “I was wrong. She's the therapist.”

“Yeah, I know,” he replied. “I'm one of her patients.”

They made themselves comfortable in the living room. They talked about the city. They talked about the zoo. They talked about nursing. This was fine and dandy, but Zac was awaiting the Big Reveal. After fifteen minutes of chitchat, he'd had enough.

“Calista, you said there's something you want to discuss,” he addressed the elephant in the room. “Don’t keep me in suspense.”

“Should I get lost?” Abby offered.

“No, it's okay,” Calista replied. “I figure he'll tell you anyway.” She took a deep breath that became a sigh. “You asked me if Mordecai really believed all the stuff he said on TV.”

“I've been asking everybody that,” Zac said. “Oliver thinks it was an act. Layla's not sure and she says she doesn't care. Wyatt Carter, the meteorologist who hopes to fill his shoes on Fox, thinks Mordecai's beliefs were sincere.”

“Well, they weren't,” she dropped a little bomb. “Mordecai wasn't dumb. He knew what he had to do to be successful on Fox. He joked about it. He said his real talent was making bullshit sound reasonable. He was always looking for stuff he could use. He'd come across something online or hear some podcast, and he'd change it up and turn it into one of his rants.”

“Can you give me an example?” Zac asked.

“There's this climate change denier guy who posts temperature charts on Facebook, supposedly proving that back in the day it used to be hotter, or there were more wildfires or hurricanes or whatever. Mordecai called him the king of the cherry pickers, because long range trends are what tell you what's going on, not isolated events. I mean, so what if it was

108 in Kansas City in July 1946? He talked shit about the guy all the time, but he borrowed his ideas."

"How do you know what he believed?"

"I lived with him," she said with a shrug. "We talked about it."

"Why are you telling me this now?"

"Because Mordecai was a very intelligent man. I don't want you thinking he was crazy."

"But if he knew what he was saying was wrong, he was a fraud."

Calista frowned.

"An *intellectual* fraud," he modified it. "He was telling people what they wanted to hear so he could make a nice living."

"If you listened to him carefully, sometimes he wasn't. He did a show about wind turbines where he talked about how much steel goes into making them, how many thousands of tons they weigh, and how much gas it takes to haul them around the country in huge trucks. He said manufacturing steel throws off more carbon dioxide than all the vehicle emissions in the world combined. The fiberglass blades wear out and they can't be recycled. By the end of the show, you're convinced wind power's a dumb idea. But if you listened carefully, he wasn't denying climate change, or even saying people aren't responsible for it. He was just mocking how we deal with it."

"But it fits with his general theme of environmentalists being clueless," Zac argued. "He spent plenty of time tossing red meat to the Fox faithful. He used phrases like *climate hysteria* and *climate madness* and *climate hoax* and *phony science* to suggest scientists and liberals exaggerate the problem for their own purposes. He preached the fossil fuel gospel."

"That doesn't mean he believed it," she countered. "Maybe it was a bogus way to make a living, but it paid for this apartment and put food on our table. We wouldn't be sitting in here now if he hadn't done it."

Maybe he wouldn't be dead either, Zac thought to himself. The journalist in him wanted her to go on the record.

"Would you be willing to do an in-depth interview with me about this?"

"Hell, no!" she reacted. "Are you kidding? I wouldn't be able to go anywhere without reporters hounding me. They'd want me on CNN and MSNBC. His fans would claim I'm making it all up or someone was paying me to say it. This thing would follow me around the rest of my life."

"Then why are you telling Zac about it?" Abby was curious.

"I thought if he knew the truth, maybe he could find a way to prove it without dragging me into it. I don't care if people know what Mordecai really thought as long as you leave me out of it. Truthfully, I don't think he would mind either. He had a project he was working on."

"A project?" Zac inquired.

"Check his notebook and his laptop," she suggested.

"If they were in the freezer with him, they're probably in the State Police evidence room," Zac pointed out.

"Can you get them?"

"Oliver would stand a better chance. They might fall in the category of personal belongings they'd be willing to turn over to him."

"Well, there you go," Calista said. "Problem solved."

"Maybe," Zac wasn't so sure.

"When are you going to Maine?" Abby asked her.

"Soon. I'm going to hang out with my family while I figure things out and wait for all this to blow over."

"You probably won't have to wait long," Zac predicted. "Mordecai's death is a major story now, but as soon as something else comes along it'll be relegated to the back pages, unless they find the person who did it."

"Maine's a nice place to hang out," Abby opined.

"My family's way up north," she explained. "I don't think they'll be sending reporters up there to find me. I hope not anyway."

"One more thing," Zac remembered something he'd meant to ask her before. "When Oliver had dinner with his father the day before he died, Mordecai said he was doing something that would make his children proud. Any idea what he was talking about?"

"I'm pretty sure it's what I'm talking about," she said. "If you get his laptop, you'll figure it out. Oh yeah, there's something else I didn't tell you."

"What's that?"

"I'm pregnant. Mordecai's going to have a third child."

The air went out of the room.

"Do Oliver and Layla know?" Zac asked her.

"No, not yet. I just found out."

Abby got up, went over to the young woman and gave her a hug. "Congratulations, Calista."

+ + +

They were riding in the back seat of an Uber, heading to LaGuardia. "So what do you think about all this?" Zac asked Abby.

"I think you know a few things the police don't know. You know about Carter. You know Mordecai's public and private personas were different. And - drum roll, please - you know Calista's pregnant with his child."

"True," he agreed. "I'm wondering what the police know that I don't."

Chapter 28 The Finger of Blame

It was time for Gunner, Round Two. Wendy didn't want to risk having a stray member of the Hoke family interrupt her follow-up interview with him, so she'd arranged to meet her Potential Person of Interest on the colonnade of The Greenbrier's north entrance, overlooking a European-style formal garden. He arrived on his mountain bike, and she watched him pedal around the circular driveway, park his bike and bound up the exterior staircase. She waved a greeting and he claimed one of the adjacent white rockers.

"Hi, Gunner. What's new?"

"I'm going to be a lifeguard," he reported.

"Where?"

"The pool at the Summit."

"Where's that?"

"Up on a mountain. It's only for Sporting Club members."

"Meaning the people who own property here, like your family?"

"Yes. There's a restaurant and a gym and an outdoor pool. My parents think it will be good for me to work there this summer so I can practice relating to people before I go to college."

"That sounds like a good idea, even though the people you meet in that setting may not be much like the ones you encounter in college. Is this your first job, Gunner?"

"Yes."

"I'm sure you'll do well. Are you nervous about it?"

"No. Why do you want to talk with me again?" he was curious. "You didn't talk to anyone else in my class twice."

"How do you know?"

"I asked them."

She'd already decided how to approach this. "When we talked before you said two things that caught my attention. One is that you have an excellent memory. The other is that your mind works logically. Maybe you can help me think through this case."

He wasn't buying it. He looked her in the eyes. "You think I killed Mordecai Oakes, don't you?"

"No," she said, wishing she sounded more convincing. "What makes you think I see you as a suspect?"

"Because I'm obsessed with the environment, I hated Mr. Oakes, I can't prove where I was, and everyone thinks I'm weird."

"Those things don't necessarily add up to murder."

"*Am* I a suspect?" he asked point blank.

"Should you be one?" she avoided the question. "*Did* you do it?"

"No."

"Would you tell me if you did?"

"No."

She laughed. "This isn't the conversation I thought we were going to be having. If you don't mind, let's go back to square one. Help me think through things. What would the person who committed this crime need to know?"

He ticked off a list. "When Mr. Oakes was getting here, what room he was staying in, when he was speaking, if he was alone or he had someone with him, how to get a bellman's uniform, where the freezer is, how to get him into the freezer, whether he could escape once he was inside, how to make a getaway, and whether any security cameras would record him."

"All excellent points. What kind of person would it take to know all that?"

"Someone who knows a lot about The Greenbrier."

"An employee?"

"Maybe. Or someone who spent a lot of time hanging around, figuring it out."

"What makes you think you're on my radar?"

"I think Mr. Bell said something to you. How else would you know our class was there? Hundreds of people were at the hotel that day, and you're questioning some random high school students, acting like we can help you. It's not logical."

This guy's too logical, she thought. "If that were true, why would Mr. Bell have come to me?"

"Either because *he* thinks I might have done it, or because *he* did it and he's trying to get you to look in another direction."

The sergeant's jaw practically hit the colonnade's concrete floor. "Wow! Do you really think your teacher is capable of murder?"

"Maybe," he said with a shrug. "He hated Mr. Oakes as much as I did. He brought us over here and got rid of us for two hours. He said he was grading papers in a room by the main lobby, but when I walked by the room, he wasn't there. He had a backpack with him and he might have had the bellman uniform in it. His wife works here and he comes here all the time, so he knows his way around."

Her head was spinning. "Do you honestly think Mr. Bell would risk his career and his marriage and his good standing in the community just to kill someone he saw on television? Or are you upset because you think he's suspicious of you?"

"He had all the same opportunities I had. Even more because he controlled our schedule. He could have figured out from his wife or somebody where Mr. Oakes was staying and if there was anyone else with him. I wouldn't have known that stuff. Maybe you should be questioning him instead of me."

And with that he got up from his rocker and headed for the staircase. He turned back. "It takes a pretty clever killer to arrive at the crime scene on a school bus and leave the same way, doesn't it?" He hurried down the stairs to the ground level, hopped on his bike and pedaled off.

Chapter 29 Home Again, Home Again

Zac and Abby were on their way back to West Virginia from the Roanoke airport. The winding trip through the Virginia countryside featured rolling scenery and the blink-and-you'll-miss-it town of Iron Gate, an infamous speed trap. They slowed to a crawl and managed to pass through without contributing to the municipal fundraising efforts. They hurried the rest of the way, crossed the state border and reached Lewisburg by 7:15.

They walked in the door and found their two mothers on the couch, watching Wheel of Fortune. Connor appeared from his bedroom.

"Welcome home," Zac's mother greeted them. "How was your week?"

"Great, but it reminded me of why I like being here better," Abby replied. "More importantly, how was your week, Debbie?"

"It was a slower pace for me, but everything went fine. Connor helped with the cooking."

"We made One Alarm Chili last night," Connor reported. "The recipe was Five Alarm, but we dialed it back a few alarms to take it easy on the grannies' stomachs. It has two secret ingredients."

"What are they?" his mother inquired.

"Pineapple and cocoa," he revealed.

His grandmother sighed. "It's not a secret anymore," she said.

"It's not a well-kept one, Mom," Zac reminded her. "I've watched you make it a few dozen times. But we'll swear

Connor to secrecy. Only the Wolfe Pack will know your recipe." He turned to his son. "How's Little League going?"

"Grandma wouldn't let Uncle Brendan drive me," he griped. "She made me walk to the park!"

"Six blocks," his grandmother pooh-poohed it. "A healthy 12-year-old boy can walk six blocks."

"You're just trying to get me in shape for farm work," he accused her. "Next thing it'll be, 'A healthy 12-year-old boy can stack 1400 bales of hay.' "

"I survived it," his father reminded him. "Do you know what position you're playing?"

"Shortstop."

"The coach must think you're pretty good. Shortstops need speed and quick thinking."

"It's not like the other positions require slow, dumb people, Dad."

"Maybe he thinks you're not quite as slow or dumb as the others."

"Whatever." He sidled up to his mother. "You know how little kids, when their parents get back from a trip, come running and ask, 'What'd you bring me?' I'm too old for the running part."

"Good," Abby replied. "Does that mean you're too old for the present part?"

He grinned. "I'm willing to accept one."

"You probably don't remember this, Connor, but when you were four, we got you a t-shirt at the beach with a shark on it that said *Here Comes Trouble*," his mother recalled. "We've never been able to find another gift as appropriate as that one. Unfortunately, they don't make them in larger sizes."

"So you got me a Yankees ball cap?"

"Give us some credit, Connor," his father said. "Your parents are more creative than that." He handed him a shopping bag. "Ideally, this will get you interested in robotics, aerodynamics, engineering, aviation, photography and videography, and improve your eye-hand coordination."

The boy eyed the bag suspiciously. "This sounds way too educational." He reached in and pulled out the box. "Wow! A drone!"

"Your first job is figuring out where you're allowed to fly it. Part of this area is in the restricted flight path for the airport, but I'm not sure where it is."

"This is GREAT! Thanks! You guys should go away more often."

"You might be able to use it to make some money," Zac suggested. "Realtors need aerial shots of their properties. You see their videos online all the time."

"Wicked."

"It's too late to get into it now, but we'll mess around with it tomorrow and get it set up. We'll have to find somewhere that's not in the flight path."

"I'll stay up all night reading the directions."

Abby smiled. "That's fine, Connor. Tomorrow's Saturday."

He headed to his room with the drone while the adults remained in the living room. "How'd the week go?" Abby asked Zac's mother.

"Your momma's such a lovely person," she said. "She knitted, we watched TV, we chatted. "One evening Connor wanted to watch a movie, so we watched it together."

"What movie?" Zac was curious.

"Moonrise Kingdom. It's a little odd for my taste, but entertaining."

Zac smiled. "I know why he wanted to see it," he said. "The other day someone told him he looked like the boy with the coonskin cap."

"I thought the same thing!" his mother exclaimed. "When it was over, he announced that he wants a shorter haircut and contact lenses. I think you'll be hearing about it."

Zac laughed. "I don't know if we're ready for Connor Version 2.0."

"I'm more worried about Version 3.0," Abby said.

"He'll be fine," Zac assured her. "He's got incredible parents."

"Grandparents, too," his mother added. "Your father always says the apple doesn't fall too far from the tree."

"That's generally true," Zac agreed. "But we've all known a few that have rolled down the hill."

Chapter 30 Summit at The Summit

Zac had asked Buzzy to arrange a meeting with Sergeant Lavender. His friend had selected one of the most remote spots on The Greenbrier property for the meeting, a mountaintop complex called The Summit, on the 3300-foot crest of Greenbrier Mountain, where Gunner was scheduled to spend his summer months as a lifeguard. They were enjoying the view from Adirondack chairs on the back porch of the lodge-style eatery, which was next door to the infinity pool, a barn-style indoor basketball/volleyball court, a firepit and a terraced amphitheater. The Sporting Club's well-heeled members often had more than one vacation home, so The Summit sometimes went days with light use, and it wasn't available to the hotel's guests. But just to make sure they weren't going to be interrupted, Buzzy had scheduled this confab for 8:30 in the morning, when no one was around. Mindful of the early hour, he'd brought along a thermos of coffee and some Danish pastries.

"I don't usually meet privately with members of the press," Wendy said to Zac as they enjoyed their continental breakfast.

"I just got back from New York," he told her. "I've been doing some research. I thought it might be advantageous if we compared notes."

"Are you asking me to share things with you that I'm not sharing with the other media outlets?" she asked pointedly.

Buzzy quickly saw where this might be heading. "Come on, guys, let's not be adversarial. Zac's come up with some interesting stuff. He met with Oakes' family and with the

NYPD, and with someone at Fox News. He's been to Oakes' apartment and talked to his fiancée."

"We'll get around to talking to the same people," Wendy assured him.

"I'm not convinced they'll be as candid with you as they were with me," Zac said pointedly. "The NYPD will, but I doubt if the family members will be as open. Face it - law enforcement officers represent a threat that journalists don't."

"We have different jobs," she reminded him. "Mine is to find the person or persons responsible for Mordecai Oakes' death. Yours is to report on it."

"Yes, but in the process, I gather a lot of information, some of which you might find very helpful, or at least intriguing. I don't mind sharing it because if you don't solve this, I don't have a story. But in return, I'd appreciate it if you'd point me in the direction of anything that might be escaping my attention."

She mulled it over. "I don't negotiate with the press."

"I'm flying blind here, Wendy. Like I told you, homicides aren't my thing. I don't know your protocols."

"For God's sake, stop doing your little dances and just trust each other," Buzzy played the referee. "As much as I hate to admit he has any redeeming qualities, Zac is trustworthy. I'd lose my job if he ever shared some of the crap he knows about me."

"All right," the sergeant caved. "What are our ground rules?"

"I'll tell you some things I think deserve your attention, but I won't go into specifics. If you interview the folks I've talked with, I trust you'll go about it in a way that doesn't suggest I supplied you with any information. I don't want them to know we've had this conversation. I'm sure you can figure out how to do it."

"And what are you expecting in return?"

"I'd like to know what your folks have come up with so I can add it to what I know."

"Fair enough," she decided. "Truthfully, we don't have much. We've ruled out the actual bellmen. I talked with the manager of the hotel's uniform shop and she told me one of the bellmen had reported his uniform missing. We're assuming the perp helped himself to it from the rack in front of the shop when no one was looking. We know our suspect is five-nine or five-ten."

"How do you know that?"

"From studying the video. We measured the size of the wheelchair and the freezer door and did a little calculating."

"Interesting, but that just makes him the height of the average American male."

"I questioned Oliver Oakes and I know about the will and their inheritance situation. That certainly makes the children and the fiancée persons of interest," she said. "And there's a more remote possibility we're looking into."

"What's that?"

"I'll tell you after you tell me what you know."

"The estate is supposedly worth about four million," Zac revealed.

"Oliver didn't mention that," the sergeant said.

"There's a glitch. The will was apparently written in preparation for Mordecai's upcoming wedding. It assumes Calista Martin is his wife and it refers to her Calista Oakes. She could end up with half the estate, or she could end up with nothing. There's some negotiating going on with the parties involved."

"Interesting," the sergeant reacted to this. "I didn't know about that either."

"You might also find it interesting that a few weeks before the murder, Layla Oakes and her boyfriend, Declan Delaney, came to see Oliver because they were struggling financially and they needed to borrow some money from him to cover their rent. Declan's a 23-year-old aspiring actor who has some of his own costumes and ready access to others. He seems like a nice guy, but he and Layla are living hand-to-mouth and he's trying to keep her off drugs. Oliver and Layla blame Mordecai for their mother's suicide six years ago. They had a lot of negative feelings toward him. All that bears looking into."

"Agreed," the sergeant nodded.

Zac continued. "One of the members of the Meteorological Association who helped plan the convention came up with the idea for the debate and invited Mordecai to participate. This same man made two prior trips to the hotel last year, one in the spring to decide if it was an appropriate site for the convention, and a vacation trip in the summer with his family. He's a weatherman at the local Fox station in New York City. He's already filling in for Mordecai on Fox News."

"Intriguing," Wendy reacted. "What's his name?"

"Wyatt Carter. He's hustling back and forth between doing weather reports at the local station and commentaries at Fox News in Midtown. Apparently, he was one of the people they tapped to replace Oakes after his car accident. He claims they never met and he was looking forward to meeting him at the convention."

"That's very interesting, Zac," she was impressed. "I'm sending a couple of our men to New York to conduct interviews and those are very helpful leads. I'm not sure I can be as helpful to you."

"While they're up there, have them drop by the 19th police precinct in Manhattan and take a look at the hit-and-run report. Okay, that's pretty much what I know. What's the other possibility you mentioned?"

She was struggling with whether she should reveal it. "This falls in the category of something that has to stay with the three of us. And I mean you can't breathe a word to anyone, including your wife. Understood?"

"Understood."

"Brendan Bell met with me and shared some suspicions he has about one of his students."

"Which one?"

"Gunner Hoke."

"The boy with autism?"

"Yes. His family lives here on the grounds. His mother's a doctor at The Greenbrier Clinic."

"I know the Hokes," Buzzy recognized the name. "Don and Luisa. Nice folks. Sporting Club members. They live in Creekside."

The sergeant continued. "When Mr. Bell was at the hotel with his students on the day of the murder, he gave them time to do whatever they wanted between 11:45 and 1:45. His wife ..."

"My sister Greta," Zac reminded her.

"Your sister Greta provided box lunches for them when they arrived. After that, the students were running around unsupervised for two hours. Gunner was the only one who was by himself, and your brother-in-law isn't sure what he was up to during that time. This young man is obsessed with environmental issues, and he knows the hotel and grounds very well because he lives here. In fact, he's the one who told me about this place up here." She pointed to the swimming pool. "He's slated to work next door as a lifeguard this summer. Mr. Bell has an uneasy feeling about him. He suggested that I question him."

"Did you?" Zac asked her.

"I've started. Gunner avoided me at the school, so I ambushed him at home a few days ago. We seemed to be establishing rapport, but then his mother came home and it didn't feel like the right time to pursue it. We met again yesterday, but by then he'd figured out that his teacher was the one who put me onto him. He surprised me by suggesting that I need to consider your brother-in-law a suspect."

"*Brendan*?"

"He pointed out that Brendan Bell shared his dislike for Mordecai Oakes, and suggested he might have arranged the class trip as a cover to commit the crime."

Zac laughed. "This kid's trying to throw you off, Wendy. Don't give it a minute's thought. I've known Brendan for years. He's a totally upstanding guy, not the murdering type. He's a vegetarian. He's probably a pacifist. When he hit a buck last fall, he was more upset about the deer than the damage it did to his truck."

The sergeant continued. "All the same, Gunner pointed out that Mr. Bell wasn't where he told his students he was going to be for those two hours, that he knows the hotel as well as anyone, that the backpack he brought along could have contained a change of clothes, and that coming and going from the hotel in a school bus makes an excellent cover."

"So you've got two pissed-off guys pointing the finger of blame at each other," Buzzy summed it up.

"I have to consider all the possibilities," Wendy said. "I want to be able to rule them out. But don't you dare mention this to your brother-in-law," she wagged a finger at him. "Or your sister. Or your wife. Got it?"

Zac took a deep breath. "Understood," he promised her.

"I'm trusting you with this, Zac. I probably shouldn't have said anything. I think both possibilities are equally farfetched."

"Do whatever you need to do," Zac said. "I'll stay out of it. But you've got me very curious about Gunner Hoke. Brendan wants me to speak to the class about an article I wrote some years ago. I'll have the chance to meet this young man and decide if he seems like an evil genius."

The Sergeant smiled. "In my limited experience with supervillains, the genius part usually helps them conceal the evil part," she said.

Buzzy had been listening to all this with interest. "Please let me know if you think we're about to hire a murderer as a lifeguard," he requested. "I know that's up to the Human Resources department, but I am the Director of Security."

"I want to ask you two more things," Zac remembered. "Did you ever enhance the video enough to figure what Oakes pulled out of his pocket and gave to the bellman?"

"It looked like pen," she revealed.

Zac smiled. "Oakes used to give people fake Montblanc pens. It was a little practical joke he liked to play. They thought they were getting a luxury item from Germany, but they were getting knockoffs from China. I saw a bunch of them on the desk in his home office. Calista told me about them. She gave me one."

"Hey, at least the guy had a sense of humor," Buzzy said. "He didn't know the last person he played his little joke on was going to kill him."

"That takes care of that mystery," Wendy checked it off her list. "What's the other thing?"

“Where are Mr. Oakes' belongings? The things from his room and the stuff he had with him in the freezer?”

“We gave his clothing and toiletries to his son,” she said. “We kept the briefcase and laptop and papers he had in the freezer because they were part of the crime scene. They're in our evidence room in Beckley.”

“Suppose Oliver wants to look through them?”

“It's fine with me, but he'll have to do it under our supervision. If he wants to look through his father's belongings, we'll have to monitor him to make sure he's not pocketing anything or deleting things from the laptop.”

“Suppose he wants to copy something?”

“He can photograph things or copy the hard drive. We're not going to print out anything for him or let him take the laptop from the evidence room.”

“Would it be an unusual request?”

“No. People keep all sorts of information on their phones and laptops and tablets that their families need to access. Since his phone is missing, this might be the only way Oliver can get some of the information he needs.”

Zac was pleased to hear this. Now all he had to do was get Oliver on board.

Chapter 31 The Turtle

He was heading home when he spotted something in the road ahead. He slowed down and saw it was a box turtle. The little creature wasn't making much progress. He knew there were heartless assholes who liked to run over turtles and squirrels for the sport of it, so he stopped on the road, put on his flashers and got out of his vehicle. The turtle saw him coming and retreated into the safety of its domed fortress.

Bending down, he picked up the turtle and held it up to his face. "Don't worry, I'm not going to hurt you," he said reassuringly. He carried it over to a patch of grass and put it down gently. "I'm pretty sure this is where you're trying to go," he said. "I hope so anyway."

He waited patiently for the turtle to emerge from its shell as another vehicle swerved around his own. Eventually it poked its head out and took in the new surroundings.

Satisfied that he'd rescued the situation, he returned to his vehicle, cut the flashers and continued on his way.

Strange, he reflected. Three weeks ago, I killed a human being and I still don't feel any remorse. Now here I am fretting over a little turtle.

Chapter 32 Flying Lessons

The State Fair of West Virginia takes place every year in August, just outside Lewisburg in the unincorporated community of Fairlea. The thousands who stream through this agricultural expo, with carnival rides and nightly concerts, enjoy complimentary parking across the road, in a grassy expanse called the Free Parking Lot.

Eleven months of the year, when the fair's not happening, these many acres dissected by paved roads and gravel lanes are a popular spot for learning to drive. Except for a couple of restrooms and a few light poles, there are few objects an inexperienced driver can hit. There's the Greenbrier Valley Aquatic Center, with three indoor pools, but its location on the far edge of the property makes the pool complex an unlikely site for an accident.

Zac and Connor decided the Free Parking Lot was an ideal place for two novice pilots to practice flying their new DJI Mini4 Pro Drone. They arrived late Saturday morning, and it was quickly obvious who had done his homework.

"Don't we need to charge this first?" Zac asked Connor.

"I already installed the battery and charged the drone and the controller," his son informed him. "I downloaded the updates, too. See these lights? All four are lit up, so it's fully charged. We'll get about 20 or 25 minutes of flight time."

"Did you read the manual?"

"No, I watched some videos on YouTube. The best one is this German dude who explains everything like he's talking to a preschooler. What did you pay for it?"

"About $300," Zac recalled. "I told the clerk we needed one that was idiot-proof, and this is what he recommended.

Supposedly everything we need came with it. He tried to sell me some extra batteries and lens filters, but I figured we'd get that stuff if we really like it. He said we don't have to register it with the FAA because it's under the weight limit."

"How does some rando in a New York shop know about the laws in West Virginia?"

"He doesn't, but if we get in trouble, we'll blame him."

"I think you got the right one," Connor said. "It has thousands of positive reviews."

"What'd you do - stay up all night reading them?"

"I looked at them this morning when I was waiting for you to get back from the hotel. The controller has a lot of settings. I already took care of some of them."

"Like what?"

"I engaged the Return to Home button, so when we push it, the drone flies back and lands where we launched it."

"What if there's a tree in the way?"

"I engaged the Obstacle Avoidance."

"Connor, you're ten steps ahead of me."

"Maybe you're ten steps behind me."

"Good point."

"What if one of us wrecks it?" the boy wondered.

"If I wreck it, I'll get you a replacement," Zac promised. "If you wreck it and you want another one, you're on your own."

"I don't have any money," his son protested.

"You can work in your grandparents' hayfield."

"There you go with the hayfield again," he griped. "It's always the damned hayfield."

"I survived it," Zac said. "You act like I want to send you down in a coal mine with a pick ax and shovel. Farm work builds character."

"I'm already a character. I think I'm allergic to hay."

"I think you're allergic to work," Zac had his own diagnosis. "Do your friends think you're funny?"

"Yeah, but the teachers think I'm a wise guy."

"It's not hurting you too much. You're a solid B student."

"Don't you want me to get A's?"

Zac thought about it. "Honestly, Connor, I really don't care. It's up to you. When I was in school there were always a few B students who were just as smart as the ones who got A's, maybe even smarter, but they weren't into the competition thing and they didn't care about keeping the teachers happy. I usually got along better with them than with the ones that were obsessed with their grade point averages. Sometimes they were into things they cared about more, like music or computers or whatever. I think you might fall in that category, and that's fine with me."

Connor smiled. "I'll get you a bumper sticker that says I'm the Proud Parent of a B Student."

"Let's just keep it between us," Zac requested. "I'm not sure Mom feels the same way."

"Are we going to fly this thing or not?" his son asked impatiently.

"Educate your old man. Teach me what I need to know."

"A couple of things before we launch. They say when people learning to fly them have crashes, it's usually because they're watching the drone when they should be watching the controller screen. We need to keep an eye on the screen."

"Check."

"See this front part with the rotating camera? It's called a gimbal."

"What's a gimbal?"

The boy rolled his eyes. "The front part with the rotating camera," he repeated. "Good thing this is idiot-proof. To turn the drone on, we hold down the power button. You press the icon on the controller to make it take off. When you push up on the left stick, it goes up. Pull down and it comes down. Push it left and it rotates counter clockwise. Push it right and it rotates clockwise. The stick on the right makes it fly forward, backwards and sideways. Got it?"

"Sounds pretty intuitive."

"See this switch in the middle? It controls the speed. C stands for slow, N is normal, and S is fast. I set it on normal. The RTH button is the Return to Home. I set a 150-foot altitude so it doesn't hit any trees on the way back."

Zac stared at his son. “You're acing this, Connor.”

“It's easy to understand if you play video games. Our generation was born with controllers in our hands.”

“It must make you feel good to be able to teach an old fart how to do something.”

“Yeah, if he can learn. These two dials control the camera's tilt and the zoom. The front left button is for video and the one on the right takes still pictures. You can control those functions with icons on the controller, too. And it's got a feature called Active Track. You can make it follow an object. Like if you walk over to the Aquatic Center, I can make it follow you and keep you in the center of the video.”

And so it continued, son lecturing and father pretending to absorb it.

“Maybe you don't need the hayfield after all, Connor,” Zac decided. “Have you ever thought of becoming a test pilot?”

The boy grinned. “Now I'll probably crash it.”

But he didn't. Zac almost did before Connor grabbed the control from him and hit the Return to Home button. The amazing little machine turned around, flew back, hovered and sat down at their feet like an obedient dog.

Chapter 33 Ashes in the Subaru

Zac had adopted The Wild Bean, a downtown coffee shop, as his office and meeting place. It was easy for people who weren't familiar with the town to find, and there was a nook in back where he could have private conversations. The only drawback was when a friend or acquaintance spotted him and wanted to catch up on the past ten or fifteen years. Even when he hinted that he was working, they didn't always take the hint. So, despite the hubbub and occasional interruptions, the Bean was his office.

This morning he was getting together with Oliver, his most valuable source, although Calista was proving to be a close second.

He looked up from his notes and spotted Oliver coming in the door. The young man saw him and made his way to the back of the coffee shop.

"Don't you ever wear anything besides your river outfit?" Zac ragged him.

Oliver grinned. "Not if I can help it."

"Remind me to get a job like that."

"Can't writers wear what they want?"

"Sort of," Zac said. "I don't think I could show up at *The Times* in flip flops, board shorts and a T-shirt, although they've probably seen worse. Can I buy you a cup of coffee?"

"Sure. If the paper's paying for it, I'll take an everything bagel."

They queued up at the counter. "What's new, Oliver?" Zac asked him.

"The autopsy," he said in a low voice. "The cause of death was heart failure and respiratory arrest from hypothermia."

"No surprise there."

"The police said the temperature in the freezer was minus 10 and he probably died in less than a half-hour. He was frozen to the floor when they found him."

"I'm sorry to hear that, Oliver," Zac commiserated. He waited until they returned to the table with their drinks to report on his trip to New York.

"I had interesting conversations with Layla and Calista," he reported. "Calista's not what I was expecting. I've got a different take on her than you do."

"Did you hear the news?" Oliver asked him. "She's pregnant! I'm going to have a brother or sister 25 years younger than I am!"

"Is that so bad?"

"It's just weird."

"It answers my question about the nature of their relationship," Zac said. "After she told me, I read up on paraplegic sex. I didn't know that some guys who are paralyzed can have erections and ejaculate."

"Yeah, me either," Oliver confessed. "You learn something new every day."

"Does the fact that you're going to have a little brother or sister change your mind about how you're going to deal with the estate?"

"It's changed Calista's mind. Now she wants a third."

"You know, Oliver, there's probably enough to go around for everybody."

The young man gave him an accusatory look. "Calista put you up to saying that, didn't she?"

"Nope, it's just a personal opinion. You don't seem like you're driven by money. Your father wanted Calista to have half of his estate. She's asking for a third. The fact that she's bearing his child would seem to strengthen her case."

He leaned across the table and lowered his voice. "How do I know she's not playing me? How do I know she's really pregnant, or if the child is even his?"

"You don't, but con artists don't usually go to the trouble to earn nursing degrees and go to work for home health care agencies. Her father deserted the family when she was young, and when she moved to New York her abandonment issues came with her. She met your dad when he was at a low point in his life. She showed concern for him and they hit it off. By the time he went back to work and she saw him on TV, she realized the guy she was living with wasn't the grandstander he was playing on Fox News, but she didn't care because it was how they were paying the bills. You've got to give your father some credit, Oliver. He went back to work when a lot of people in his situation would have stayed home and felt sorry for themselves."

"You can't live off disability and health insurance in an Upper East Side apartment," Oliver countered.

"True," Zac agreed. "It sounds like he wanted more in life and he did what he needed to do to make it happen. He went from being just another talking head to being a minor celebrity."

"He craved attention," Oliver said. "That's why he went into TV and what got to him about Mom. She looked great and she had charisma. People were drawn to her. She sucked all the air out of the room and didn't leave enough for him. He wanted to be celebrated like the bride at every wedding and the corpse at every funeral, but he couldn't compete with her."

"Speaking of funerals, have you given any more thought to a memorial service?"

He let out a sigh. "Yeah. I know he would have wanted us to have one so people could talk about him like he was the second coming of Jesus."

"Where would you have it?"

"We'd have to do it in New York because that's where he worked. He didn't really have friends, but he had coworkers and acquaintances and they keep asking about it. I don't know if Layla could deal with it, and she'd pretty much have to be involved."

"Maybe Declan could prep her. Memorial services are kind of like shows and he's an actor."

"Yeah, but she's not. What you see is what you get with Layla."

"One of the few good things to come from COVID is that people don't think you have to have services right away anymore," Zac pointed out. "Sometimes they're six months later."

"Maybe if I stall long enough people will forget about it," Oliver said. "I can just say we're planning one. I've got his ashes in my Subaru. I don't want to keep them where my friends can see them because it might freak them out or they might think it's funny to mess around with them."

Zac pointed to the coffee shop's window. "Mordecai's outside?"

"Yep. We're spending more time together now than we did when he was alive."

His bagel arrived and they lapsed into silence while he scarfed it down with the appetite of a man who burned 5000 calories a day. Zac often gauged people based on whether he felt comfortable with them during long silences. Oliver was passing the test.

"You really think we should give her a third?" Oliver asked after he'd polished off the bagel.

"That's what I'd do," Zac said. "Calista seems like a decent person and now she's got to raise a kid. She'll probably go back to her family in Maine and have the baby there."

"I'll think about it," he conceded. "This is the only inheritance we'll ever get. I don't know if we should give up a big chunk of it."

"You know how you thought your dad didn't really believe the shit he was shoveling on Fox?" Zac changed the subject.

"Yeah."

"According to Calista, you're right. He was candid about it when it was just the two of them, but she doesn't want to go on record about it. She thinks there's proof in the notebook he kept with him and the files on his laptop. I don't know how you feel, but as a writer I'd love to take a look at them. They're in the State Police evidence room in Beckley. Sergeant Lavender told me she'd let you have access if you do it under their supervision. They won't let you take anything out of the room."

"What good is his laptop if I don't know his passwords?"

"He might have them in his notebook. A lot of people keep lists of their passwords. Even if he didn't, we have resources at the *Times*, techies and cyber security experts. They can probably tell you how to break into it. Wouldn't you like to know what your father really thought?"

He nodded slowly. "Yeah. It might change my opinion of him."

"I know you don't want the publicity that would come with a revelation like that," Zac said. "If I break the story, I'll take the heat."

He thought about it for a long moment. "Let's go for it," he decided. "Tell me what I need to do."

"Get in touch with Sergeant Lavender and let her coordinate it," Zac instructed him. "When you're there, look for anything that suggests he knew that what he was telling people wasn't true. If you can make a copy of his hard drive, I'll go through it with you. If you can't figure out how to get into the computer, I'll call the techie cavalry at *The Times* and get their advice."

"Okay," Oliver agreed. "Now it's my turn to tell you something. When I was in New York before you went up there, I went through his desk. I thought there might be bills or stuff about his finances that I need for the estate. I grabbed all his files and folders, tossed them in a couple of boxes and brought them back with me. I've been going through them. I found something that totally blew me away."

"What?"

"Mom wrote two - I guess you'd call them suicide notes - the day she died, one to Dad and one to us. He never even told us about it."

"Did you bring them with you?"

"No. They're pretty short. I'll take pictures of them and text them to you."

"When we first met and you told me about your mother's death, you were pretty adamant that you don't want me writing about it. Are you sure about that, Oliver? I can handle it sensitively. I think it's an important part of your father's story. Your family story, too."

"Read the notes and then we'll talk about it."

"Have you told Layla?"

"No. I just found them yesterday. I probably need to be with her when she reads them. They were in one of those file folders that has a bunch of pockets. I don't know if he forgot to give it to us because he was so upset or if he didn't think we could handle it."

"Did you learn anything new?"

"Read the notes."

"Okay. I appreciate your willingness to share something so personal. And thanks for coming over here today."

He stood up to leave. "Are the police getting any closer to figuring this thing out?"

"Honestly, Oliver, I don't know. Unfortunately, they don't tell me everything."

Chapter 34 Punchbowl Cop

In six years of chaperoning the senior prom, Brendan had seen every take on formal dress the teenage imagination could dream up. Most of the students favored the traditional look and made their entrances in elegant evening gowns and stylish tuxedos. But there were always the creative types in ruffles, lace, sequins, feathers, leather, denim, tie-dye or duct tape. Gowns that looked like tiered wedding cakes. Sleeveless dinner jackets that showed off tattooed arms. Rainbow jumpsuits. Marge Simpson beehives. It seemed fitting to Brendan that prom was short for promenade; this high school rite of passage was largely a costume parade.

The faculty chaperones functioned as undercover cops. His assigned station: the punchbowl. His assignment: make sure nobody spikes it. He could tell from the disappointed faces of several young men who approached the bowl that he was doing his job.

The prom was in Colonial Hall, the same cavernous space at The Greenbrier that had served as a venue for events ranging from Congressional meetings to boxing matches to the infamous debate debacle.

Hudson arrived at the punchbowl with a young man Brendan didn't recognize.

"Hello, Hudson," he greeted his student. "You look pretty in pink. Who's your date?"

"We're not dating," his companion objected. "We're just friends."

"At least that's what we told my parents," Hudson added with a wink.

"Your coordinated outfits and boutonnieres kind of give you away," Brendan pointed out.

"This is Lance," Hudson introduced his friend. "We've been seeing each other for a couple of months. The cat's probably out of the closet after tonight, but we don't care."

"Good to meet you, Lance," Brendan offered him a handshake.

"Is this punch alcoholic?" Lance asked hopefully.

"Come on, boys," Brendan chided them. "Is a bear Catholic? Does the pope shit in the woods? The Greenbrier's not going to make the mistake of serving alcohol to minors."

"Damn."

Hudson turned to Lance. "Let's find someone with a flask," he suggested. "We'll doctor our own."

Brendan put his hands over his ears. "I didn't hear that."

"You know I'm just joking, Mr. Bell. Right?"

"Of course, I know you're joking, Hudson. High school students would never drink. It's against the law."

"You're cool, Mr. Bell," Hudson paid him what teenagers thought adults considered the ultimate compliment.

"Get out of here before I report you to the authorities," he threatened them.

"You are the authorities," Lance reminded him. They ladled two cups and vanished in the crowd.

Students drifted on and off the dance floor, handing Brendan phones to take their pictures, some of which might have turned out better if the girls weren't sweating their makeup off.

Hayley and her escort Gabe Peters, the editor of the school paper, approached. Crowned monarchs, they were the prom queen and king.

"Hi, Hayley. Hey, Gabe. Are you enjoying your reign?"

"I keep thinking of *Carrie*," Hayley said. "I'm waiting for the bucket of pig's blood."

"If I remember the movie, the bucket was rigged in the rafters of the school gym," Brendan said. "I think you're safe here because this ceiling's really high and I don't think the hotel would have loaned anyone their scissors lift for the project."

"Good. I'd hate to have to use my telekinetic powers to wreak vengeance on everyone."

"You don't have much reason to be vengeful," Brendan offered. "Carrie wasn't her class valedictorian, she wasn't dating the state tennis champ, and she wasn't heading to Duke with a scholarship."

"Just between us, being an overachiever's a pain in the butt, Mr. Bell," Hayley confided. "I want to be reincarnated as a slacker."

"Me, too," added Gabe, who was bound for Yale.

"You're both going places where you'll meet a bunch of other overachievers," Brendan pointed out. "I have a feeling you'll fit right in."

"Sorry I didn't take your classes, Mr. Bell," Gabe said. "It never fit my schedule. They say you're a great teacher."

"I'm sorry, too, Gabe. I'm sure having you in class would have been one of the highlights of my career. But you seem to have made it through without the benefit of my wisdom and guidance."

"Somehow," the boy said with a shrug.

"I meant to thank you for the article you wrote about the Teacher of the Year award."

"It was Ms. Bishop's idea," Gabe confessed. "We were short on articles and she thought it would make good filler."

"Still, you did a nice job."

"See you later, Mr. Bell," Hayley raised her cup as they headed off. "Gotta go be fake royalty."

Brendan was fetching a drink for himself when he noticed Gunner making a beeline in his direction. Social occasions weren't Gunner's natural habitat and he'd been hanging on the fringes all evening, visibly uncomfortable.

"Hi, Gunner. Would you like a drink?"

"Why did you tell Sergeant Lavender you thought I killed Mr. Oakes?" the boy demanded to know.

Brendan nearly dropped his cup in the bowl. "I didn't tell her that," he denied the accusation. Technically it was true; he'd just suggested she look into his whereabouts at the time of the murder.

"Then why did she come to my house to talk to me? Why did she want to talk to me again? She didn't go to anybody else's house or talk to them twice."

"You'll have to ask her," he said. "I can't speak for the sergeant."

But Gunner smelled a rat, and the rat was his teacher. "You think I killed that man, don't you? You think I'm some kind of weirdo, just like everyone else."

"I don't think that, Gunner," he tried to put the boy's mind at ease. "I think you're letting your obsessive tendency get the better of you. You're the best student I've ever had. You know more about the subject matter. You care more, too. You could probably teach the class. If the sergeant has concerns, all you have to do is tell her where you were when the incident happened. It's called an alibi."

"I don't think she'll believe me," he said. "I don't have any witnesses."

"Someone must have seen you over the course of two hours."

"A bunch of strangers. I don't know who they were or where they are now."

"If you're innocent, which I'm sure you are, you don't have anything to worry about," Brendan assured him.

"Innocent people get accused of things all the time. You know what I told her?"

"What?"

"I told her I think you did it."

"Now why would you tell her something like that?"

"Because I think you did."

"Come on, Gunner. *Really*?"

Gunner started to leave, but he turned back. "Am I really the best student you've ever had?"

"Absolutely."

"Thanks."

"There's no reason to be mad, Gunner."

"I'm not mad. Getting mad is stupid. I don't get mad."

"That's good to know," Brendan said.

"I get even."

He headed for the exit.

Chapter 35 A Voice from the Past

Zac was enjoying his morning coffee on the deck when a text from Oliver arrived with photo attachments of his mother's two handwritten notes. He hadn't added any commentary, and the messages spoke for themselves.

> Dear Mordecai,
>
> It's been quite a ride for a couple of kids from Indiana, hasn't it? Married for 20 years, 2 teenagers, 5 homes, the passing of your mother and both of my parents, ups and downs, successes and failures. Whatever's held us together all this time was gradually unraveling, but the past three months have helped. I'm sorry it took a terminal illness for things to get better.
>
> We're all dying, I'm just doing it faster than most people. I'm trying to be philosophical about it. I don't like the way this is unfolding, and the agony and expense it will mean for you and Oliver and Layla. I'm taking matters into my own hands. I see this choice differently than some others do. Life is a temporary journey and I don't think choosing how the journey ends is wrong or sinful. I know you'll understand. I hope the kids will, too. The trauma will be short-lived compared to what you and the kids

would have had to endure if I let nature take her course.

I couldn't be prouder of Oliver and Layla. I'll miss them terribly. Please nurture them along. It's going to be hard with your work, especially since you're finally starting to achieve the success you always wanted. As you know, I'm not thrilled with the way you're doing it, but you're in a tough situation at your place of work.

They say when people lose a spouse, women mourn and men replace. If you find someone else, please make sure she's someone our children can accept and respect.

When the end is near, some people claim they don't have any regrets. I've always thought only saints or idiots could think that way. I'm neither, and I'm full of regrets. The main one is that we didn't find a better way to resolve our differences. We're both good people and we should have been able to recapture the optimism and enthusiasm of our youth. Those were the days, weren't they?

If you don't think Oliver and Layla are ready for the note I'm leaving them, please hold on to it until they are. I trust your judgment.

I'm going peacefully, with nothing but good memories of my brief time here, and of you, Mordecai, the only man I've ever loved.

All My Love, Marianne

The note to her son and daughter was just as straightforward and heartfelt.

Dearest Oliver and Layla,

How do I say goodbye forever?

Three months ago the doctors told me the severe headaches I was having were being caused by glioblastoma, a rapidly growing malignant brain cancer. It's called the Emperor of All Cancers and they don't know what causes it. The treatments are surgery, radiation and chemo, but so far there's no cure and nearly certain death. Medications can help relieve the headaches and pressure, but they cause bloating, fatigue, disorientation and a few other things I don't want to spend my last days enduring and putting you through. I don't want to leave you with that memory. I'm exiting this world on my own terms, going to sleep peacefully. I hope you understand my choice. If not now, maybe someday.

You two have been my greatest joys, and for the rest of your lives I'll always be with you in spirit. From your tender moments to your silly antics, you gave me a reason for living. Bringing you into the world and doing my best to raise you and point you in the right direction has helped me look at my own short life less selfishly. I thought I'd be around for your next chapters, but it's not to be. Feel free to make me a grandmother if it ever seems right.

You're both aware that your father and I have our differences. Before my diagnosis we were talking about getting a divorce and sharing custody of you. Please know that he has been more attentive, gentle and understanding these past few months. Single parenthood is going be a challenge for him. He's got to figure out how to try to balance his career with a home life. Please show him some patience. In some ways he's more of a family man than he's willing to admit.

In a cosmic sense none of us are very important. We'll all eventually be forgotten, washed away in the vast ocean of people who have come and gone from this planet. I'm not sure I've made much of a contribution in my short time here, except for you two. Thank you, thank you, thank you for being so wonderful and making my life worth living.

How do I say goodbye forever?

With eternal love, Mom

Zac set his phone aside. The notes were as elegant and beautiful as the woman Oliver said his mother was.

Chapter 36 Family Conference

Oliver had borrowed a tripod from one of the Adventures on the Gorge videographers and affixed his phone to it. He sat down on a log, with a quiet stretch of the New River and the dramatic cliffs as a backdrop. This was going to be a tough conversation and he thought the tranquil setting might help.

It was five o'clock and he gave his sister a call at the agreed-upon hour. Layla and Declan appeared on FaceTime with a background that couldn't have been more contrasting, sitting on the sofa bed in their cramped Hell's Kitchen studio.

"Well look at the Nature Boy," Layla reacted to her brother's staging.

"It's just my workplace," Oliver indicated his surroundings. "Think of it as a teaser for the rafting trip I promised you the next time you're down here."

"Your text sounded serious," Declan said. "What's up? Did they arrest somebody?"

"No, I don't have a clue where that stands," he said. "I get more information from Zac Wolfe than from the police. At least he treats me like a normal person. The cops act like they think we were behind all this."

"They were here yesterday," Layla revealed.

"Who?"

"Two cops from the West Virginia State Police. They took one look at this shithole and saw we're obviously broke, so they asked us a million questions. They were here two hours. They were going to see Calista next."

"Was one of them a lady?" Oliver asked.

"Nope, two guys," she reported.

"They were doing the good cop, bad cop routine, but they weren't very good at it," Declan said. "They were way too obvious. They might as well have said, 'We're Officer Nice 'n Friendly and Officer Mean 'n Harsh.' I don't know how they train them at the police academy, but they should give them acting lessons."

"Good cop, bad cop only works if people are dumb and guilty," Oliver said. "We're only one of those things. What did they ask you?"

"I taped them," Layla disclosed. "They were taping us, so I taped them. I'll send you the file. They asked a lot of stuff about our family and where we were the day it happened. They wanted to know if we'd ever been to West Virginia or the hotel. When I told them we went to see you a couple of months ago, they looked at each other like we'd just confessed."

"I don't think they believed us when we said we'd never been to the hotel or ever heard of it before this happened," Declan added.

Layla took a vape drag and continued. "They acted like we should have known Dad was going there. Like we kept up with his travels. Officer Mean 'n Harsh said, 'Are you telling us you didn't know your father was speaking at that conference and getting together with your brother? You didn't know they were discussing his will?' I said yep, that's what I'm saying."

"The strangest thing they asked was how tall I am," Declan said. "I said, 'Here you go,' and I gave them a headshot with my stats."

"What are you, about six feet?" Oliver estimated.

"Six-one, bro. Every inch counts."

"Leave sex out of this," Layla said, and they all laughed.

Oliver's expression grew more serious. "Listen, I'm working on a little project. Supposedly, Dad didn't really believe all the crap he said on TV and put in his books. At least that's what Calista told Zac Wolfe. She thinks there's proof on Dad's laptop and in his notebook. They're in the police evidence room and they let me go in and copy the hard drive and photograph the notebook. There was an officer watching me the whole time. I thought they might make me wear gloves or something, but they'd already dusted everything for fingerprints, so they didn't care."

"What'd you find?" Layla asked.

"We haven't gone through it yet. I say we because Zac put me up to this. He thinks it's a big deal. Maybe it is."

"Too little, too late," Layla had her opinion.

"Think about it, Layla," Oliver disagreed. "If he knew scientific evidence proves the climate really is changing for the worse and his notes show that he knew it, where does that leave all the deniers? I'd like to feel better about him. Wouldn't you?"

"I suppose."

"If he was acting, he was a lot better paid for it than I am," Declan said. "He bailed us out twice before he realized some of it was going for other activities." He glanced at Layla.

"Back off, Declan," Layla reacted. "I've been clean 13 weeks."

"And I'm proud of you."

"Me, too," Oliver said. "If you can stay clean through all this crap, you're probably going to make it."

"Just don't piss me off, Oliver," she threatened him. "I'll relapse and I'll blame it on you."

"There's another reason I wanted to talk with you today," Oliver switched gears, feeling he'd been dancing around the real subject. "When I was in New York I cleaned out Dad's desk and I took his files and papers."

"You said you were doing that," Layla remembered.

"He had a file folder with a bunch of miscellaneous papers. I started going through it and I found two notes that Mom wrote the day she died. I guess you could call them farewell notes. One was to Dad and one was to us. He never told us."

"Oh, my God," Layla reacted. "Maybe he thought we couldn't handle it."

"I want to read you the notes. I've got them here."

"I'll go for a walk or something," Declan offered.

"No, stay here," Layla gave him a pat. "You're my emotional support animal."

He nuzzled her. "I try."

Oliver disappeared off screen while he opened his backpack. Declan put an arm around Layla and they watched the river flow until Oliver reappeared holding the notes. He took a deep breath and he read the well-chosen words from the mother they hadn't seen in six years, speaking to them from beyond the grave.

By the time her brother stopped reading, Layla was crying, overwhelmed by memories and the revelations her mother's notes contained. She collapsed in her boyfriend's arms.

"I know you miss her," Declan said softly.

Oliver waited for his sister to recover and dry her tears. "Mom's death was always a mystery to me," he said. "I remember Dad saying she had cancer or a tumor or something and she wasn't in her right mind. She'd been sleeping a lot and she didn't have any energy, and we thought she was just depressed because she was unhappy with him. Turns out she really did have cancer. These letters sound like she was thinking pretty clearly. We always thought Dad was the bad guy, but maybe not so much. I mean, he didn't exactly turn into the world's greatest father after she died. He always thought his job was providing for us, but providing meant a financial thing to him and he wasn't any good at the rest of it. He wasn't really interested in what we were up to in school or with our friends. He couldn't cook, he wouldn't clean. He thought Mom was supposed to handle all that stuff, and even after she was gone, he didn't see it as things he needed to do. He had an old-fashioned idea of his role and he couldn't adapt. When he was home, he was either watching sports or the news, or digging around in books for things he could use on TV."

"The Emperor of All Cancers," Layla repeated her mother's words. "Do you think we could inherit it?"

"No. She said they don't know what causes it, remember?"

"She had such a high opinion of us. If she could see us now, she'd be proud of you and disappointed with her crazy, fucked-up daughter."

"Don't say that," Declan chided her.

"How would you describe me, Declan? I barely squeaked through school and I'm an addict. I don't have a job and I've been sponging money off my father and brother."

"Somehow you landed a great boyfriend," he pointed out.

"He's humble, too," she said.

Oliver offered his viewpoint. "I figure the years between twenty and thirty are given to us to figure out what we want to do with our lives," he said. "You're only twenty-one, Layla. If you get to thirty and you still don't know what you want to do, you probably never will. I'm doing the Great Outdoors bit. Declan's playing starving artist. You just have to figure out what your thing is and go for it. If it doesn't work out, then try something else."

"I tried drugs and they didn't work out," she said. "I can't decide what comes next."

"Just look at the things that have always interested you," he suggested. "That's what'll make you happy."

"I have the curse of the disinterested," she said.

"Write a blog about having the curse of the disinterested," Declan suggested. "Maybe you can monetize boredom."

"I can write a blog where I give people bad advice," she considered. "I have a lot of expertise in making bad choices. All they have to do is read it and do the opposite of whatever I recommend. I could call myself Miz Guidance."

Oliver saw the look on Declan's face. "Oh shit, I see the wheels turning in Declan's head. He thinks it has potential."

"You read me like a book, Oliver," Declan admitted. "It sounds crazy, but it's the kind of crazy that would probably pay better than what I'm doing."

"Migrant farm labor pays better than what you're doing," Oliver said. "At least their substandard housing is free."

"While you guys are planning my new career, keep in mind that I can't write and I can't spell," Layla tried to bring them back to earth.

"Not a problem," Declan assured her. "That's why God made Spell Check and A.I."

"Maybe Mom's note means I'm supposed to get off my ass and do something," Layla reflected. "Maybe it was meant to come now instead of six years ago, like it's been lost behind some dusty shelf at the post office. Would you mind sending it to me?"

"I'll text you a screenshot," he offered. "I don't want to put the original in the mail."

"I don't believe in sudden conversions," she said. "I don't think something happens and, ta da, you're a new person like Scrooge on Christmas Day. I think change happens slowly. Maybe this is the start of mine."

Declan gave her a hug. "I'm honored to be your emotional support animal."

"Keep me posted, Miz Guidance," Oliver requested. "The light's fading, so I'm over and out. Love you both."

He turned off his phone, sat down on the log again and watched evening fall on the New River Gorge.

Chapter 37 Conversation in a Cemetery

Zac had given up on getting the simple Yes or No he requested from Wyatt Carter when a surprise phone call came from the meteorologist. He was working in his nook in the back of the Bean when he saw who was calling. It was lunchtime, the shop was slammed and he didn't want to compete with the chaos.

"Wyatt!" he greeted him enthusiastically.

"Hey, Zac, I wanted to ..."

"Listen, I'm in a noisy place. Can I call you back in five? I'll go someplace quiet where we can talk. Okay?"

"Sure."

He hurried to his Jeep and headed a few blocks away to the most secluded spot in town he could think of, the Confederate Cemetery, where the remains of 95 soldiers slain in the Battle of Lewisburg, a Union victory, were interred in a cross-shaped common grave. The little cemetery was tucked in the woods near the library and community college, and visitors to it were few and far between. He climbed out of his vehicle, took a look around and decided the only eavesdroppers were the ghosts of the South Carolina regiment that hadn't fared well in the battle. He sat down in the grass and returned the newsman's call.

"Hey, Wyatt, good to hear from you," he said. "I thought you might shoot me a text, like we talked about."

"I'm no idiot, Zac. If I had something newsworthy, I'd share it with my employer, not *The New York Times*."

"I gather you didn't uncover any death threats?"

"Sorry to disappoint you, buddy. Nowadays people express their outrage online, and they can be as vicious as they want because they're anonymous. Oakes had plenty of haters who said all kinds of shit about him, but the closest thing I could find to a death threat was the guy who said whoever ran over him should have backed up and finished the job."

"And this is the person you want to replace, huh?"

"He got a lot of positive comments, too," Carter said. "Mordecai's problem wasn't his content, it was his delivery. Some people just couldn't take his personality. Viewers think I'm clueless, but I don't get the reactions he did. The worst thing anybody's called me is the Fox Wasteland's Village Idiot. Actually, it has a nice ring to it."

"You're not calling me to talk about death threats," Zac guessed.

"True," Carter said. "I had a visit from a couple of West Virginia's Finest. They gave me the fifth degree."

"How'd that go?"

"I'm not sure. They asked a lot of specifics. If I'd ever been to The Greenbrier before, how well I knew the place, how I felt about Oakes, why we chose him for the debate, his travel and accommodations arrangements, what we were paying him, what the other attendees were doing on that day. If they come around again, I'm lawyering up. I don't mind being helpful, but I'll be damned if I'm going to let them treat me like I'm guilty of something."

"I'd react the same way," Zac said.

"I'm through planning the AMA conferences," he declared. "Although I must say it was a success, except for the fact that one of our headliners was murdered."

Zac laughed at the gallows humor. "A minor hiccup."

"On the bright side, we're getting a lot of press," Carter added.

"If you can work that wry humor into your commentaries, you'll have a successful career," Zac predicted.

"Whatever his virtues, Mordecai didn't have much of a sense of humor," Carter opined. "He came up with good one-liners, but it always felt like he was trying to drive a knife into the people who disagreed with him."

"Fanning the flames of hate rarely ends well," Zac said as he eyed the grave of the young soldiers who died for the Southern Cause.

"Do you think the police consider me a suspect?" Carter pressed him. "They sure as hell acted like it."

"That's why you're calling, isn't it?" Zac voiced his suspicion.

"Guilty as charged, my man. What do you think?"

"I don't know, Wyatt. Were you at the banquet when Oakes was murdered? Are there people who can vouch you were there?"

"Everybody saw me there. We did a half-and-half drawing for a charity and I was running it."

"Sounds like it would have been hard for you to be playing bellman at the same time."

"What would I know about freezers at some hotel in West Virginia?"

"Hopefully, not much."

"They weren't on the itinerary when we scouted the place for the convention."

"Yes, but you brought your family back in the summer," Zac reminded him. "They can interpret that as your opportunity to case the joint."

"The freezers weren't on the family itinerary either. Infinity pool, check. Golf, check. Spa, check. Casino, check. Restaurants, check. Bunker tour, check. I don't remember a freezer. If I was scouting someplace in preparation for a homicide, I wouldn't bring my wife and daughters along."

"I'm not the one you have to convince."

Carter hesitated. "You think I need a lawyer?"

"I'd give it a little longer," Zac suggested. "You might not hear from them again."

"Okay, but if they show up while I'm on the air and haul me away in handcuffs, I'm counting on you to go my bail."

"You'll need someone with deeper pockets," Zac informed him. "Call the Murdochs."

"Yeah, right. I thought you said I have a friend at the *Times*."

"The job doesn't pay as well as you might imagine. However, the good news is I am willing to visit you in prison."

"I can see this was a wasted call."

"Let's waste another one sometime."

"Later."

"Later."

Abby's right, Zac thought after they hung up. *I'm the world's worst investigator. I like all these people and I can't imagine any of them killing Oakes. The only one I probably wouldn't have liked is the victim.*

He stood up, faced the cross-shaped grave, gave the soldiers a salute and he turned and headed back to the Bean.

+ + +

"There's someone waiting in your office," the barista informed Zac when he returned to the coffee shop. She pointed to his usual table, where Sergeant Lavender was nursing a mug of something.

"I heard a rumor you hang out here," she greeted him.

"And I heard a rumor a couple of your officers were in New York."

"Word travels fast," she was impressed. "They aren't even back yet. They're following up on leads some guy from *The New York Times* gave us."

"I just had a call from Wyatt Carter. He seemed a little shaken by the pointed nature of the questions your men were asking him."

"They talked with Oakes' daughter and her boyfriend, too," she said. "Despite his acting and costuming experience, we've ruled out Declan Delaney as our bellman."

"Why is that?"

"He's taller than the person in the video," she said simply. "Short people can make themselves look taller, but it's pretty hard for tall people to look shorter. My guys say Delaney's taller and hunkier than our mystery man. That's not to say he couldn't have hired someone and supplied the uniform. Apparently, he and his girlfriend are hurting financially. An inheritance could solve a lot of their problems, but so far all the evidence we've gathered is circumstantial. I'm not even sure I'd call it evidence."

"I beg to differ, but an inheritance isn't going to solve their problems," Zac said. "You're probably aware of Layla's history of drug use. Financial windfalls don't solve addiction problems, they complicate them. According to Oliver, Layla's portion is going into a trust managed by a bank. I doubt if the trustees will be giving her large sums. Besides, estates take a couple of years to settle in New York, so anything she's getting is pretty far down the road. Unless Declan lands a big payday, they're still going to struggle. I know a lot of workaday actors and they all hold two or three jobs and live on the edge of financial ruin. I don't get the vibe that Layla or Declan were involved in this."

"We don't base our conclusions on vibes," Wendy said.

Zac smiled. "People base friendships and marriages on them."

"What's your take on Carter?" she asked him.

"I'm still trying to figure him out," he admitted. "He seems like a straight shooter, but it's hard getting past the fact that he planned everything. He knew when and how Oakes was getting there, where he was staying, and the specifics of his schedule. Except for Oliver, Layla and Calista, he seems to be the main beneficiary of Oakes' demise. He's almost too obvious."

"We questioned him at length," Wendy reported. "He claims people saw him at a banquet at the time the crime took place. We're checking it out. Just for fun, we had the DMV run a check on his vehicle registration history. At the time of the hit-and-run he owned a navy-blue Toyota Rav4."

"Holy shit."

"To be continued," she promised.

Chapter 38 Playing the Mediator

The sergeant's next order of business had the potential to be messy. She'd gotten a call from an upset Brendan Bell, who reported that Gunner Hoke had threatened him. She'd asked both of them to stay after school.

She arrived at the campus at 3:30 to find a line of yellow buses and student vehicles exiting, and parents waiting to turn into the entrance. She didn't want to flip on her blueberries and cherries and pretend there was an emergency, so she waited patiently in the line of cars. In the process she witnessed several teen drivers executing bold traffic maneuvers, but she resisted the temptation to pursue them.

Fifteen minutes later she walked into Brendan Bell's room. Teacher and student were in opposite corners, trying to ignore each other. "Hear ye, hear ye, hear ye," she announced. "Court is now in session. The Honorable Wendy Lavender presiding. Why don't we all sit up here?"

Gunner came to the front of the room, pulled a chair up to Brendan's desk and awaited instructions.

"Gunner, Mr. Bell told me you came up to him at the prom, accused him of suggesting to me that you might have murdered Mordecai Oakes, and threatened him. Is this true?"

"The first part is," the young man admitted. "But the part about threatening him isn't true."

"You said, 'I don't get mad. I get even,' Brendan quoted him. "I call that a threat. What do you call it?"

"I was trying to freak you out," Gunner said. "I heard it in a song in an anime."

"Well, it worked," Brendan admitted. "That's why you're sitting here right now."

The officer reminded herself that she was talking with a young man on the spectrum. "Gunner, even a vague statement like that can be construed as a threat. It doesn't matter if a student says it to a teacher or a teacher says it to a student. Normally something like this would be handled in-school, or it might even involve the Board of Education. But given the fact that it relates to a homicide investigation that we don't want to have to discuss with the principal or the school board, I hope we can talk it out here."

"Am I under investigation?" Gunner wanted to know.

"No, and I'm sorry if I gave you that impression. The fact is you're the only one of Mr. Bell's students who hasn't provided a satisfactory explanation about where you were and what you were doing during your free time at the hotel. You said you were looking at meteorology exhibits, but that doesn't sound like something that would keep you occupied for two hours, even with your interest in the subject."

"I looked at the exhibits and then I went home," he told them. "We weren't supposed to leave the hotel, so that's why I didn't tell you where I was."

"Why did you go home?" Brendan asked him.

"I didn't like the lunch, so I didn't eat it. I went home and I had a peanut butter and jelly sandwich and a Pellegrino and watched YouTube videos."

"How did you get to your house?" Brendan pried a bit more. "Seems like it would take a while to get over to Creekside from the hotel. Did you call a shuttle?"

"I walked. It took 15 minutes. I knew I couldn't walk back and make it on time, so I rode my bike back and left it on the porch of one of the empty Spring Row cottages. I came in the north entrance, went upstairs and then I came down the stairs by Colonial Hall, where you told us to meet you."

"Do your parents know you went home?" the sergeant asked.

"No. They wouldn't like it because it was a school activity and I was supposed to be at the hotel. They would say I was taking advantage of living here."

"It sounds like you were," she said. "Can you prove you were at your house?"

"No."

"Did you say hello to anyone, maybe a groundskeeper or someone, when you were going to and from your place?"

"No. I don't know the groundskeepers. I wouldn't talk to them anyway."

"Well, just because you can't prove your whereabouts, it doesn't mean I think you're guilty of homicide," the sergeant let him know.

"Am I a suspect? Did Mr. Bell ask you to question me?"

"I had concerns about some of the things you said in class the week after the murder," Brendan admitted. "You had some exceptionally detailed information about walk-in freezers and hypothermia and death by freezing. It's not the kind of thing the average high school student knows about."

"I'm not the average high school student. I researched it."

"So did the person who committed this crime, Gunner," Sergeant Lavender reminded him. "You may be perfectly innocent, but you seem to have done the same kind of research the guilty party would have done. Don't you see why that might raise a red flag?"

"I didn't think about it because I'm not guilty."

"When I tried to talk with you on the colonnade, you said you thought Mr. Bell committed the murder. That's a pretty serious accusation about a teacher you supposedly like."

"He had the same reasons to do it and the same opportunities I did," Gunner said with a shrug. "If I'm a suspect Mr. Bell should be a suspect, too."

"What reasons and opportunities are you talking about, Gunner?" Brendan wanted to know.

"You didn't like Mr. Oakes and the way he was influencing people. You have access to the hotel and you hang around there a lot."

"My wife works at the hotel and sometimes I meet her after work, or wait for her to get off."

"You said if we needed you, you'd be grading papers in the Victorian Writing Room. I walked by when I was leaving the hotel and you weren't in there. Neither were your papers or your backpack."

"I left twice, once to get coffee from the gourmet shop on the lower level another time to go to the bathroom," he explained. "You must have gone by one of those times. I took my backpack with me because it's an expensive leather pack that was a gift from my wife and I worry someone might take it. You may have noticed I always keep it with me. I don't even leave it in the classroom. When we have class outdoors, I bring it out there."

"It's big enough for a bellman's uniform," the boy pointed out. "And because your wife works here so you could have found out where Mr. Oakes was staying."

"Gunner, Santiago's parents work at the hotel, too," Brendan said. "They might even have cleaned Mr. Oakes' room. That doesn't mean Santiago killed Mr. Oakes."

"Santiago didn't hate him like you did."

"Gunner, that's enough," the sergeant intervened. "I get your point. You're saying you shouldn't be considered a suspect any more than the teacher who brought you to the hotel. You're upset with Mr. Bell because he told me what you said in school. You're upset with me because I followed up on it. Can we find a way to erase the board and go back to the way things were before? You've done well in school and you're about to graduate. You're obviously a nice young man from a decent family, and Mr. Bell is an outstanding teacher who's had a positive influence on you and a lot of others. Don't let this incident ruin your relationship. I don't intend to pursue this. All these suspicions and accusations only amount to weak circumstantial evidence that wouldn't make it past a grand jury. Even if they did, it would be a cakewalk for most defense attorneys. The victim had a lot of people who didn't like him, and a number of them were running around The Greenbrier. So please stop worrying about it. Okay?"

"I'm not a suspect?"

"No, and neither is Mr. Bell. Do you have any other questions?"

"Yes."

"Go for it."

"What's a cakewalk?"

Their laughter signaled that, at least for the time being, the situation was defused.

"A cakewalk is something that's ridiculously easy," Brendan explained. "I'm not sure, but I think it dates back to the time of slavery, and it had something to do with slaves doing dances to mock the fancy ones the white slaveholders did. The winner got a cake as a prize. But I might not have the story right."

"I'll look it up," Gunner said. "Research is a cakewalk for me."

"Gunner, did you just make a joke?" Brendan asked him.

"Yeah. Was it funny?"

"On the scale of mildly amusing to leaving people collapsing on the floor in laughter, I'd say it was closer to mildly amusing. But if you're considering a career in comedy, it's a start."

"I'm not considering a career in comedy."

"I gather we're okay now?" Wendy asked them.

"Yeah," Gunner said.

"Absolutely," Brendan agreed.

Chapter 39 A Professional Liar

Connor and Zac were riding the Adventures on the Gorge shuttle bus down to the spot on the New River where they were launching their 8-person raft.

"Are they trying to terrify us?" Connor asked his father.

"This is the standard safety briefing they give everyone," Zac explained as they hugged a hairpin curve inches from the edge of a sandstone cliff. "They're trying to impress on us that white water rafting isn't a theme park ride. There's an element of danger if we aren't careful."

"I'm not talking about the safety speech," Connor said. "I'm talking about this dude's driving."

"He could go a little slower," Zac agreed. He studied his son's new haircut, short on the sides, tousled on top. He'd swapped his prescription glasses for polarized sunglasses, one of Oliver's suggestions for the outing. "You look good, Connor," he said. "You've morphed from a tween to a teen overnight."

"Thanks."

The excursion was a makeup for the trip Oliver had cancelled, and a chance for Zac and Oliver to get together afterwards and take a look at what he'd retrieved from the evidence room. Rafting the Lower New River would fill the morning, and Oliver had promised to find something to keep Connor busy in the afternoon while they went about their business.

The company had furnished personal floatation devices, helmets and paddles. Oliver had instructed them to wear synthetic clothing and sandals with straps that would stay on their feet, like Tevas or Chacos, and bring along dry clothes, towels, gloves, sunscreen and sunglasses with neck straps.

"Can I go talk to Oliver?" Connor requested.

"Sure."

He made his way to the back of the bus and claimed the seat next to the river guide. "Hi, Oliver."

"Hey, Connor."

"So this is like a real job you get paid for?" the boy asked.

"Yep."

"You get paid to have fun?"

"There's a little more to it than that," Oliver explained. "I have to guide the raft through the rapids, keep everyone safe, deal with any injuries or medical issues, explain how to navigate each set of rapids - we'll have 17 on this trip - talk about the history, geology, flora and fauna of the gorge, and entertain the rafters. Occasionally I get someone who's scared to death and I have to deal with that. It may not look like work, but it really is. I guarantee you'll have more fun today than I will."

"Shit. I thought I'd found an easy career choice."

"Yeah, I thought the same thing. A river guide is a coach, an athlete, a teacher, a counselor, a medic and an entertainer all rolled into one without being paid as well as any of them."

"Some of the guides have nicknames like Rowdy and Dan-Dan," Connor had noticed. "I asked Dan-Dan why he's called that and he said it's because he's twice as good as you. But you go by your real name."

"I'm open to suggestions," Oliver said.

"I'll work on it."

"You know, Connor, you and I have something in common," Oliver pointed out. "We both grew up in New York City and we both moved here."

"Yeah," the boy said. "Now I understand two languages - English and West Virginian. Maybe someday I'll learn to speak it."

Oliver gave him a fist bump.

"Your river name could be Yankee Dude," Connor suggested.

"I think I'd get tired of that one."

"How about Mighty Oakes?"

"That's better. Keep working on it."

They arrived at the put-in site and Oliver made sure his eight passengers were snug in their PFD's before he pressed them into service hauling the 16-foot raft down to the water. He assigned Zach and Connor the front positions and warned them they were going to get soaked.

They were sharing this adventure with a honeymooning military couple and a family of four from Michigan. The couple had prior experience on the Salmon River in Idaho, but the parents and their teenage daughters were newbies who had a lot of trepidation about the whole thing. Zac and Connor watched Oliver work his magic, chatting it up with his crew and getting a feel for their personalities. He demonstrated the proper paddling technique and estimated that at the river's current level the 8-mile trip would take less than three hours. He illustrated how to swim out safely if they fell out of the raft. He explained how rapids are classified, and promised to tell them how to navigate each one they would encounter. His confidence was infectious, and by the time he finished, his ragtag crew was ready to go.

The next two-and-a-half hours were spent flying over rippling waves and navigating rapids with whimsical names like Piece of Cake, Double ZZ, Greyhound Bus Stopper and Thread the Needle. Oliver sat in back, steering the raft with long oars and issuing orders. The daylong version of the same trip featured two sets of rapids where the rafters could hop out and float through, a boulder where they could test their nerve by jumping 17 feet into the water, and a catered lunch. Oliver had signed up to guide the shorter trip so he and Zac would have time later for their private matters.

During the quieter stretches he provided commentary on the forces of nature that had created the thousand-foot gorge and history about the mining towns that had dotted the banks a century earlier. Whenever the roar of an approaching rapid became audible, he switched to giving navigation guidance.

Connor liked to take a knee when he was paddling - he thought of it as the superhero crouch. He expected Oliver to tell him to sit down, but the guide didn't admonish him. Besides, he knew what to do if he fell out: try to grab the raft so the others could help him climb back in, and if that didn't work, float on his back through the rapids, feet first with his feet up so he didn't get snagged in the rocks. Fortunately, he didn't have to test this and they made their way downstream safely, soaked to the bone but exhilarated.

Once they'd cleared Greyhound, named for the bus-size boulder in the middle, they spent the last stretch admiring the bridge 900 feet above them. They arrived at the takeout point and hauled the raft back up the hill. The honeymooners stripped out of the rented wetsuits they hadn't needed.

"This is the most fun I've ever had," Connor enthused. "I wish I could do it every day."

"Welcome to my life," Oliver said.

\+ \+ \+

After lunch Oliver dispatched Connor with a coworker named Kai to spend the afternoon on a guided rock climb. "Rock climbing sounds hardcore, but the way we do it, it's pretty softcore," Kai reassured Zac. "The other day I helped a 77-year-old grandmother do it."

Zac wanted to pay for this activity, but Oliver wouldn't let him. "Maybe you can just write an article about it," he suggested.

"I don't write travel pieces," Zac said. "Even if I did, our editors wouldn't want you comping me for it because it could be interpreted as paying for a favorable review."

"Okay, whatever," Oliver said. "The climbing's still a freebie and I don't want to hear any more about it."

They retreated to a picnic table in the shade with Oliver's laptop. He pulled out a flash drive.

"You cloned the hard drive on that?"

"No, I bought a new MacBook Air and I copied his whole laptop on it. It took a couple of hours. I thought I'd find password-protected files and we'd have to call your hacker friends. But like you suggested, Dad had his passwords in his notebook. He wasn't big on security. His Apple ID was the year he was born. Whenever he needed a password, he used his name and the year he was born. If it needed a symbol, he'd add a dollar sign. That's his whole damn security system. He probably thought passwords were a pain in the ass. I took some pictures of his notebook while the hard drive was uploading. He used it for random ideas. This notebook covers the past four months. If he had older ones, they're probably on a shelf in his home office. They weren't in his desk."

"I carry a notebook, too," Zac said. "A lot of writers do. I guess I could make voice memos, but it's easier to flip through pages than listen to recordings, and sometimes you're in situations where you can't talk."

"The notebook has some stuff that contradicts what he was saying in his TV commentaries," Oliver revealed. "Whenever he made a note like that, he wrote CPL next to it."

"Curious," Zac commented.

"It gets curiouser and curiouser," Oliver quoted *Alice in Wonderland*. "There's a file on his computer desktop labeled Current. It's all Word documents and none of them are password-protected. A lot are his commentaries. He's got the eulogy he gave at his father's funeral. There's a list of his medications. There's a file with the passwords for his bank account and his Schwab account, and all his subscriptions. He's got the manuscripts for his three books, and a new book he was working on. Are you ready for it? The new one is called *Confessions of a Professional Liar*."

Zac put two and two together. "CPL."

"He dedicated it to Layla and me, and it's a mind blower. He admits he's been bullshitting and there really is a climate crisis. Remember when I told you he said he was going to do something that would make us proud of him?"

"Yes."

"This has got to be what he meant. He knew it would get him fired and he says in the introduction that when the book is published he won't be working for Fox News. I guess he thought he could make enough off it that when he added it to what he already had, he could live off it. Or maybe he was planning some new career. Guess we'll never know. But the manuscript is pretty damn interesting. I copied it on this flash drive."

"Holy shit," Zac reacted. "How much did he finish?"

"Dunno. I think he was just winging it. The file's about 65,000 words. There's no outline or table of contents."

"Are you going to out him?"

"Hell, yeah. I'm thinking a memorial service might be a good place to do it, with all the Fox people sitting there. I'm also thinking you'd be the perfect guy to do it."

"I didn't even know your father," Zac reminded him.

"No, but you're going to read the manuscript and you're going to get up there and tell everyone about it. I talked to Layla and she totally agrees. We want you to edit it and add the story about how you got involved, and get it published."

"Oliver, the *Times* has writers who specialize in environmental issues. Don't you think it would carry more weight if someone with that kind of expertise handled it?"

"I don't know those people. I know you and I trust you. That counts for more."

"Are you sure about this, Oliver?"

Wordlessly the river guide picked up the flash drive and handed it across the table to Zac.

\+ \+ \+

On their way home Connor was going on about his climbing experience when he noticed his father was only half-listening.

"Is something wrong?" he asked him. "We had a great day but you're acting weird."

Zac realized he should be paying more attention to his son. "Sorry, Connor. Oliver told me something this afternoon and I'm thinking about it."

"What did he tell you?"

"It's about his father. I can't really talk about it."

"I hate secrets," Connor complained.

"Yeah, me too. Lately I seem to be dealing with a lot of them."

Chapter 40 A Guest Lecturer

The halls of Greenbrier River High School looked oh-so familiar to Zac, and when Brendan described his room's location, he remembered having a biology class in the same room. He and Abby hadn't attended the reunions, and this was the first time he was setting foot in his old school since they graduated seventeen years earlier.

His brother-in-law had pranked him, telling him the school was inviting him to serve as this year's commencement speaker, with a $2500 honorarium. A few minutes into their phone conversation he started laughing and admitted he only wanted him to talk to his seniors. After a few choice expletives, Zac had agreed to meet with them.

"I understand Mr. Bell had you read my story about the three Virginia students who went on a rampage in the name of the Earth Liberation Front," Zac said to the class after Brendan had introduced him and the students had introduced themselves. "Bear in mind I wrote that story a few years ago, and the incidents that led to their arrest and prosecution happened long before that, in 2002. From my perspective it's a distant memory, and from yours it's ancient history. I might have a hard time remembering all the details, but you're welcome to ask questions. Fire away."

Jude raised his hand. "Do you think those guys should have been prosecuted as terrorists, or were they just making an example of them to discourage people from doing that kind of stuff?"

"You asked the hardest question first, Jude," Zac reacted. "I don't usually insert my personal opinions in articles, but to be honest with you, no, I don't think they should have been prosecuted as terrorists. At the time people were sabotaging property around the country in the name of ELF and very few of them had been caught. These teens weren't exactly slick operators, and the FBI managed to nab them. I agree with what you're saying - labeling them terrorists was a convenient way to discredit them and discourage others from engaging in similar activities. Unfortunately for those three guys, the laws relating to terrorism had legal consequences far beyond what they would have faced otherwise. I think the laws were misapplied in their case. I couldn't come out and say it in the article but I hinted at it. Does that answer your question?"

"Totally," Jude said.

"Let me add a disclaimer," Zac said. "Environmental issues aren't my area of expertise. The *Times* has writers who are true experts on the subject. You name the topic and they can talk all day about it - federal regulations, air and water quality, toxic waste, deforestation, coal mining, EPA permits, legally mandated public meetings. I'm not that guy. I write people stories and I'm not the ideal speaker for a class like this. I'm only here because I happened to be in town when Mordecai Oakes was murdered, and I'm working on that story now."

"What have you found out?" Gunner wanted to know.

"A lot about Mr. Oakes, thanks to his family. But as far as the homicide goes, you'll have to talk with Sergeant Lavender."

"She's not going to tell us anything," Gunner was convinced.

"I'm not sure she's telling me much either, Gunner," Zac said. "Believe me, I've tried. Some police investigators enjoy the limelight, but I think Sergeant Lavender and her team like to work quietly behind the scenes. She holds her cards close to her uniform."

"You're kind of an investigator, too, aren't you?" Joseph asked him.

"Kind of is a good description, Joseph," Zac admitted. "My ability in that department is pretty limited. But let's get back to Short Pump. When Mr. Bell asked me to talk with you today, I did a little research and discovered the three teenagers who went on the rampage, who are now middle-aged guys, are leading perfectly respectable lives. At least two of them graduated from college after they finished their prison terms. The Richmond City Council appointed one of them to serve on a committee. I don't know if they're still bosom buddies because one of them turned state's evidence on the other two in return for a lighter sentence. They still seem to care very deeply about the natural world. I'm not sure what shipping these three young men off to prison accomplished, except making the folks whose property they damaged feel some sense of vindication and closure. I'm not fond of the way we handle crime and punishment in this country."

"I like that you're not afraid to say what you think," Hudson said.

Zac smiled. "Thanks, Hudson, but I don't think it's that brave to express my opinions in front of a handful of high school students in West Virginia. I don't think any of you are going to alert the news media."

Hayley raised her hand. "Mr. Wolfe, if it was your house or your business they vandalized, or your new SUV, wouldn't you feel differently?"

"Whew. I thought Jude asked the hard question. Can I plead the fifth?"

"No, you've got to answer it," Hayley stood her ground.

"You've got me there. It's easy to talk about this in theory, but if I were one of the victims, I might want retribution. But let me turn the table on you. Suppose it was your son who'd done this. Would you think he needed to serve three years in prison to learn his lesson? Do you think it would help him at age 19 to live with drug dealers and rapists and child molesters and con men, when he should be starting work or going off to college?"

"No," she admitted.

"Don't you think it would be better if these guys had been sentenced to do community service and get started on paying the restitution they owed? Don't you think they suffered enough from all the negative publicity and embarrassment they caused their families and their school?"

"Yes."

"We're not talking about hardened criminals. We're talking about teenage vandals."

"Misguided idealists," Santiago labeled them.

Brendan smiled. "Santiago, you never cease to amaze me with your ability to come up with the right words. For a self-described lazy student living with parents who speak Filipino at home, you have a surprising command of the language."

"Salamat, Mr. Bell. That's thanks in Filipino. I'm not all that smart, but I read graphic novels and I hang out with Jude. I think some of his intelligence accidentally rubs off on me."

"Maybe you need to take him to college with you," Brendan suggested.

"No, thanks," Jude declined the invitation. "I'm taking a gap year. Or two or three. The gap might turn into a canyon."

Zac looked at Brendan. "Are the conversations in here always this interesting?"

His brother-in-law nodded.

Gunner spoke up. "Do you think the person who killed Mr. Oakes should go to prison?" he asked him.

"Premeditated murder's a little different than vandalism, don't you think, Gunner? If the point you're making is that both things were done to make a statement about the way we're destroying the environment, we can't really say that for sure in Mordecai Oakes' case. It might turn out to be true, or his murder might be some completely unrelated personal vendetta. The culprit didn't leave a manifesto, so we're left guessing. The Short Pump boys left a note in the mailbox of the owner of a construction company accusing him of creating 'revolting sprawl'. The note was one of the things that led the FBI to them. The Unabomber published a manifesto that led to his arrest. Luigi Mangione had handwritten notes that ranted against the health care system and said, 'these parasites had it coming' and 'you whack the CEO at the parasitic annual bean-counter convention'. The moral of the story is, if you don't want to get caught, don't leave a written explanation for your crime."

"Don't you think the freezer was a statement?" Gunner asked.

"Maybe. On the other hand, it could just have been a clever way to get rid of someone without leaving much physical evidence."

"I still can't believe we were there when this happened," Zoey said.

"While I'm here, let's talk about something I know more about," Zac suggested. "Are any of you interested in writing careers?"

For the first time, the room fell silent.

"That would have been the same response back when I was in high school," he said with a smile. "But just for the record I'll share a few things I've learned about the writing business after doing it for a few years. I like to say that writing's just edited thinking. Some people aren't very good thinkers. Their thoughts are hazy, or paranoid, or they have a poor vocabulary or a limited attention span. When those people try to write, it doesn't turn out well. But if you don't have those challenges, you might have the potential to be a good writer. Have you ever noticed that when we talk, no matter how hard we try, sometimes the wrong words come out of our mouths?"

"Amen," Hudson said.

"Hearty agreement from the Amen Corner. The thing about writing is you can keep working at it until you find the right words. Editing your thoughts takes patience. It takes the humility to accept that all the crap that pops into your head isn't necessarily brilliant. But if you keep playing around with words, you can make them better. That's the gift that writing allows us. Humans are the only creatures who have that advantage."

"I write poetry," Skylark told him.

"A lot of writers start with poetry, Skylark," Zac said. "And then they often move on to longer forms - essays, short stories, books."

"Poems are easier to write," she explained. "That's probably why people start with them. I used to write poems about my feelings, but that got boring, so I started writing about other things and the writing got better. You want to hear one? It's called *Fall*."

"Share your masterpiece, Skylark," he invited her.

She recited from memory:

“When leaves slowly turn in time
hopeless shades of brown,
finally taking journeys to fall
listless on the ground,
I fear I am a leaf.”

“That's actually very good,” Zac congratulated her. "Do you have another one?”

“Sure,” she appreciated the positive review. “This one's called *More*.”

“And though you think
you've got me figured out
there's more to me
than you will ever know.
I'll always leave you
with a nagging doubt
even when you think
you've got me figured out.”

"You can say that again," Joseph said.

“You say meaningful things in a few words,” Zac praised her. “That's a talent. You can tell people that a writer from *The New York Times* likes your poetry.”

She beamed. “Thanks.”

“You've got a good name for a poet, too,” he added. “You don't even need to use your last name.”

“Good. It's Polish and when people try to pronounce it, they sound like they're trying to read an eye chart.”

Hudson raised his hand. “Does writing pay well?”

“It depends on what you mean by well, Hudson. None of my coworkers have private jets or yachts. Obviously, Steven King and J.K. Rowling can afford them, but 99.9999% of writers can't. If money's your object, there are avenues you can pursue. Take a writer/producer like Vince Gilligan, who created *Breaking Bad* and *Better Call Saul*. Vince grew up in Virginia, he went to college in New York, and then he headed to Hollywood and went to work in television. If he'd stayed in Virginia and been a reporter for the Richmond Times-Dispatch, would he have done as well? Definitely not. If he'd stayed at home and written novels instead of screenplays, would he have done as well? Possibly, but probably not."

"Will you tell us how much you make?" Hudson followed up.

"You shouldn't ask people that," Brendan chided his student. "It's inappropriate."

"I don't mind," Zac said. "What do your parents do, Hudson?"

"My dad's a preacher and my mom's a dental hygienist."

"Unless your father's one of those televangelists who specializes in fleecing the flock, it sounds like your family's middle class. That's what we are. We pay our bills and we're comfortable, but we're not going to be packing our son off to a $60,000-a-year prep school."

"So if I want a personal assistant and a private chef and a villa in Italy, I need to go into another line of work?"

"That would be my suggestion."

"Hudson," Brendan said, "you have delusions of grandeur."

"No, Mr. Bell," Hudson disagreed. "I have grandeur."

"If you don't have any more questions for Mr. Wolfe, we'll let him get back to his day job," Brendan said to the class. "Thanks for coming by, Zac."

"I have a question," Skylark spoke up. "Can I get in touch with you? I'd like to get my poems published, but I don't know how to do it."

"I'm not sure I can help you much with that, but I can put you in contact with someone who knows more about it," he told her. "Some magazines accept poetry, but they might only accept submissions from agents, and I'm guessing you don't have an agent. I didn't bring my business cards, but I'll give you my email and you can send me a reminder to look into it."

"Thanks."

He turned to Brendan. "Do you have a scrap of paper and a pen I can borrow?"

"Sure," his brother-in-law said. He tore a yellow sticky note from the pad on his desk, picked up a pen from his desk and handed it to him.

Zac felt a jolt of electricity.

The black pen with the gold band that he was holding was identical to the fake Montblanc Calista Martin had given him, and, presumably, the one Mordecai Oakes had given to the bellman.

Chapter 41 An Unfinished Symphony

Zac had been hunkered down for three days at The Wild Bean, poring over *Confessions of a Professional Liar*. Oliver and Layla were pinning their hopes on seeing this book published, and they were expecting him to make it happen. Some of the rough ideas in their father's notebook had morphed into entire chapters in his manuscript. Despite Mordecai's many shortcomings as a human being, Zac had to give him credit - the man could write. He estimated the manuscript would translate into about 250 book pages. He could pad it with a Forward and an Afterward. The only problem was the material building to an unstated conclusion; the manuscript was an unfinished symphony. He decided that would make a good title for the Afterward.

Try as he might to focus on his task, his thoughts kept straying to his brother-in-law. He tried to think of some way besides the obvious one that Brendan would have come to possess a phony Montblanc pen.

He'd known Brendan Bell for eight years, ever since he and Greta were an item. He was a stellar guy - a loving husband, an upstanding community member, a gifted teacher beloved by students, trusted by parents, respected by coworkers. Could the same Brendan have planned and executed a cold-blooded murder? It didn't make sense.

Or did it? How passionately did Brendan really feel about the subject matter he taught? Why had he introduced his students to Mordecai Oakes and his TV commentaries? Why had he taken them to the debate? Why had he let them roam the hotel unsupervised for two hours? After Oakes' body was discovered in the freezer, why had Brendan called him at the crack of dawn the next day to talk about the murder? Why did he ask his students if Oakes deserved to die? Was he looking for validation? Why did he cozy up to the lead investigator and point her in the direction of the Hoke boy? Why did he introduce his students to the subject of eco-sabotage and groups like ELF? Thanks to Greta's employment, his brother-in-law knew The Greenbrier like the back of his hand. He even knew the code the emergency responders used to open the Sporting Club's private gates.

He kept trying to banish these thoughts. Surely, it was just his imagination in overdrive. Wyatt Carter seemed a more likely suspect, especially after learning that he'd owned a navy-blue Rav4 at the time of the hit-and-run. But Wendy had informed him that three people had verified that Carter had been present at the AMA luncheon while Oakes was on route to the freezer. Could Carter have been in cahoots with the person who did the dirty deed and set it up? If so, who was his mystery collaborator?

His thoughts were trapped in a vicious circle. He'd even been waking up in the middle of the night and thinking about it. Sooner or later, he'd have to confront Brendan. It was the only way he could put this thing to rest. But how would he start this conversation with his brother-in-law?

+ + +

It was late afternoon and the crowd at the Bean had dwindled to a handful when he got a call from Oliver.

"There's no such thing in New York as an inexpensive venue," the young man said.

"What are you talking about, Oliver?"

"The memorial service," he explained. "The one you've been hoping I'd forget about."

"Are you really going through with this? Do you really expect me to get up in front of people and talk about what we found on your father's laptop?"

"Absolutely. That's the main reason I want to have it. Every day I look at where I'm working and I think about how beautiful the world is. Then I think of all the fat cats and corporations that don't give a rat's ass and are only interested in lining their own pockets. I thought my father was one of those people. But he was planning to redeem himself and we're going to help him. Aren't we?"

Zac issued a deep sigh. "I guess so. I had no idea I was going to end up knee-deep in this thing. I didn't know your dad, and now I'm a featured speaker at his memorial service. I don't remember signing up for this, Oliver."

"You didn't, you were drafted. You know The Tavern on the Green?"

"You mean the restaurant in Central Park?"

"Yeah. They rent out rooms for private events. They have six different spaces, depending on how many people you're planning on. I don't have any idea how many folks are going to show up for this thing, but I don't think it's going to be a big crowd. The room I'm renting holds 150."

"Isn't The Tavern kind of pricey?" Zac asked.

"Yeah. I spent three hours calling venues and I discovered they're all ridiculously overpriced. But I talked to Fox and I talked to The Greenbrier and they're making contributions to help out."

"The Greenbrier? Really?"

"They offered me their 500-seat chapel for free, but Dad didn't have any connection with the place except for dying there, and nobody's going to travel from New York to West Virginia for a service. The people he worked with are probably going to have a hard time getting away from their jobs anyway. The Greenbrier's kicking in some on the rental, and so is Fox, and the estate's paying for the catering."

"Who's speaking at this thing besides me?"

"I'm not sure yet. The service is three weeks from Friday, so I have until then to get it figured out. It's probably more like two weeks because we need to get programs printed up. It'll be simple, I guarantee you that."

"What would you like me to say?"

"You're the writer, man. You figure it out."

"Are you expecting me to out Mordecai as a closet environmentalist?"

"Why not? He was planning to do that himself."

"This thing has the potential to make me rue the day I met you, Oliver Oakes. Do you want to read what I'm going to say ahead of time so you can suggest changes?"

"Nope. If you can write for the *Times*, you can write this."

"Did your dad have relatives?"

"Two brothers. One's a school administrator in Bloomington and the other's in the wine business in Sonoma. Dad wasn't big on keeping in touch with them, so they weren't close. I seriously doubt they'll come. They'll probably just send flowers. My guess is it'll be mostly Fox folks and his publisher and maybe the agent that booked his speaking gigs. I asked Calista if she thought her family would come. She said her brothers might come and bring their mom, and then take her back up to Maine."

"That doesn't surprise me," Zac said. "From what she said, it sounds like her family's pretty close and they probably want to be supportive, especially now that she's pregnant."

"I'm taking your advice about giving her a third," he revealed.

"Good. What made you come around?"

"I was having a hard time making up my mind, and then I remembered that one of our college profs showed us a method for making decisions called the OODA Loop. I sat down with a piece of paper and worked it out."

"I've never heard of the OODA Loop," Zac said. "It sounds like a Dr. Seuss book."

"Look it up, man. I don't know if it helped me reach a decision or forced me to make one, but I'm okay with it. Calista is, too. We could fight this out in court, but none of us have the stomach for it. I'm sort of coming around about Calista. She's not as bad as I thought. Not that I would have wanted her for a stepmom, but she seems okay."

"Things seem to be moving in the right direction," Zac observed. "I'm bracing for a setback. Watch it turn out that Calista and Wyatt Carter were having an affair and they were behind this whole thing."

"Who's Wyatt Carter?" Oliver asked him.

“A meteorologist at the local Fox station in New York. He was tapped to fill in when your dad was in rehab, and now he's back on Fox News and he's hoping to make his gig permanent. Turns out he owned the same kind of vehicle as the one that hit your father. He was on the planning committee for the Meteorological Association conference and he was the one who came up with the idea for the debate. He invited your dad to participate, and he booked his travel and room. And he made two prior visits to the hotel before the convention.”

“Wow," Oliver exclaimed. "Why haven't they arrested this dude?”

“They haven't connected him to the accident yet, and he can prove he was elsewhere when the murder happened. It's pretty damning, but it's all circumstantial. He might show up at the service. He claims he admired your father.”

“I don't want to meet these Fox people. If Dad hadn't gone to work there, he might not have become a hypocrite.”

“Oliver, that was entirely his choice. I don't think Mordecai was the kind of person who let himself get shoved around. You're hosting this event. You don't invite people to a memorial service and act hostile when they get there. You need to be cordial to his coworkers.”

“I'm hoping after they hear you, they'll all walk out.”

“Well, there's always that possibility.”

Chapter 42 Altitude, Attitude, Gratitude

It was their fifteenth wedding anniversary and Zac and Abby had left Connor in charge of his grandmother while they went out to dinner. Zac had considered a number of restaurants, and even a catered picnic, before having an inspiration and calling Buzzy.

"Friday's our anniversary and I want to surprise Abby," he said to his friend. "What would it take to get a dinner reservation at that place on top of the mountain?"

"Membership in the Sporting Club," Buzzy explained. "The Summit's private, Zac. It's not open to peons like you and me. The hotel guests can't even go there. You have to belong to the Sporting Club, which usually means owning property there."

Zac wasn't giving up. "There's got to be a workaround, Buzzy."

His friend pondered it. "You can go there if you're a guest of one of the members."

"How well do you know them? Does someone owe you a favor?"

"Let me work on it. What time do you want to eat?"

"I'm picturing watching the sunset over the mountains."

"6:30?"

"Perfect."

"I'll call you back."

A half-hour later his phone rang. "Done," Buzzy proclaimed victoriously. "There's a South Carolina couple with a chain of furniture stores who have a place here. I've golfed with the guy a couple of times when his regular buddies weren't available. I explained your situation and he called and made the reservation. He gave them his credit card number, so you'll have to repay him."

"No problem."

"I'll tell you something about the folks who own houses here," Buzzy continued. "They're all successful executives or business owners, and when they want something done, they don't screw around. They're used to making things happen and they won't take no for an answer. He called me back in two minutes with your reservation."

"I really appreciate your help with this."

"Tip generously."

"Buzzy, my generosity is legendary up and down the eastern seaboard. When I call restaurants for reservations, fights break out with the waitstaff about who gets to serve my table. Two servers retired after receiving my gratuity. One bought a condo in Cozumel."

"Make it at least 20%, okay?"

"Okay. Abby and I are at the point where we'd rather spend money on experiences like this than buying more crap. She's not into expensive jewelry and clothes. She's more practical."

"Yeah, that's what I thought about my last ex when I gave her a vacuum cleaner for Valentine's Day. She served me with divorce papers the next month."

"Oh, Romeo."

"It was a cordless Dyson, for Chrissake! You know how much those babies cost? More than your dinner, I'll tell you that. And she kept it as part of the settlement!"

"There might have been other issues," Zac speculated.

"Yeah, whatever. Enjoy your dinner. The only thing I've ever had at that altitude is complimentary airline pretzels. I'll lend you a card that opens the Sporting Club gate on Route 60."

"Thanks, man. We'll have a drink in your honor."

\+ + +

"It feels like we're going to a ski resort," Abby said as they negotiated the hairpin turns on Greenbrier Mountain. "Why haven't I ever heard of this place?"

"Because we're not one-percenters," Zac replied. "We're pretenders. If anyone asks, we recently added a Sporting Club home to our portfolio of vacation properties."

"And what does our new home look like?" she wanted details.

"Rustic elegance. Timber frame, with high ceilings and exposed rafters. Massive fireplace and stone hearth. Gourmet kitchen with an Italian marble island, a butler's pantry and a wet bar. Jaw-dropping views from our cantilevered decks, which are Trex, of course, so we don't have to worry about insect or weather damage. Our driveway and sidewalks are heated, and we melt the snow with the flick of a switch. And we've tastefully landscaped the property with native shrubs like mountain laurel and rhododendrons that require little or no maintenance."

"If all these things require little or no maintenance, what's our staff going to do?" Abby wondered.

"We can have our groundskeeper cut and stack firewood."

"What do you think has kept us together for fifteen years besides obscene wealth and the pre-nup you made me sign?" she asked.

"Possibly our warped senses of humor," Zac speculated.

They eventually reached the 3300-foot mountaintop. The restaurant was a more elaborate version of the imaginary home Zac had described, an Adirondack-inspired oak and timber lodge with a stone terrace that offered a sweeping view of the valley and distant mountains.

"Wow," Abby reacted.

"I thought you'd like it. I'm sure the food's great, but with a view like this, I'd be content with peanut butter and jelly."

On Zac's prior visit to the Summit, he'd met with Wendy and Buzzy on the back porch, so he and Abby were seeing the restaurant's interior for the first time. An impressive double-sided stone fireplace divided the dining area from the bar. Their South Carolina patron had reserved a table on the terrace so they could enjoy an unobstructed view of the Alleghenies.

"We've got to watch how much we drink," Abby said. "I don't think we can call an Uber to take us home."

"One of us can be the designated driver and the other can be the designated drunk," Zac proposed. "Want to flip a coin?"

Soon they were enjoying raw oysters and glasses of pinot noir while they waited for a Wagyu steak and local trout.

Zac had been giving the future a lot of thought, and he'd chosen this setting for a conversation he wanted to have with Abby. He'd considered having a family meeting and including Connor, but he decided they could rope him in later.

"How do you like being back in Greenbrier County?" he asked his wife.

"More than I thought," Abby admitted. "The surprise is that Connor likes it, too. I thought he'd miss his New York buddies and city life, but he's adapted pretty quickly. He's got a new group of friends. Caring for Mom limits our mobility, and it's only going to become more challenging as her Alzheimer's progresses. But she needs me more than the patients at Sloan Kettering do. I thought not having a regular job would bother me, but it's kind of nice not to have to get up at 5:30 and ride the subway into Manhattan. I'm liking this lifestyle."

"It's what we grew up with," Zac said. "I guess if we'd grown up in a city, urban life would feel normal. Even though I've only been here a few weeks, this feels right to me, too."

Abby studied him pensively. "What are you saying, Zac?"

"I want to move back," he let the cat out of the bag. "I know it's an absurd idea with my job. Journalists all over the world would love to work for the *Times*. We've got over ten million online subscribers and the number's always growing. Features like Games and Wirecutter are the industry's gold standard. I'm unbelievably lucky to have landed a job there. But Dad's always said you can't beat working for yourself, and I'm starting to think maybe he's got a point. New York comes with a way of life I've never fully embraced. I'm tired of trying to convince myself I love it. The city has its own complicated set of rules, and even after 12 years I'm still trying to learn them. Life here feels comfortable."

"There are the small matters of paying our bills, health insurance, putting Connor through college and saving for retirement," Abby reminded him. "Can we afford for you to quit your job?"

"Maybe," he said. "I've got an idea."

"How many times have I heard those words in the past fifteen years?"

Zac sensed it was the right time to share his thoughts. "Quite a few, but hear me out. The manuscript I'm editing has the potential to be a big deal. Oliver's proposing we split the royalties, half to the estate and half to me. I'm going to have to find an agent and see if we can get an auction going for the rights. If things unfold the way I hope they will, I could end up with an advance that's the equivalent of what I'd make at the *Times* in the next two or three years, maybe even more. That's enough to let me live here while I try to get a different kind of writing career going. I could help my folks with the farm. Greta and I are going to end up owning it someday, and we'll have to decide if we want to keep running it, lease it or sell it. I need to learn more about the cattle business, and the best way to do it is by helping Dad."

Abby smiled. "I think you've always known that land's going to be part of your future, even if you didn't want to admit it."

"Farming's just never seemed that creative or exciting to me. But there are lots of folks around here who have farms and jobs, too. They seem to make it work."

"Zac, if it works financially, I'm all for it. Mom could have Alzheimer's for the next ten years. I really don't want you 500 miles away all that time."

"Me either. So do we have a plan?"

Abby raised her glass. "Sort of," she said, and they drank to it.

"Remember when you said I don't make a very good criminal investigator because I like all the suspects?" Zac switched subjects. “You're right. Making matters even worse, I've pretty much stopped caring who killed Mordecai Oakes. Someone did it for some reason, and it's over and done and life goes on. I know that's not the right attitude about a homicide, but with the people I've met, it almost seems like his death was a catalyst and their lives are getting better. Even Mordecai himself is turning out better in death than he was in life, thanks to his manuscript. Who knows - if he'd lived, he might have changed his mind and dragged his manuscript into the trash icon. But we're resurrecting him! Whoever wheeled him into that freezer is going to be surprised when he emerges from it in the form of a book that disavows his supposed beliefs.”

“You're really into this, aren't you?”

“Totally. Mordecai's Second Coming is more interesting to me than finding whoever killed him.”

“Is this your midlife crisis, Zac?”

“God, I hope so. I don't need a Maserati and I've still got my original trophy wife.”

They realized the view from Greenbrier Mountain faced the wrong direction for the sunset, but as their food arrived, they were framed by an orange and pink watercolor sky in the southeast. Abby pulled out her phone and preserved the memory with a selfie.

Chapter 43 A Hit-and-Run Revisited

Zac had been working on untethering himself from his phone, so he'd left it in his Jeep while he was in the Bean laboring over two projects - getting the manuscript ready and figuring out what he was going to say at the memorial. The projects dovetailed, and he'd been toggling back and forth between them all morning. When he went out to his Jeep to go home for lunch, he looked at his phone and saw he had 26 text messages, including ones from his editor and Oliver. His editor's read, "Congratulations, Zac! Call me when you have time." Oliver had attached a link to a *Times* article.

Fox 5 Meteorologist Arrested for Hit-and-Run

> Police have arrested a local Fox 5 meteorologist and charged him with an intentional hit-and-run three years ago, which left the late Fox News commentator Mordecai Oakes partially paralyzed. Wyatt Carter, 33, of Brooklyn, was charged with leaving the scene of a personal injury accident, failure to render aid, failure to file an accident report, and attempted evidence tampering. He is being held on $500,000 bond.
>
> Oakes, whose mysterious death two months ago in a West Virginia hotel walk-in freezer remains unsolved, was

temporarily replaced by Carter on Fox News after the hit-and-run, and again following his death in April.

CCTV footage indicated Oakes was hit by a Toyota RAV4 while crossing East 75th Street, sending him flying 25 feet into a parked vehicle. An NYPD investigation revealed that two days later Carter took his RAV4 to a Brooklyn body shop to have front-end damage repaired. The technician who worked on the vehicle recalled that it was equipped with a privacy blackout plate, enabling the driver to obscure his license by remote control. CCTV footage suggested the vehicle involved in the hit-and-run had a similar license concealer. New York law prohibits license plates that are covered, coated or altered to obscure readability.

Reached for comment, Oakes' 24-year-old son, Oliver Oakes, said, "This brutal attack left my father wheelchair-bound for the last three years of his life. I think Carter's motive was obvious, but that's for the legal system to decide. Speaking for our family, we're grateful to the NYPD for reopening the investigation, and to *New York Times* reporter Zac Wolfe and the West Virginia State Police for bringing this man to their attention."

"Holy shit!" Zac reacted. He speed-scrolled through the other messages. They were all related to the article. He called Oliver but the call went to Voicemail. He called Emma Penn, his *Times* editor.

"Well, if it isn't the man of the hour," she said. "It not every day one of our world-class journalists solves a cold case."

"The West Virginia State Police and the NYPD solved it, Emma," he insisted. "I just put them on to the guy. There's a lot more to it. Carter was at the convention at The Greenbrier. Not only was he there, he planned the debate and recruited Oakes to participate. On the surface he looks guilty as sin, but he wasn't the mystery bellman. Witnesses swear he was attending a function when it happened. I'm not convinced the accident and the murder are related."

"I'm sure you'll get to the bottom of it," she said.

"I'm lousy at this investigation stuff, Emma. I wasn't suspicious of Carter. I happened to catch him on TV and I decided to interview him. I was trying to find out if Oakes had ever gotten death threats. I mentioned him to the State Police's lead investigator and she took the ball and ran with it. They coordinated with NYPD, and they contacted the DMV and discovered Carter had the same kind of vehicle as the one that hit Oakes. Then I guess they checked the collision shops in his neck of the woods and hit a bull's eye."

"Hit-and-runs are one of the most common crimes in New York," his editor said, speaking from years of experience at the paper. "Half the time they don't find the driver. It never happens years later like it did with this man."

"It was blind luck on my part," he assured her.

"When will we see you again?"

"In a couple of weeks. The Oakes family asked me to speak at Mordecai's memorial service. You might want to send someone to cover the service. I think you'll find it newsworthy. It would be nice to have a perspective besides Fox's and the New York Post's."

"Send me the date, time and place. Come by the office when you're here."

"Will do. Thanks, Emma."

He tried Oliver again without any luck. He called Calista.

"Hello, Zac," she answered. "I hope they're giving you a raise."

"I just talked with my editor. She didn't bring it up."

"Speaking of raises, thanks for talking with Oliver about the will. He respects your opinion. I think that's why he came around."

"Common sense made him come around, Calista. He realized you could end up slugging it out in court he prefers outdoor adventures to courtroom drama. Oliver's sort of a neo-hippie. He wants to give peace a chance."

"Did you find what you want in Mordecai's things?" she was curious.

"Yes, and if you come to the service, you'll hear all about it. It was in his notebook and laptop, like you thought. I appreciate your putting me onto this. I'd like to give you credit, but I know you don't want your name connected with it."

"Did Carter kill Mordecai?"

"He may have been behind it, but the bellman's identity is still a mystery. Hopefully time will tell."

"What kind of asshole runs over someone, leaves him for dead in the street and then fills in for him at work?"

"An ambitious psychopath," Zac characterized him. "He must have been eaten up with jealousy of Mordecai. Remember asking me if I believed in karma? I think it's caught up with Wyatt Carter. And I think Mordecai's manuscript has the potential to redeem him in some people's eyes, so maybe karma's at work there, too. I still don't know if I believe in it, but I'm definitely a fanboy."

"How's Abby?"

"She's fine. I'll tell her you asked about her. We just celebrated our fifteenth wedding anniversary."

"Congratulations. Maybe I'll have one of those someday."

"Maybe you will. I'll see you at the memorial service."

"Am I sitting with Oliver and Layla?"

"I don't have a clue, Calista. That's probably up to you. But you are family. You're going to be the mother of their half-sibling. It would be nice if you can all get along."

"One big happy family," she considered it. "That's us, all right."

Chapter 44 A Memorable Memorial

Robert Moses's vision for New York's Central Park didn't include grazing livestock, so in 1934, under his supervision, the flock was evicted and their sheepfold became an eatery called The Tavern on the Green. Featured in movies as far-ranging as *Ghostbusters*, *Wall Street* and *Mr. Popper's Penguins*, the restaurant is a popular spot for weddings, bar mitzvahs and other celebrations. The owners were taken aback when Oliver Oakes requested to use it for a memorial service, but when he explained it would just a be private gathering with a few words of remembrance, with the deceased present in spirit only, they came around.

Oliver had tapped Jeff O'Malley, one of his father's Fox associates, to serve as Master of Ceremony. His assignment was to thank people for coming, and invite those who wanted to share a few thoughts about Mordecai to speak. The final speakers would be Zac and Oliver. Seventy or so people had shown up, including a handful of media reps, some lugging TV cameras.

The Tavern's manager wasn't pleased. He cornered Oliver. "I thought you said this was a private affair," he said with a frown.

"It is," Oliver insisted. "We didn't publicize it."

"Why are all these television people here?"

"My father worked for Fox News," he explained. "He was murdered, so I guess they consider his service newsworthy."

"Oh, sorry," the man backpedaled. There was an awkward pause, and he slipped away.

Mordecai's favorite musician was the late jazz pianist Bill Evans. Oliver had asked Declan to find some of his music and have it piped over the sound system. Evans's ivories were tinkling unobtrusively in the background, drowned by conversation.

Zac had walked by this restaurant many times and admired its conservatory greenhouse style, but this was the first time he'd been inside. The room was attractive but noisy. The buffet looked appealing, but he didn't have much of an appetite.

In addition to the media, Mordecai's family, his Fox colleagues and his literary associates rounded out the crowd. The family included Oliver, Layla, Declan, Calista, who was accompanied by her mother and two brothers, and Mordecai's brother Elijah, who had flown in from Indiana.

As the service got underway, O'Malley described Mordecai's indomitable spirit and his triumphant return to Fox News after his accident. He elicited a collective sigh when he mentioned that a week before his death, Mordecai had asked him to serve as best man at his upcoming wedding. As others stepped up and shared their own remembrances, Zac noticed their personal anecdotes weren't very personal. He gathered that Oakes had been an intelligent, clever man who wasn't particularly warm or demonstrative, cast in a role designed for someone with a more outgoing personality. Mordecai had apparently created his bombastic TV persona out of whole cloth, but in private he was more intellectual. This matched Calista's description of her fiancé. It also fit with what Oliver and Layla had said about their father enjoying attention but lacking natural charisma.

Elijah Oakes stepped forward and, choking up, he described their hardscrabble childhood and Mordecai's emergence in high school as an academic star. The memories that he shared dated from this era, suggesting that once Mordecai and his young family left Indiana, the brothers hadn't remained close.

After fifteen or twenty minutes, it was Zac's turn. He rose from his seat in back and made his way to the microphone in the front of the room.

"Unlike most of you, I didn't know Mordecai," he said as he scanned the sea of faces. "I never saw him on television or on YouTube until after his tragic death. I grew up in the West Virginia community where he died, and I was visiting my family when it happened. I work for *The New York Times* and my editor asked me to cover the story. Since then I've spent time with his family and learned more about him."

"I've learned that Mordecai Oakes was a complex man. The memories you've been sharing have reinforced that impression. He was obviously a gifted writer and speaker. He was an evangelist of sorts. You might even call him a televangelist since broadcasting was the primary way he spread his message that the climate crisis is a hoax. In addition to his commentaries, he wrote three books that expanded on the things he said on TV. He gave his books creative titles and subtitles. *The Gospel According to Chicken Little: Why the Left Wants You to Believe the Sky is Falling. Macarena Meteorology: Why El Niño and La Niña Are Forecasting Figments. Apocalypse Postponed: Don't Pack for Mars Quite Yet.* Titles guaranteed to grab the attention of, and warm the hearts of, Fox viewers."

The Fox contingent laughed appreciatively. They knew it was true.

"At the time of his death Mordecai was working on a fourth book, and he'd completed probably 75% of it. Oliver found this unfinished manuscript on his father's laptop. He'd given this one a catchy title, too: *Confessions of a Professional Liar.* Mordecai was dedicating this book to his son and daughter. Below the dedication he quoted a Native American proverb: We do not inherit the earth from our ancestors, we borrow it from our children."

"I've had the privilege to read the manuscript, and at Oliver and Layla's request, I'm editing it, adding a forward and an afterward, and getting it ready for publication. I could describe the contents in more detail, but instead I'll let Mordecai do that himself. I'm going to read you his Preface."

He took a fortifying breath.

> "For the past eight years I've been a hired gun. I don't use the term lightly.

According to Webster, a hired gun refers to an expert hired to do a specific and often ethically dubious job. I've appeared regularly on TV, on a network whose motto could be Loud Voices, Closed Minds. I've often been the loudest and the most closed, and believe me, it's a tough competition. When this book appears, I'll no longer be working for Fox News.

I've been preaching what the fossil fuel companies want you to believe: the climate crisis is a manufactured, non-existing problem, and attempts to address it will wreck the global economy and ruin life as we know it by adding onerous regulations to our businesses and daily lives. I've decided I'm not preaching this message any longer. I've changed my mind, and in the following pages I'm going to try to change yours. Most people hate to change their minds, but when you change your mind, it means you've learned something.

I like to put things plainly, so let me put this as plainly as I can: I've been paid to bury you in an avalanche of bullshit. If the climate isn't changing, why are insurance companies raising their premiums or pulling out of large markets like Florida and California? Why are cliffside homes sliding into the Pacific and beach houses washing out to sea on the Outer Banks? Why is the Earth getting warmer? Why are forest fires occurring more frequently than in the past? Why are glaciers and permafrost and ice caps melting? Why are coral reefs bleaching out and eroding? Why are extreme weather events wreaking havoc in so many places around the world?

I've come to the conclusion that whether we accept it or not, climate change is real. I've made fun of former Vice President Al Gore for some of his more dire predictions, but *An Inconvenient Truth* is an excellent three-word description of what we're facing. Of course, environmentalists can get things very wrong. In 2016 Professor Guy McPherson at the University of Arizona predicted that by 2026 there wouldn't be any human life left on the planet. I think he missed that by a few years. Wildly inaccurate forecasts like this are entertaining, but they don't negate the reality of what's happening.

In the beginning, despite my degree and training in meteorology, I half-believed the misinformation I was sharing with you. I tried to believe it because I didn't want to admit to myself what I was doing. I described environmentalists as alarmists, catastrophists, doomsday cultists, radical nut jobs, purveyors of doom and gloom, climate freaks, green crazies, elitists with private jets who don't have to worry about affordability. Actually, most of them are just sincere people who care about our planet and

> are worried about what it's going to be like if things keep heading in the wrong direction.
>
> I've been lying to you, and this book is my confession. It's an apology to all my meteorological brethren who've been telling you the truth. And it's an attempt by a father to be less of an embarrassment to his children, to try to leave them a more positive legacy.
>
> As Jane Goodall once observed, what we do makes a difference, and we have to decide what kind of difference we want to make. After all these years, I've finally decided. Read on."

Zac looked up from his paper and he saw a roomful of stunned faces staring back at him. He was going to continue with his remarks, but something told him to let Mordecai's words hang in the air and speak for themselves. He returned to his seat, his footsteps echoing in the room's dead silence.

Awkward seconds ticked by before Jeff O'Malley returned to the mic. "Well, that was certainly interesting. Now Oliver would like to say a few words, and then you're all invited to stay for the reception, enjoy the food and drinks, and take the opportunity to visit with each other."

Oliver strolled to the front of the room with the calm demeanor of a young man who'd dealt with rafters having full-blown, screaming panic attacks, demanding to be let out in the middle of raging rapids. He adjusted the mic and smiled at the assembly.

"Dad always liked to have the last word," he said, "but today we're not going to let him. I know some of you were surprised, maybe even shocked, by what you just heard. Believe me, you're no more surprised than I was when I read those words. He seems to be telling us that he's not quite the man we thought he was. Zac called my father complex. After hearing what we just heard, I don't think anyone's going to argue that point. If I could have designed my own father, there were a lot of tweaks I would have made to the one I had. We didn't always get along, and there were probably a few things he would have changed about his son and daughter, too. It's been a journey for us, like it is for most families, but I think in the end it's kind of turning out okay, despite the very unusual circumstances of his death."

"With Zac's help we're going to publish *Confessions of a Professional Liar* and let people make of it what they will. I'm sure that in death, as in life, Mordecai Oakes will continue to be controversial, a hero to some, a villain to others. That's just the man he was."

"Don't let what you just heard scare you away. We'd really like for you to stay and visit with us. If you have a strong reaction, say so. If you're confused, say so. We can handle it. We need to be prepared for what we're going to hear about Dad in the coming months and years. Besides, somebody's got to eat all the food here. Thanks for coming. Belly up to the bar. It's on us."

If there were ever people who looked like they needed drinks, it was the Fox crowd, who'd just heard their moral and career choices called into question by the deceased.

The media pack made a stampede for Zac, but the rep from Mordecai's publishing house arrived first. "Angie Wilson," the woman stuck out her hand. "I worked with Mordecai on his books. This one won't appeal to the same readership, but we're definitely interested in it."

"I'm working with a literary agent who's planning to hold an auction for the rights," he broke her the news.

"Well," she reacted, looking crestfallen. "We may be interested in bidding."

"I'll let him know," he promised her.

The rest of the reception was a blur. Journalists wanting quotes. Videographers wanting footage. Calista introducing her brothers, who for some reason invited him to go ice fishing with them in Aroostook County. Declan handing him a mojito and whispering, "Oliver said you need this."

Zac sipped his drink and watched the Fox folks muttering among themselves. He was thinking about joining them when Ginny Donnelly from the *Times* sidled up. "Hey, Zac."

"Hi, Ginny."

"Emma sent me here to cover this. Am I writing about it or are you planning to?"

"Be my guest," he invited her. "I can't be the newsmaker and the reporter, too. Just say some nice shit about me, okay?"

"Talk about tough assignments."

"Grab a drink, Ginny. I won't tell anyone you were drinking on the job."

She gave him a thumbs up and headed for the bar.

A woman in a power suit strode up purposefully. "Anastasia King," she introduced herself.

"Hello, Ms. King. Are you with Fox?"

"I'm the General Counsel," she said.

"Nice to meet you."

"You're not really serious about publishing that book, are you?"

"Absolutely. I think a lot of people will be interested in it."

"What you read is defamation, pure and simple."

"Um, I'm no lawyer, but it seems to me I was reading one person's opinion about his job, which he has every right to express."

"Mordecai Oakes was treated extremely well by Fox News."

"I'm sure he was. He did an excellent job for you. But apparently somewhere along the line he decided it was a charade."

"You realize there's probably going to be a lawsuit over this?"

"One thing I've learned at *The New York Times* is that people threaten to bring suits against writers and their employers all the time. Sometimes they even follow up. The interesting thing is they very rarely win because of a little thing called the First Amendment. If I were you, Ms. King, I'd let this play out and hope it goes away quietly."

"I don't need advice from you," she said curtly. She wheeled and stalked out of the room.

Zac wound through the crowd to Oliver, on the opposite side of the room, and relayed his conversation with the Fox lawyer.

Oliver reacted with a grin. "This thing's going to be more fun than I thought," he said. He raised his glass. "To the old man," he toasted him, and they killed their drinks.

Chapter 45 A Trail Ride

The Greenbrier River Trail starts just outside Lewisburg and shadows the river to the Cass Scenic Railroad State Park, 78 miles to the north in Pocahontas County. The longest trail of its kind in the state, the scenic path is popular with hikers, bikers and equestrians, and anglers and kayakers use it to access the river. Passing over 35 bridges, through two tunnels and two towns, the limestone path gradually rises only a thousand or so feet, making it an easy hike or bike ride.

Knowing his brother-in-law was up for anything outdoorsy, Zac had suggested they take a ride on the trail. They dusted off two mountain bikes in Brendan's garage, hauled them down to the river in Brendan's pickup, and set off from the parking lot.

They had only pedaled two miles when they reached a place where a large, flat boulder jutted out in the river, overlooking an island and offering a tempting spot for sunning, picnicking or daydreaming. They left their bikes on the trail and made their way down to the boulder.

The scene was unfolding like Zac had envisioned it.

"I've noticed you like to ask your students hypothetical questions to get conversations going," he said to his brother-in-law. "Sometimes they're kind of off-the-wall, like when you asked them if Mordecai Oakes deserved to die."

"Yeah, sometimes it takes a little drama to engage them," Brendan shared his rationale. "I knew that seemed like a harsh thing to ask them, but they had opinions."

"You think they would answer any differently now that it's come out that Mordecai was about to repudiate his body of work?"

"We'll never know," Brendan said. "They've graduated and gone on their ways."

"Do you think Oakes has redeemed himself?" Zac pressed the subject.

"It's like Shakespeare said in *Julius Caesar*," Brendan reacted. "The evil that men do lives after them. I seriously doubt if the folks who read his other books are going to rush out and get this one. That's not what the Fox demographic does. I think your readers are going to be the people that are already convinced of the message."

"Preaching to the choir?"

"Exactly."

"Would you use *Confessions of a Professional Liar* with your students?"

"I don't know. I'll have to read it and see what I think."

"At least you're not boycotting it."

"You're editing this, Zac. If the school buys a bunch of copies, at least some of the money stays in our family."

"Music to my ears," Zac said. "All right, I've got a hypothetical question for you."

"Fire away."

"If you killed Mordecai Oakes and I asked you if you did it, and I promised it would stay between us, would you tell me?" He studied the mix of confusion and amusement on his brother-in-law's face.

"Why would you even ask me something like that?"

"Just answer it."

"Of course I wouldn't tell you," Brendan replied. "If I were clever enough to hatch a plan like that and execute it successfully, I'd be a fool to tell anyone. If the murderer is as smart as he seems to be, he knows not to take risks. Telling someone he's guilty is as foolish a risk as he could possibly take."

"Good answer," Zac agreed.

"A logical one," Brendan said. "Why did you ask me that?"

Here we go, Zac thought. "Because something's been bothering me, Brendan. The day I came to your class and the girl who wrote the poem asked for my contact information, I borrowed a pen from you. Do you remember?"

Brendan thought back on it. "Yeah. So what?"

"The pen you handed me was identical to one Mordecai Oakes pulled out of his coat pocket and gave the bellman before they went in the freezer. I'm just wondering how you happened to come by it."

Brendan thought about it. "I think I found it on my desk that morning. When the janitors clean the rooms in the evening and they find something on the floor that a student might have dropped, they put it on my desk so I can try to get it back to its rightful owner. No one in my morning classes claimed it. I didn't ask my seniors because you were there and we had all that going on. Is there something special about it?"

"It's a fake Montblanc."

"I hate to be ignorant, but what's a Montblanc? I'm not a pen expert."

"A luxury writing instrument from Germany," Zac elaborated. "They cost several hundred dollars. I saw a bunch in Oakes' apartment and his girlfriend told me they were knockoffs from China that he gave away as a little joke. A fake Montblanc isn't something a high school student is likely to have. It just seemed very curious to me that you had that one. I took one from his apartment in New York, and the one you loaned me looked identical to it."

"Ah - that's why you asked me that supposedly hypothetical question - you think I offed the dude. I only wish I was that clever."

"I don't know if you did it, but I do think you're that clever, Brendan."

"Thanks for the compliment, but I hate to disappoint you. You haven't found your man yet."

Zac smiled. "You just said if you did, you'd never admit it."

"True. So I guess you'll never know until they catch the person who did. Then I'll be off the hook."

"Honestly, I've stopped caring," Zac admitted. "I've reached the point where I'm more interested in Mordecai's life and his change of heart than I am in his death. When I say I don't care if you did it, I sincerely mean it."

"So you forgive me?"

"Really?"

"I'm joking, Zac. I think it's strange that after all the years you've known me, and all the times we've shared, you've decided your sister is married to a homicidal maniac."

"Think of it as the ultimate compliment, Brendan. If anyone could pull off the perfect crime, you could because you're smart and no one would ever suspect you. Even if you posted a video confessing to it, people wouldn't believe you. But the fact remains that you had that pen. Facts don't lie, but people do."

Brendan looked him squarely in the eye and made what would be his final pronouncement on the subject. "I think a certain student put that pen on my desk. I think he was smart enough to make sure there were no fingerprints on it. And, personally, I think this case will never be solved."

They walked back up to the trail, hopped on their bikes and pedaled north.

Chapter 46 Dreamwork

For weeks Wendy Lavender had been plagued by a gnawing suspicion that she was overlooking something. Oddly, it came to her in a dream. She usually had trouble remembering her dreams, but this one had awakened her, and it was crystal clear.

The hotel's security camera had captured the bellman wearing black athletic shoes. The bell captain had flagged this as unusual footwear for a bellman at The Greenbrier. The enhanced video had identified the shoes as Converse Shai 001's in triple black.

In the back of her mind she vaguely remembered seeing a pair like the ones in the video, which were sleek and futuristic-looking, laceless with a zip-up closure.

While she was sleeping her subconscious had been working overtime. She knew where she'd seen them.

Chapter 47 Cakewalk

He'd run across something interesting online the other day. A prison warden who was being interviewed had said he would rather have a murderer clean his office than a thief, because most murderers are just murderers one day in their lives, but a thief is a thief from the day they're born to the day they die. It was true, he supposed. He'd only been a murderer one day in his life.

Now he had all the time in the world to mentally replay his perfect crime. Two months had gone by and, as far as he knew, they weren't any closer to solving it. All in all, ridding the world of a problem called Mordecai Oakes had been a cakewalk. Interesting word, cakewalk. It sounded a lot better than perp walk.

He blew his whistle. "Cut it out, you guys!" he yelled. "Stop the horseplay or I'll put you out of the pool!"

His phone vibrated. He glanced down and saw that his mother was calling. She was probably just checking up on him, making sure his first day as a lifeguard was going okay. She was such a worrywart, always treating him like a little kid.

"Gunner, Sergeant Lavender was just here," his mother reported, a bit breathlessly. "She had a search warrant."

"A search warrant?" he puzzled.

"She took a pair of your shoes."

"My shoes? Which ones?"

"I don't know the brand. The black ones with the zipper. What on earth does she want with your shoes?"

"I have no idea."

"She's on her way to the pool right now to talk with you."

Obviously, there were going to be more pesky questions. It was a good thing he had a spongy brain and a high IQ.

Afterword

The Greenbrier has been celebrated in any number of books, none better than *The History of The Greenbrier* by Dr. Robert Conte, the resort's official historian for more than forty years. This sprawling, awe-inspiring property holds magical remembrances for many visitors, memories of weddings, honeymoons, family celebrations, vacations, sporting events, unexpected celebrity encounters, and retreats from a complicated, messy world. Knowing The Greenbrier means so much to so many people, I hesitated to set a murder there, but fiction likes intriguing settings, and it's an endlessly interesting place. Hopefully no sacred memories were trampled.

I'd like to add a word about my use of a character with autism. I realize some readers, or the autism community, might take issue with this portrayal. In my 30-year career as a social worker and therapist, I knew many young people who had been given this label. The character in this story is a composite of three I knew especially well, particularly one rather self-centered, conniving young man who was convinced he was a genius and didn't have much tolerance for the rest of us. Gunner isn't meant to represent people with autism any more than Mordecai is meant to represent paraplegics. Saints and sinners come in a variety of packages. In any event, my sincere apologies to anyone offended by this character.

Our society can't seem to make up its mind about many things, and climate change is one of them. Conflicts and wars come and go, but this is something larger, with more far-reaching implications for all of us. I set out to create a murder at The Greenbrier, but as the story evolved the hotel became a scenic backdrop for a tale that might be a bit of a parable.

Greg Johnson
March 2026

www.ingramcontent.com/pod-product-compliance
Lightning Source LLC
LaVergne TN
LVHW100524110826
845146LV00002B/763

* 9 7 9 8 9 9 4 3 2 0 0 0 6 *